Dragon's Domain

LORENZO ANTONIO HALL

Illustration by Tostantan

Published by CaryPress
International Books www.CaryPress.com

Dedicated to:
Anna Hall
Who taught me how fun
reading can be and the
power of a fun story

Special Thanks
My father, Oakrie Jordan
Michael Joyce
Nicholas Murgio
Scott Weingartner
Taras Yanovskiy
Ted Bishop

Wynveria, a nation of the proud and strong, also known as the land of the dragons. The nation evoked a feeling of quiet, understated dignity. The verdant lowlands plain and humble, a stark contrast to the great mountains that surrounded them. For any outsider, it would take weeks to climb the mountain range and reach the larger settlements of Wynveria, but for the natives, born aloft on the wings of dragons, travel was far easier.

Nearing the clouds and stretching high into the sky was the great mountain of Excelsis; upon its pinnacle, where it had rested for countless centuries, was the castle of Wynveria's ruler. The onyx-colored bricks that the castle was composed of seemed to blend into the mountaintop, creating a unique, breathtaking image of seamless strength and unity.

As the sun rose over Excelsis, rays of light crept through the windows of the castle, basking its insides with radiance. This woke the castle's ruler from her slumber, shifting out of her covers and swinging her legs over the bed's edge as she yawned tiredly. She was used to being tired when she woke up, but she was never pleased with having to rise this early.

Now awake, she was soon dressed and prepared for her day ahead. She noted that her servants had prepared her finest clothes, as befitting the occasion, considering she was to entertain important company.

Once she dressed, she admired what she wore. Her outfit consisted of a dark orange dress with yellow embroidery and a rich brown bodice and matching boots, with her gold necklace and crown rounding out the ensemble. The necklace had a single cerulean gem nested into its center. As she inspected herself, she found nothing amiss. Her clothing was pristine, her boots and necklace were all well-polished.

Soon, there was a knock at the door.

"Who is it?" asked the queen, an air of authority and power clear in her voice.

"Delys, Your Majesty," came back a voice from the other side of the door. "The Heofonite Guardians are scheduled to arrive in four hours."

"I am aware," replied the queen, an undertone of weariness creeping into her voice. "Please wait outside; I will be with you shortly."

"Yes, Queen Zelina."

Queen Zelina sighed as she strolled to her wardrobe, carefully opening its antique doors. Within its mahogany confines rested a Wynverian relic, the royal crown. Its gold finish gleamed in the morning sun as she donned her symbol of regency. Her outfit completed and her mind prepared, Zelina exited her chambers.

"Delys, I am ready," spoke the queen as she looked at her tan-skinned assistant.

"Oh, good. I'm glad to see you prepared so quickly," said Delys as she smiled at her queen. Delys had glossy, light red hair that was cut short, and bright yellow eyes. She was shorter than the queen, and had a curvy, somewhat ample frame. Her friendly disposition and disarming smile endeared her to many.

"You say that as if I waste time in the mornings," Zelina joked, a childish pout quickly flashing across her face.

"You don't, but you do have a tendency to rest longer than you are supposed to," prodded Delys, half-attempting to hide her giggle with her hand.

Zelina rolled her eyes. "If you are done making jokes at my expense, please tell the others to prepare brunch and be ready to welcome our guests. We want to be sure a good first impression is made."

"Of course, Your Majesty. My apologies." Resuming her role as Zelina's assistant, Delys bowed before hurrying off to deliver the message.

After seeing Delys off, Zelina walked through her castle, taking her time to admire the morning's light and watch her servants amble here and there on their business. She eventually came to her castle's courtyard; she decided to take a moment for herself as she sat down on one of the courtyard's many stone benches. She wanted to be utterly composed for her meeting with the Heofonites later.

Instead, she took her time and enjoyed the few moments she had to herself. These moments were precious to her, for her busy life as queen often kept her on her toes, making days of rest feel better earned. She bathed in the rays of the sun, feeling its warmth upon her fair skin. Closing her eyes in bliss, her mind drifted, thinking of other places and other times. This high in the mountains, the sunlight was particularly warm and welcomed in the cold kingdom. Snapping out of her reverie, she frowned slightly, remembering that she would later have to hold an audience with the nobles of Wynveria, if they had any issues with how she ruled. The life of a Wynverian ruler was not as restful as many assumed.

After her moment of rest, Zelina decided to see if Delys had done as instructed, and from there she proceeded to help. Although Zelina indeed did have servants who were meant to take care of such things, she felt things usually went more smoothly if she directly oversaw and helped with any ongoing tasks; for important matters such as the upcoming meeting, everything had to be perfect.

Within a matter of hours, preparations had been made and everything was perfectly set; all that was left was the arrival of their guests. Zelina was approaching the front gates of the castle when Delys spoke up, her hand raised in attention.

"Queen Zelina, you have a slight smudge on your face. I'll clean it," she said as she reached up to her queen.

"No, allow me to," said the queen as she gently brushed Delys' hand away. "I would rather handle it myself." The queen backtracked into the castle until she came across a mirror. It hung in one of the castle's grand halls and was large enough to accommodate her large figure. Once there, she observed her reflection with a slight smile.

Zelina was a young woman, early into adulthood. As she looked at her face, she noticed the spot of dirt that Delys had mentioned and wiped it a way with a cloth produced by one of her nearby servants. She decided to look over the rest of herself to be sure no similar blemishes remained.

Zelina was sure to check her hairstyle, as well. Her long, golden blonde hair was tied with wrappings on both sides, while her eyes were a brilliant sapphire color, and her gaze was sharp as she scrutinized herself. After making certain not even a single hair was out of place, she was satisfied; the Wynverian Queen wanted to appear warm and welcoming to her guests. Heading back out to the front gates, she met with Delys and others. As she arrived, she spotted two, unusually small figures flying nearby as they descended towards the gates.

"They're so short," Delys commented as she squinted at the figures.

"Delys, please remember your manners."

"Yes, Your Majesty, my apologies." Delys looked down in chastisement. "I'll try to be more tactful."

"Please see that you are. Your actions reflect upon our people," scolded the queen as she turned towards the visitors.

"Understood." As Delys finished speaking, the Heofonite Guardians landed. The first was none other than the Sovereign, leader of the Heofonites. The majestic being landed gracefully, his sandaled feet touching the black, stony walkway as he approached. Directly behind the Sovereign was another Heofonite, although this one appeared significantly younger. His landing was a bit less majestic; whereas The Sovereign had gently glided into a soft landing, the young man landed at a more of a jog before he stopped himself.

The two were tanned due to their closeness to the sun, and they each possessed a pair of angelic, feathered wings. Compared to The Sovereign, who appeared to be in his early forties and exuded an air of calm serenity, the young man had a far more energetic disposition and was wide-eyed. He looked to be barely over seventeen, though he might have been older; Heofonites tended to look younger than they truly were.

"Lord Sovereign, I am glad you have deigned to grace us with your company," said the queen as she greeted the ambassador.

"The honor is mine, Queen Zelina." The silvery-gray eyed man bowed slowly, his companion following suit. "I have not seen you since the Titan's Trial Tournament in Ahsira."

"Yes, I remember." Zelina smiled as the memory flitted through her mind. "Your Guardians did well in the tournament; their performance honestly influenced my decision to accept your offer."

"I am glad to hear it. Your own followers were impressive, as well; I believe only one of them actually lost against one who was not of your kind."

"Yes, Cassera. She was disappointed by her loss, but such things happen," the queen said. "She will have another chance when Wynveria hosts the next Titan's Trial Tournament. Then again, I may participate myself."

"Then I fear for any who has to face you, young Queen," said the Sovereign, looking at his companion and motioning for him to come forward. "It was rude of me to take so long to introduce him, but this is Markus," he said with a slight smile of pride. "He is one of our finest Guardians. He is young but holds promise."

"You're embarrassing me, sir." Markus began to blush and look down, his sky-blue eyes facing the ground.

"I merely speak the truth," chuckled The Sovereign as he reassuringly patted Markus on the shoulder. "Regardless, I am sure that he will serve you well."

The queen nodded in affirmation. "This is my hope as well, but I must ask you to explain the nature of Guardians to me. I learned precious little of them from our prior exchange. We can converse inside, should you desire a place to rest."

"Of course, Your Majesty. By your leave." He bowed slightly, motioning for the queen to lead the way.

At Zelina's motion, the others followed her inside, guiding them to the dining room so that they might eat. Once there, the Heofonites and Zelina began to dine before Delys departed to give the queen privacy in this foreign affair.

"Sovereign, would you please explain once more what Guardians do?" Zelina asked. "I would like to have a full list in mind before I decide." Zelina spoke between morsels of food, having already cleared her plate twice while somehow maintaining her table manners. She noticed that though Markus also ate, his eyes were constantly on her unless she met his gaze. She could tell the Heofonite was nervous.

"Of course, Queen Zelina," the Sovereign said warmly. "The Guardians work as liaisons with willing kingdoms and act as allies during any and all conflicts between people. Our organization's duty is to maintain peace and foster good will, as well as aid those who will have us during times of strife and conflict." The Sovereign had completed his plate of food, but had not touched anything after.

Zelina nodded before a thought came to mind. "And if you are allies with two nations who decide to war with one another? It may cause a conflict of interest."

"A fair point, but in such a situation we will try to facilitate peaceful negotiations. If not, then we shall abstain from the conflict itself if both sides are adamant about fighting."

"Hmm...Very well." The queen was satisfied with that answer. She didn't like the idea of third parties interfering when two nations were set on doing war. "What are the general benefits of a Guardian, then? I am sure your followers are powerful, but we of Wynveria are certainly formidable in our own right."

"I am very much aware of that, but Guardians have access to certain ancient scriptures, information channels, and more. Our talents aren't just strength of body, but strength of the mind and wise counsel to those who would have us. Markus here shows particular promise in those regards."

"Is that true?" Zelina faced Markus, trying to gauge if the Heofonite agreed with his superior.

Markus nodded, still nervous, but at least self-assured. "Yes," replied the timid Heofonite. "I can seal and cancel magic, among other things. I can control it, so it should not be a hindrance."

"It would not be, anyway," said the queen with a quick handwave, attempting to not sound too prideful. "The royal family does not dabble in magic, save for that which is related to our clothing and armor."

"Why would you need to charm clothing?" Markus curiously inquired. "Is it so you don't outgrow them?"

"Not quite," chuckled the queen. The chuckle quickly faded as she turned more serious. "I would also like to ask if I have a choice in who is left with me, or is Markus my only option?" she asked as she turned towards The Sovereign.

"I chose Markus because I believe he can bring your kingdom certain benefits no one else can. Please trust that my intent was merely for the improvement of Wynveria."

Deadly serious now, Zelina put down her utensils for the first time during the meal before authoritatively addressing the Guardian. "While your gesture seems to come from a good place, I must remind you that I am ruler of Wynveria, not anyone else. Whatever your intentions, it is my decision who will and will not serve with me. Is that understood, Sovereign?"

The Sovereign smiled thinly for a moment before replying. "Of course, my apologies. All I ask is that you humor me. Keep Markus with you for a month or so, and if he proves unsatisfactory, then please send him back and I will allow you your choice of any Guardian you desire."

Considering this for a moment, Zelina nodded. "Very well; that is amenable."

Softly clapping his hands together, The Sovereign smiled widely. "Excellent. I suppose my work here is done, then." The Sovereign stood and bowed. "Queen of Wynveria, I must depart, with your permission."

Zelina frowned slightly at this. "Do you plan to go so soon? You could rest for the rest of the day, if you so desired."

"Are you certain?" The Sovereign asked. "Absolutely. I would be a poor host if I did not allow either of you a respite in our castle."

The Sovereign nodded and gave an appreciative smile. "We thank you, sincerely."

"It is the least I can do. Please wait and I shall have my attendants guide you."

After, a couple of minutes, the attendants arrived, guiding the Heofonite Sovereign off, leaving Zelina and Markus alone in the grand dining hall. The soft clinking of utensils on plates was the only sound for several minutes as Zelina finished her fourth plate and Markus picked at his first. Seeing his reluctance to finish, Zelina began to look at the young man, noticing that he was still looking at her.

"You have stared at me for some time. Is something amiss?

"Please, forgive me, but I've never seen someone so..." Markus began, before trailing off nervously.

""So" what?" Zelina asked, a hand on her hip and an eyebrow raised.

Markus seemed to realize his blunder and looked down. "Um...Most Heofonites are slender, as are the select few humans and Ellons I've met, but your people seem...big."

"Well, of course," Zelina said plainly. It was no secret that she had a wide body type; if Zelina was any other race, she would have been considered tall and overweight. Wynverians were naturally taller than other races and had hefty bodies. Zelina was a full head taller than Markus and at least twice as wide. Her body was curvaceous and ample, but in excellent shape; beneath the layers of fat were muscles that had power beyond what most races possessed.

"I'm sorry, Your Majesty," spoke the Guardian as he flushed red and gazed towards the floor. "This is new to me, and I will try to be more mindful."

"Please do. I will assume you mean well, but if you let people see your ignorance, they will get the wrong impression."

"Of course, my apologies." Markus bowed his head.

"Apologies accepted," smiled the queen as she finally finished her meal. "Now, when you finish your meal, I will have Delys escort you to your quarters."

"Yes, Your Majesty. Thank you."

Zelina smirked inwardly. She could tell the awkward young man meant well. He was honest, at the least.

* * *

Wynveria, an ancient and storied land, filled with powerful opponents and vast mountains to climb; it was a perfect place for the warlord from a foreign shore to begin a new campaign. As his warship drifted closer to the craggy shores, the immense mountains they had seen from further out were far more imposing, and the monument in front of them was even more impressive.

It was a large statue, crafted of steel that rose just as the mountains did; it was a female figure with long hair and posed in a way that depicted grace and strength. It gleamed in the afternoon sun, its steel construction reflecting light towards the lands around it.

The warlord turned, his dark eyes upon one of his men. "Fetch the bibliognost. While you're at it, tell Shary to prepare the men. We will disembark soon."

With haste, the man left to obey his master's will. It was a few minutes before he returned with a thin, pale man in tow. He was dressed in a shabby coat and tattered hat, clutching a bag of books while he shook with fear.

"Bibliognost, what is before us?"

"A monument, Lord Raleigh," stuttered the smaller man as he quivered before the muscular warlord.

"I am aware it is a monument," hissed the warlord in annoyance. "Tell me why it was made."

"I believe that is the alternate guise of Aurah, ancestor of the Wynverian dragons, claimed as a goddess..."

The warlord scoffed. "Enlighten me, why would a supposed goddess-dragon take human form?"

"The legend states that she did so for the love of a man."

"How sickeningly sweet," Lord Raleigh said with mock sincerity in his voice, then turned to his men. "It is time to send a message. Everyone mobilize! We will let them know that Lord Raleigh's army has graced their shores."

"Yes, sir!" The myriad of soldiers readied their weapons and grabbed their few belongings, one preparing the way for their master to disembark.

Before long, all were prepared, with the warlord stepping off first. One of his underlings escorted the bibliognost and the rest followed, marching towards the grand statue. Raleigh halted his band with an outstretched hand as they arrived at the foot of Aurah's monument.

"Men, before us stands a legend of the land, one which embodies its old culture so much so that they made it to rival their mountains." The warlord pulled forth a great sword from the sheath on his back, the metal stained a haunting blood red color and the edges jagged and chipped, letting it slowly swing down to rest in the ground. It was wide, heavier than most blades and far too unwieldy for most, yet he wielded it like it was little more than a twig in his hand.

"Today, we shall build a new legend, a legend of our glorious might. The ways of these dragons… their land, their gold, their history, their lineage; all of it is worthless. All that will matter is who is strong and who will fight. Spare none save those who shall embrace our message, accept brothers-in-arms, and allow them to have a foretaste of the new world's message; a message of struggle and valor, of fire-forged bonds, brothers of blades, and of a world unified by strength!"

The multitude of mercenaries cheered at their master's message, and before long they watched as the warlord used his blade to strike the monument. Raleigh swung his sword with one arm, cutting through the wide expanse of steel as if it was naught but more air before his weapon. There were sparks and a crimson glow as the steel gave way to the foreign metal of Raleigh's sword. Once he had cut the statue across its chest, leaving a deep slash mark, Lord Raleigh signaled his men.

They began to rage against the monument, those wielding hammers pounding their mighty weapons against the statue. Others readied battering rams and struck in coordinated rhythms. The force of their blows, the strength of their arms, and their own savagery gave them the power needed to topple the ancient statue and all it stood for.

The once great monument, now battered and broken, teetered as if it was still attempting to stay upright, but the army's work was thorough; the statue collapsed under its own weight, falling to the earth with a sound like thunder. The shockwave that ensued shook the land, as if in empathy to the fallen monument, ringing like the bell of war's approach.

With the idol having fallen, Lord Raleigh led his men forward, beyond it and towards their true targets. The campaign had begun, and war was to be waged.

* * *

The days since Markus first arrived in the capital of Arachon were filled with many new sights for the visitor from afar. The Heofonite was in awe of the simplest things, from the sight of snow to the number of Wynverians flying high and walking upon the ground. Even the sheer variety in clothing and food amazed him and made him want to see more. While Zelina rarely had a chance to move about Arachon as much as she used to, she was glad to show Markus his new surroundings and make him more accustomed to life in Wynveria, especially since she had business to tend to.

The Heofonite Guardian was astounded by much of what he saw, looking around with wide eyes and curiosity. "This country really is impressive. I have never seen so many people out at once before."

"Is it so uncommon?"

Markus nodded. "There aren't very many of us in the Guardians, or Heofonia in general. It's a new experience for me."

"Hopefully one you will grow accustomed to. I will not be able to escort you around the kingdom after today, so if you have anything you would like me to personally explain, now is the time."

Markus pondered the offer. "Do Wynverians still have warring clans?"

Zelina raised her eyebrows in surprise. "You know about that?"

"Yes. I read some texts about your people. It said that leaders of the Wynverians gain that position by fighting in battles," Markus said, as if reciting a text he had just read.

The queen nodded. "That is correct, but we have established more order since those days. There are now formal challenges and there are Noble Clans and Errant Broods."

Markus looked confused. "What are Noble Clans and Errant Broods? I don't recall them from my studies."

"Noble Clans work with the ruling Wynverian family and promote the society we have made and receive aid and support in return from Wynveria and their allies. Errant Broods are not affiliated with the kingdom, but unless they cause trouble, we leave them be."

"So, are they not your subjects?"

"No, but they stay in our nation. Wynveria was founded by our ancestor, Aurah. She wanted all of her children to have a place to stay, and we have respected this for all but the cruelest of our kind.

Speaking of such, I have a meeting with one brood today."

"You do? Is that wise?"

"They have their own form of honor, so I doubt they have anything treacherous planned." Zelina could see Markus considering what she had told him. He obviously still had much to learn about Wynveria, but he would be as good a student as he could. It was then that both of them noticed the sound of flapping wings was growing louder and more intense.

It appeared as though a number of dragons were flying in the air, far more than usual, and a whole group were on the approach. "Queen Zelina…"

"Hm? Ah, it seems I spoke at just the right time. It appears the Relia Brood is on their way.

Immediately, five white-scaled dragons landed, each of them with four horns and bright, golden eyes. It did not take long before they transformed, shrinking down as their bodies went from dragonic to human, dressed in white leather clothing. The tunics they wore had teeth of what appeared to be beasts sown into them, along with thick fur from mountain bears.

As far as Markus could tell, the group appeared to be family of some kind. He looked and saw Zelina stepping ahead to greet them.

"The Relia Brood. May I ask why you have chosen to come here as a group? It is rare to see you in Arachon."

"We wish to challenge you, Your Majesty. It is time for new rulership in this land."

Zelina smiled. "Very well. Please, inform me which of you will be challenging me?"

From the group, a man stepped forth, his shaggy hair was cut short and a sooty black color and his brow furrowed. He was very tall and muscular, taller than the queen and bearing many scars on his body. He stared intensely, his expression serious. "I shall. I am Hemon Relia, current heir of our clan. I have come seeking a duel with you, Queen Zelina."

"Very well. As queen, I accept your invitation to battle." Zelina then directed her attention to Markus. "Come with us, this is your opportunity to see how Wynverians conduct themselves."

Slowly, Zelina began to grow larger, her hands becoming clawed. Her body expanded and covered in scales as her clothing disappeared. The ruler of Wynveria was the size of a house, with large, shining claws as sharp as scythes. Brilliant, golden scales covered her body, each one glistening in the light as darker, sharper scales also emerged, running along her newly emerged tail and wings.

Zelina began roaring, fire erupting from her open maw. After revealing her ivory colored fangs, Zelina then faced Markus who stepped back, awed. With some effort, Zelina began to speak to Markus, as if to bring his attention back to the moment. Her voice was deeper, reverberating with a force and authority exceeding that of her human form. "Markus, come with us." Taking off, Zelina flapped her wings and flew, and soon, the Relia Brood followed suit.

Zelina, Markus, and the Relia brood all stared on as they approached a tall plateau, some distance away from Arachon.

Unlike the many mountaintops, the plateau had been made flat from many duels between Wynverians and ancient dragons even before that. Next to the castle grounds, it was the highest point in the area and it was massive enough to house the grand coliseum. The plateau was covered in snow, yet there was still grass growing through the white covering. A paved stone path paved the way to the gray, stony arena. There was a faint chill as Zelina stared at it, but not from the cold so much as her many memories of time spent in her youth training.

"Queen Zelina, what brings you here?" The guard asked, approaching as Zelina and the Relia Brood resumed human form. "Are these challengers?"

"Yes. I decided to have a public showing for this bout, something for our newcomer to witness."

"I see," one of the guards replied. "Shall we arrange for messengers to announce this to the people, Your Majesty?"

"Please. In three hours' time I would like to begin, so there will be a chance for the people to observe if they so desire."

The guard smiled cheerfully, excited at the thought. "Of course they will, after all any match of yours will be an event worth attending."

"Thank you. Please, ask the other guards to ready the arms and the announcers to move swiftly."

"Yes, Your Majesty!" Quickly, the guard went to his colleagues, spreading word and commanding the others to do call for messengers. Within minutes, many had left, and in time it was evident that word spread as Wynverians flocked to the arena and into the stands.

Zelina could see some members of the Relia Brood, on the other side of the coliseum grounds, were talking with Hemon and observing the assembly that came for the competition. They were standing at the opposite side of the arena while looking up to the stands. A few thousand people had managed to find seats and wait with curiosity, while others tried to find seating. She had a strong feeling they were relishing a chance to show their family's might to other Wynverians, which was understandable. Even so, she would have to remind them why she was queen.

Steeling herself on the opposite side, Zelina stood at ready and smiled slightly while two guards entered carrying a large, weathered looking cabinet. Once it was set down, she approached.

As Zelina arrived at the cabinet, she opened it to reveal that it was an arsenal, with each weapon within well maintained and made of intricately decorated steel. The contents were vast, ranging from swords and spears to axes and daggers, even a bow and a quiver of arrows were stored inside. Soon, she smiled as she considered using them against a worthy opponent and took a sword.

Once she had a chance, she then turned and addressed the crowd. "We shall begin our duel, with the position of Wynveria's leader as the stakes!" Zelina shouted, listening as the audience, now crowded and full of eager onlookers, cheered on. She listened to them express joy for a few moments before she raised a hand for them to be silent. Before long, they were quiet and she continued. "The rules are that it shall be one member of the Relia Brood and myself. The victor shall be the first to disarm the opponent, though either of us may yield as well. You may choose your weapon, as I have chosen my own."

Hemon, walking forward, chose a large, imposing axe. With one hand he gripped it and held it aloft, swinging in order to familiarize himself with its weight. "Then I choose this."

Zelina took a sword from the arsenal and walked to the center of the arena. She stood there, the area hushed while they waited for her opponent to ready himself.

Hemon motioned for his kinsmen to step aside before he continued to the center of the stage. Putting his weapon forward, he waited for Zelina to tap hers against his, signaling the beginning of the duel. When she did, the two backed away before they took their battle stances, ready to face off against one another.

Zelina gripped the handle of her blade tightly, calming her mind and observing her opponent intently. She could see him clutching his axe with one hand, his eyes upon her figure.

"Whenever you are ready, I am." Hemon stood perfectly still, waiting for his opponent's move.

Zelina made the first move, thrusting. The forceful strike was narrowly deflected, though Zelina continued her assault. The queen of Wynveria attacked, rapidly and relentlessly, focusing on light blows to keep Hemon on the defensive. Zelina could tell he lacked finesse based on how he clumsily blocked the strikes, nearly losing grip of his weapon twice. She continued to pressure Hemon, pushing him back with her relentless assault until she saw that he was growing tired.

Zelina stepped back, easing her offensive strategy until she saw her foe had brought up his axe and stepped aside when he swung it down, crashing into the earth with extreme force. Taking the opportunity, she slammed the flat of her blade against his hand, causing him to drop his weapon. As Hemon cried out, Zelina stepped in and pressed the blade to his neck as he recoiled.

"This duel is over!" One of the knights bellowed loudly, causing thunderous applause and shouts of adulation to erupt from the audience. The cries of praise caused the victorious queen to smile while her admirers looked on.

Hemon gave a frustrated, bitter groan, but maintained his composure. "I concede. Your skill is remarkable, I will admit..." His tone was oddly dark.

"Just as you show promise. Continue to practice and you'll grow far better." Pulling back her practice blade, Zelina watched as Hemon rubbed his injured hand gingerly. "Perhaps next time I will be able to show you more of my skill." Zelina turned her back on Hemon, unaware that he was picking up the axe again and hoisting it high.

Zelina was only made aware when Markus shouted a warning from afar. "Queen Zelina, turn around!" The queen of Wynveria saw the rest of the Relia Brood drawing closer, along with Hemon while the audience and soldiers took notice. Not relaxing her guard for even a moment, she stared them down. The four approaching Wynverians came at once, attempting to attack Zelina. For the first, Zelina hit him in the nose with the butt of her sword before shoving him into another with a single push. For the female member of the Relia Brood, Zelina caught her fist and backhanded her with her sword hand.

Zelina saw the guards and Markus also come on scene, the Heofonite visibly impressed, while Zelina felt a rush listening as the crowd cried out. They cheered as if it was a display that their queen was putting on for them, and despite the danger she appreciated the praise. Zelina had managed to best three enemies in one strike each, but two remained.

None of the guards were making a move to restrain the downed enemies, or even stop them from attacking. While Zelina was well-trained and possessed skill, she had to stay wary and focused on her opponents, so she was taken aback when Markus intervened, flying next to her.

"I'm here to help, Queen Zelina!"

"Markus, wait, I-" Zelina stopped when she noticed that Hemon transformed, going into his dragon state, while his remaining relative did the same. The two foes roared, approaching Zelina.

The queen of Wynveria held her sword at ready and went ahead so Markus would not be caught in the fray, facing both down fearlessly. She turned her attention to Hemon first and attacked him, though the second was inching closer. Zelina moved back as both of them tried to bite again, managing to dodge the first, but she felt Hemon's teeth sink into her arm, attempting to crunch her bones until they broke.

The second member of the Relia Brood tried to bite Zelina's sword arm, but Markus intercepted, flying into the dragon and restraining its neck with a crushing bear hug.

Markus wrestled with the scaled menace, his strength and sudden action causing it to struggle as Markus deprived it of air while the audience went from cheering to talking in hushed tones.

Meanwhile, Zelina was still grappling with Hemon, trying to free her arm as his teeth sunk deeper into her flesh. The pain from his fangs sinking into her arm was great, but Zelina had learned to block out suffering. With a mighty thrust, she plunged her sword into Hemon's eye, making him reel back and release his hold on her. Acting as quickly as she could, Zelina took the blood-soaked blade and started slashing downwards, hitting a weak spot on Hemon's neck. "Enough! Change back or I will kill you now."

Without any further coercion, Hemon obeyed, slowly shrinking back down to normal, grunting in pain while he did. Blood flowed down from his wounded eye and neck, while he struggled to remain conscious.

Turning to the guards, Zelina spoke. "Go fetch shackles for these dishonorable scoundrels. I want them imprisoned for attempted regicide."

The guards did as commanded, picking up the defeated members of the Relia Brood, escorting them away. Once all of the members of the Relia Brood were taken away, Zelina was approached by Markus. "Queen Zelina, please let me see your arm. I need to make sure nothing is broken," Markus stated urgently.

Zelina, however, was furious, moving away from Markus. "You intervened in combat! Perhaps the finer points of why what you did is wrong escape you, but rest assured that you will learn. Now leave while I finish here!"

The Heofonite was taken aback. "Why? I helped save your life!"

Zelina was all too aware that a Wynverian royal was expected to succeed, even in the face of underhandedness. While her title was no longer endangered, her people's belief in her as their queen and champion certainly could be, a fact she was sorely aware of. Even with his good intent, Markus had undermined her. "You will go to the castle immediately and await me in the courtyard. You will speak with no one, you will be silent, and you shall listen when I speak to you."

"But, Queen Zelina, I-"

"Shall do as I command, not anything less!" Zelina glared daggers at Markus, standing over her. "You are here to serve me, so do so!"

For a moment Markus froze, startled by the ferocity in Zelina's eyes and the harshness in her tone. Part of him wanted to argue, but he could tell Zelina was in no mood. "Yes, Queen Zelina."

Zelina watched as Markus flew off before she left to get her wounds treated. She noted the cheers by some, but others seemed to stare and whisper as she left.

* * *

The bodies of defeated warriors and slain Wynverians were strewn across the ground, the red trails of blood dyeing the earth, while fire consumed every building in sight; the village had fallen under the onslaught of Lord Raleigh's men.

As the warlord watched his men defeat the last members of burning settlement, he tightened his grip on his great sword. "Are there no more Wynverians here who can challenge us?"

"Sir, we are almost done and I have good news," one of the soldiers said with glee. "Another dozen or so Wynverian stragglers were found. They've managed to keep a whole squadron at bay all by themselves."

"Ah, it sounds like you've answered my prayers!" Lord Raleigh cheered and placed a hand on his subordinate's shoulder, the joy within his eyes reassuring the messenger. "Lead me to them."

Obeying, the soldier led his commander, with Raleigh drawing his sword before lifting it up and approaching the front lines and the site where many powerful, transformed Wynverians were waylaying their comrades.

As a large, yellow scaled dragon flew through the smoke and near him, Lord Raleigh beamed with satisfaction before he swung his blade. The edge of his sword sank into the neck of the incoming enemy. Once his weapon had sliced the dragon's neck, a spray of blood came out before the Wynverian fell to the ground with a mighty crash. Unfazed in the least, Lord Raleigh continued on, more Wynverians flying towards him. Raleigh loosed a war cry and attacked. In a single blade stroke for each, Raleigh ensured his opponents met their end.

The ease of his victories displeased the warlord. Each Wynverian faced him singularly, but they were merely large targets for him to pick off. "Come on!" He roared, his voice heard even above the cries of battle and the clash of steel. "Can none of you harm me? I thought Wynveria was a land of warriors and dragons! Will my men not face one worthy of standing before me?!"

"Why?" a voice coughed, it was weak and strained, but clear to Raleigh.

"Hm?" Raleigh looked down, seeing one of the Wynverians he struck down was still alive.

"Why seek out simple villagers?" The fallen dragon's eyes were upon Raleigh, half glazed over.

"So, you use your last words to tell me that not a single challenge lived in this pathetic burg? Pitiable." Lord Raleigh then lifted his blade and swung it down, ending the life of the maimed Wynverian. Then, looking at the remains of his victim, he continued to wonder about the stronger Wynverians he had heard of. Still speaking to the departed, Raleigh mused aloud. "Perhaps I will find some of your kinsmen here in this fine country to join me. If pawns of the kingdom are so powerful, I would love to make the talented among you into my allies."

* * *

The day after Zelina's duel against the Relia Brood was tense, especially for Markus. The Heofonite Guardian had been in his room since Zelina had dismissed him; the queen was too tired from her wounds to reprimand him. Sitting on the expansive, firm bed, Markus had already done all he could within the room. There was little to read, save the Saga of Aurah, and Markus was already familiar with the love story of the ancestral dragoness.

After the better part of the morning passed, Markus decided to exit his room. Although he had been ordered to wait, he was worried about Zelina's health. Making his way to the infirmary, Markus found Delys there.

"Excuse me, you're Queen Zelina's attendant, right?" Markus asked.

"Yes, Delys is my name. You're Markus, right?" Delys smiled warmly at him.

"I am. It's good to make your acquaintance," Markus replied politely.

"Likewise. What are you doing around here?" Delys asked.

"I came to check on Queen Zelina, how is her arm?" Markus asked, his concern evident.

Delys nodded. "Of course, that wound was bothering her for awhile, probably will still be sore for the next week or two, but she's up and about now."

"What a relief," Markus sighed, feeling calmness wash over him.

Delys nodded. "The queen is definitely hurt, but she's not bedridden. It'll take more than that to slow her down."

"That's more good news," Markus sighed. "I was worried her injuries would leave her in need."

"You shouldn't be. That sort of thing is par for the course, especially for a Wynverian ruler."

"Still, these traditions are dangerous. Isn't there a chance she'll die from a duel?"

"There are rules in place for a reason and Zelina is aware of the risks. Besides treachery isn't standard for a duel," Delys stated.

"Oh, right." Markus felt a bit foolish. "To me, trial by combat is intense; I'm not sure I could pull it off myself."

"Queen Zelina has trained for over half her life, so it's a simple, but important task for her. The same is true of every ruler of Wynveria since the last millennia," Delys said before looking at Markus closely. "I thought you studied information about our people."

"To be honest I mostly read books about your ancestor, Aurah, the alliance your kingdom made with the nation of Lurion, and a couple of old legends, but little else." Markus sighed, feeling self-conscious. "It's clear I have to learn to respect your ways too."

"Well, if there's anything our people respect, it's being able to acknowledge mistakes. You are our guest, but you're still learning our customs. Remember that and don't make any rash judgments," Delys said softly. "Maybe you should apologize to Her Majesty and try to learn more."

"But isn't Queen Zelina angry with me?"

"No, just annoyed with what you did. I'd just apologize and listen to her if you want to smooth things over, trust me." Delys began walking away. "Good luck, Guardian. Let me know how it goes!"

"Thank you, Delys." Markus replied gratefully before walking to Zelina's throne room, hoping the handmaid's words were true. It didn't take long for him to reach the throne room. Once he was there, he saw the guards. Clearing his throat and attempting to muster courage, Markus spoke. "Is the queen available for audience?"

"No, but she did request that one of us fetch you after her meeting now. You may wait here until the time comes."

Nodding, Markus waited, hoping that Zelina was not still cross with him. After a short time the guards opened the doors, letting out a few nobles. Markus stepped aside, bowing slightly to them before they left and he was told to enter. Quietly, he did as instructed before the guards closed the door behind him. "Queen Zelina?"

The queen was seated upon her throne, her eyes directly on the Heofonite. She looked at Markus with a cross expression on her face, one hand covering her newly applied bandages briefly before she spoke to him. "You arrived sooner than I anticipated."

"I did. I thought I would come to speak with you as soon as possible and apologize." Markus took a deep breath to calm himself. "I'm sorry for interfering with your match the other day, I was just trying to help."

Zelina stared at him a few more moments before nodding and speaking. "I accept your apology. I hope you will refrain from acting during any official duels."

"Of course, Your Majesty. May I ask why what I did was wrong?"

Zelina sighed. "You interfered in a duel before a whole crowd. While I understand your intent and that I was beset by the whole Relia Brood at once, Wynverians are expected to succeed, even in the face of underhanded opposition. We are to rise above and show our ability to overcome anything that challenges us with fairness and honor." Zelina then raised her injured arm and looked at Markus. "When you aided me, it showed others that I would need help to overcome enemies, and that was unacceptable."

"But no one succeeds at anything alone, not all the time. Anyone who insists on being alone and willingly faces bad odds isn't a hero; it's just risky and dangerous."

"I am not a hero, Markus, nor am I trying to be. I am a symbol of my kingdom, of Wynverian Pride and all we stand for. As I wear this crown, I cease to simply be myself, but I am also an envoy of my land and culture, all we represent and stand for. For that reason, Wynveria cannot fall to deceit or unfavorable odds, no matter how great." Zelina stared at him. "While the gesture is appreciated, limit it to non-personal duels, will you?"

Markus nodded but couldn't help but get coy. "But as you said, your conflicts cease to be personal as you wear the crown."

Zelina smiled, amused by Markus' statement. "True, but it is my personal body doing the battle. You do not see the whole of Wynveria literally fighting in these duels, do you?"

"I suppose not." Markus folded his wings inward and bowed, placing his hand over his heart. Regardless of earlier, he wanted to show her his desire to be truly helpful. "I shall respect your desires, Queen Zelina."

Zelina rose and gave him an approving stare. "Good, then you may rise. Consider our previous issue resolved."

"I am relieved to hear it," Markus said earnestly. "Is there any way I may serve you?"

"I suppose you could converse with me for awhile longer, if you don't have any more pressing matters. It grows boring waiting here with none to keep me company."

"It would be an honor." Markus smiled and stood to her right.

* * *

During the next week, the two grew more friendly, with Markus asking Zelina about her life experiences, while Markus told her stories about his time in Heofonia and some of his missions as a Guardian.

On one particular occasion, the time for Zelina to accept audience had reached its end and Markus entered when a knight entered the room. "Your Majesty, I apologize, but I have urgent news."

"Regarding?" Zelina asked, facing the knight. "There was an attack on a small village close to the coast. Reports say that the village was burned down, and bodies of both our people and an unknown force were found."

Zelina's eyes widened in shock. Gripping the arms of her throne, she kept herself composed. "Do we have any idea who may be responsible?"

"Yes, Your Majesty; there some who say they saw several unknown figures heading inland en masse, possibly towards Arachon. We have reason to believe these may be the invaders."

"Then we must act. Deploy one squadron for reconnaissance purposes. We need to know as much as we can about these invaders and oust them before they cause any more damage."

"Yes, my queen. It will be done." The knight bowed and left quickly, leaving Markus and Zelina alone again.

"Queen Zelina, will you go and face this foe?" Markus asked in concern.

The blonde royal shook her head. "No, we need to know what we are dealing with before anyone goes rushing in. My men can handle this and gain whatever information necessary before too much time passes. In the meantime, I will focus on getting well again."

"Alright, if you wish." Markus bowed, pleased by her response.

"I should hope so. For now, let's hope it is no major concern." Zelina began to think over the recent news of conflict, her expression growing grim. Her tension did not go unnoticed by Markus, who was silent for some time as he looked to Zelina.

After a few more moments of uncomfortable silence, Markus spoke. "Queen Zelina, do you have more business to tend to?"

"No," Zelina replied with a heavy sigh. "I should probably do something to ease my mind. There's nothing I can do until I gain more information."

Markus, noticing the faraway look in Zelina's eye, spoke up. "Your Majesty?"

"Yes?" Zelina replied, her hands clasped together as she thought.

"I know it's your duty to worry about your people, but I know they would not want you to stress over matters you can't deal with immediately."

"I can't exactly disregard the situation, Markus," Zelina replied tersely. "To get news like this and try to put it out of my mind is...Wrong."

"You have to take care of yourself so you can care for your people," Markus said adamantly, taking a step forward. "Please, at least consider something so you won't stress. When the time comes you'll be able to stop whoever the troublemakers are."

Zelina thought on Markus' words; she did need to keep her mind on important matters, but she couldn't let stress control her. "A small bit of relaxation can't hurt, but I will rest when I have time to myself tomorrow."

"Very well. I hope you find something to do that will ease your mind."

"You'll know because I will be having you come along," Zelina replied. "I may need you to keep an eye out for me."

Markus smirked. "I look forward to it, then."

Zelina nodded before rising from her throne. "I am glad. In the meantime, I must go. I will meet with you later."

Markus bowed, still smiling. "By your leave."

Leaving from each other, both Markus and Zelina left, each tending to their own business before the next day came.

* * *

By late morning the next day, both Markus and Zelina were both in Komah, a mountain village not far from Arachon. Zelina could tell that Markus was enraptured by how Komah looked. It was a smaller village with curving roads cut into the mountain path and a large number of houses carved from the mountain's sides. The dwellings had snowy roofs as well a few tall, leafy trees growing between the houses. The villagers were walking around, going about their business and conversing while others were stationed at several stalls with food and drinks for sale.

"It's not as big as Arachon, but it feels…Calm, more restful." Markus smiled softly as he continued to look at Komah. "It's so beautiful."

Zelina nodded in agreement, sharing the sentiment of her companion. "It is part of Komah's charm. It isn't the largest settlement, but there is a good deal of nature here and life is simple." The queen looked at the gathered crowd, noticing how varied it was, gesturing to them with one hand. "People from afar often come here to watch the performances."

Markus looked to the crowd and noticed several people who were shorter than the Wynverians. Some appeared to be normal humans, more bothered by the cold, bundled up for the weather in Wynveria and taking in sights, while others included the Ellons, the people with animal traits, who were also present. There were a few with horns and some with long ears, followed by another strange group wearing full black garments.

Zelina smiled, glad people from afar were coming to enjoy the event. Staring on, Zelina pointed ahead in a direction where other people were going. "If we follow the crowd, we will see the Stage of Devotion."

"What's that?" the Heofonite asked, brimming with curiosity.

"Where those who act in Wynveria have performed for little over a millennium. It's our oldest and most famous stage," Zelina explained. "It's been home to some of the greatest plays in Wynveria, if not the continent of Aelyr."

"Oh, I've never actually seen a play. How do they usually look?" Markus asked with excitement.

"Absolutely beautiful. Words cannot do it justice. If you want to see for yourself, follow me." With an eagerness in her step, Zelina went ahead, with Markus following behind her as they went into the crowd. A few stared in awe and bowed, realizing Queen Zelina was in their presence before making room, with Zelina greeting them and thanking them as she and Markus proceeded.

Before long, they reached their destination, a small clearing, the area had a large stage with polished stones, and behind them was a craggy wall leading further up the mountain. The flat area before the stage was laden with organized stone benches, with each arranged in a semi-circle around the stage with intricate carvings on them. Like the others around them, Zelina and Markus took a seat and waited for the play to begin, though Zelina was led to the front, given her choice of seat, with Markus sitting nearby.

Towards the central area, just offstage of the beautiful, roughhewn stone stage, musicians carrying stringed instruments, flutes, and drums gathered, playing a gentle prelude while the audience waited. The music enticed Zelina, who closed her eyes and listened, humming along with the tune.

Markus watched her, impressed by her humming, but he was more surprised by how melodious her voice sounded; It was different from the more reverent way of singing in Heofonia, but it was very pleasant.

Soon, the actors made it on stage and the play began, the duo watching it with vested interest. The story of tragic love unfolded, one rooted in Wynverian culture. It was the tale of Caeto, the Wynverian hero who had founded the monarchy of Wynveria. It detailed his humble life before destroying the foul Primordial Dragon, Myllius and marriage to the maiden Chadra. The two of them had led a happy life until a Colossus and the mage controlling it took Chadra away from Aelyr to another continent, believing her to be a Maiden of Myth who would bring peace to their land.

As Zelina, Markus watched they could feel the passion of the actors and followed the plot, hanging onto every gesture and word with deep interest. The whole audience laughed at every comedic moment between the action and tragedy and murmured at the end of drama, where Chadra had to stay to lead the lost people, despite the evil mage and his Colossus being vanquished. Caeto was duty bound to protect Wynveria, unable to remain with his beloved. The two lovers were separated by the ocean and by duty, their tearful farewell bringing the play to a close.

By the end, the Stage of Devotion was filled with the sound of the audience's applause and cheers. While Zelina clapped steadily with a smile on her face, Markus was just utterly awed.

"That play was amazing," Markus said, his mind abuzz with excitement from the show.

"I'm glad you enjoyed it as well." Zelina was still elated after the great performance.

"I did, but I didn't expect them to get so into character. I almost believed the play was real."

Zelina smiled softly. "That is the great thing about being an actor. Even for a few moments, you can be someone else, or even live another life. When I was younger, I came here often to watch their performances. I entertained the notion of maybe becoming an actress myself."

"Really?" Markus considered Zelina's statement. "As much passion as you have for it, maybe you could."

The queen shook her head before looking at the now empty stage. Even after the act was complete, the stage held a strong allure, one that made her heart stir as she gazed upon it. "When I was younger, perhaps barely ten, I dreamed of becoming an actress. I spent many days here watching the actors and trying to learn the craft. At first my parents thought it was a phase, but after some time they realized I was serious and even allowed me to take lessons."

"It must've been difficult. I know I couldn't act to save my life," Markus replied.

"I was told I had the gift for it. By the time I was fourteen I was even offered chance to act on this very stage." Zelina's eyes began to water as she looked up, a small, sincere smile forming as she reminisced.

"But why didn't you?"

"Royal duties. My father was undefeated and it came my turn to try to prove myself a worthy heir. Being so young I was not expected to best him in combat for another few years, but I had to train and hone my technique, as well as learn politics and decorum. It was hard to tear myself away, but I had a duty as a princess to become a strong queen for my people. Once I gained the throne, I grew so busy I could no longer entertain the notion of becoming an actress."

Markus looked to Zelina sympathetically. For a time he was silent before speaking up meekly. "Still, maybe during a time of peace you could, or perhaps you could put on your own production sometime."

"Perhaps someday, perhaps not, though I can always dream. Still, I am always happy to watch another perform." Zelina noticed the audience was dispersing as they continued to speak, most of them giving the queen space. "We should probably leave now before the path gets too crowded, otherwise we may be here awhile longer."

"Very well."

Exiting the audience area, the two followed a path that would lead back to Arachon, while most others stayed in Komah. They walked and discussed the play for a short time later, before talking about some of the books Markus had been reading and some of Zelina's favorite sites nearby, the two passing many along the way.

"So this is why you wanted to walk rather than fly?"

"Sometimes a walk is good for conversation, and clearing the mind."

"Especially of woes," Markus replied.

"Right. The same happens for me when I am in the middle of a rousing spar or lost in character during a brief act. I've actually dabbled in writing scenes out, though my plotlines need work."

"Oh? I'd enjoy you showing me your acting prowess if you would honor me so."

Zelina shook her head. "I don't much feel up to it right now, or even carving. That's probably my second favorite activity."

"You carve?" Markus asked. "I didn't take you for the artistic type, acting aside."

"Yes, but I'm not very good. It is more of a hobby for times when I can't travel or practice anything else." Markus nodded. "I see. Still, I'd like to see what you make sometime. I'm sure you've made at least a couple of figures that you're proud of."

"Perhaps one or two. I'll show you another soon, after all there is still plenty of time left in the day."

Markus nodded but looked conflicted as a thought came to mind. "True. Free time is nice, but I've never had much, really."

Zelina looked at him, noticing the pain in his voice. "Training to be a Guardian must have been busy."

"Life in Heofonia is always busy, but it's an orderly kind of business," Markus explained, almost defensively. "If someone isn't a Guardian or a scribe, they're an inquisitor, chorister, or a messenger. There is always something to do and we don't have much time to ourselves when we can work to make everyone's lives better."

Zelina grew more unsettled. "I can understand that, but at the same time shouldn't one be allowed time to explore one's self?"

Markus shrugged. "It is just our culture's way. Besides, the Sovereign teaches that idleness leads to time lost."

"Is the Sovereign a lifestyle leader as well as the leader of the Guardian force?"

Markus nodded. "He's one of the Heofonite authorities. There are four others, but each of them is equivalent in power. Together they lead our people in many ways."

Zelina somehow felt uneasy at the revelation. "Perhaps you should take more time to relax every so often. It might be nice, you know?"

Markus looked up to her, giving a wide, practiced grin. "I don't know, you seem to keep yourself busy and you aren't bothered."

"Yes, but I take time to relax, too," Zelina replied genuinely. "There is more to living than one's station, you know."

"I know." Markus seemed slightly contemplative while he and Zelina continued to travel, his thoughts weighing on his mind as he travelled with the queen back to the castle.

Zelina smiled, hoping she would end up teaching him about more than Wynverian culture while he was in her company.

* * *

The next few days were filled with tension as news regarding the invaders had yet to come. It was obvious Zelina felt tense and was doing her best to prepare her forces for the worst, with Markus at her side when allowed. The one positive development was Zelina's treatment was going well, as was Markus' understanding of Wynverian culture.

The blond haired Heofonite was reading about Wynverian history devouring information on the culture and trying to better acquaint himself with their ways. He was in his quarters, a stack of recently finished books on his bed along with some carefully taken notes, all done after he had made contact with Heofonia once more for a report. There was quite a bit of information that would help him better understand Wynveria and how to adapt to the culture. As Markus was getting engrossed in his research, his attention was caught when he heard a knock at the door. Standing to answer, Markus opened the door and saw Delys there, looking a touch disheveled.

The maiden's hair was out of its usually perfect updo from her rush to arrive. "Guardian Markus, Her Majesty requests your presence in the throne room, immediately," Delys huffed, almost out of breath. "The recon squad has returned, bearing urgent news."

"Is it bad?" Markus asked, already guessing that was the case.

"I'm not sure, Guardian, but they did look pretty grim." Delys took a deep breath. "Give me a moment to catch my breath...I still have four people to fetch."

"Oh, sorry! Then I'll find out for myself, if that's okay."

"Yes, please. I'll be...by later." Delys continued to rest while Markus went off.

Shortly after, Markus, several guards, a few members of Wynveria's military, and some advisors were in Zelina's throne room. Markus noticed several among them speaking, one a woman who was a captain with snow white hair, speaking with an older, more decorated Wynverian who had jade green eyes. There was a nervous tension in the air for all who had gathered until the leader of the scouting group returned with Delys, his expression dour and solemn. "Queen Zelina, I have some troubling news."

The queen sat, her posture firm as she spoke officiously. "Tell me what it is."

"The invading force is more capable than first expected. We did our best to stay from sight and we noticed that they were an army of considerable size. There were roughly fifty men to a group, and they wore strikingly red uniforms. Each man was armed, and it appeared that majority among them were human, though reports state there were a number of Flor and Ellon under their command, some followed by large war machines coming from their ships."

A frown creased Zelina's features. "No armed forces nearby wear red. Perhaps mercenaries?"

Markus also thought on the given information. Ellons from the region primarily lived in Lurion, but the island nation was further south and a known ally of Wynveria. They were also one of the biggest powers in terms of naval might.

"I doubt they belonged to any known country, Your Majesty. They spoke with accents we couldn't quite place. I would say they came from across the ocean."

"From another continent?" Zelina surmised.

The leader of the reconnaissance group spoke pensively. "We know nothing of their origin, but we found that they had destroyed two more villages since we were dispatched, and they were heading in the direction of Arachon. We even received reports that they had assistance."

"From who?" Zelina questioned, now looking more serious.

"The Justar Brood, and the Geol Brood, Your Majesty."

"They had Errant Broods helping them?" one of Zelina's advisors, an elderly woman, asked.

One of the guards nearby also spoke, taken by surprise. "Why would they ally themselves with someone trying to destroy Wynveria?"

"Could it be self-preservation?" Markus asked.

For a moment the speculation continued until Zelina raised a hand, signaling they were to be silent. Once they were, she spoke again, though the fact that she was hurt and shocked by the news was evident. "Perhaps the errants are being coerced, or perhaps they chose to follow these invaders but either way, we can't afford to waste any more time waiting." Zelina turned to one of the generals gathered before her. "General Nersel?"

"Yes, Your Majesty?" the General asked, bowing as he did.

Zelina gave him a long, serious stare as she spoke. "I hereby charge you with leading our initial assault. Marshal your men, as you are leading our opening assault."

"Yes, Your Majesty!" Rising, he departed quickly, to do as he was ordered.

Turning her gaze to the rest of the room, Zelina continued to speak. "The rest of you will await further orders while we plan for this war. I will send for those I need, but until then you are all dismissed."

With everyone in the room bowing, they soon departed, leaving Queen Zelina alone with her advisors.

It was hours later when Markus was called back for a private audience with Queen Zelina, walking in nervously. He could see Zelina was no longer acting as formally, but she was obviously tired, with one hand on the shoulder of her injured arm as she rolled it a couple of times. "Your Majesty, will you be going yourself or sending someone else?"

"Of course I'll be going, Markus." Zelina rose up, her expression serious and stern. "I have to support my people and be there to fight alongside them; It is my duty, after all."

"Queen Zelina, can you not stay? I know you have your duty, but you're still injured," Markus reasoned. "No one could blame you if you took time to heal before joining the fray."

"You're right, but I would not feel right if I sat here and waited and my subjects died for lack of my help," Zelina said, her sincerity as intense as her passion. She took a moment to breathe before she calmed herself, regaining her composure. "Besides which, I am healing well and I won't thrust myself into battle recklessly like a fool."

Markus paused. He could see the fierceness and passion in Zelina's eyes, but he was also worried due to her injury, despite her words.

"Your Majesty, I understand, but the situation might be over before you even need to get involved. What if another force and myself were sent out, merely to engage them? If they prove to be too much, we'll come back and muster the full force of your army."

"Very well. I shall send you and a few others, but you must act in tandem with General Nersel's force if you meet," Zelina said. "Is that clear?"

"Yes, I understand."

Zelina sighed tiredly. "Good. Then go prepare. You will leave first thing tomorrow after I give the orders."

"Yes, Your Majesty." Bowing, Markus departed, too, leaving Zelina alone to make plans. He could tell she had much to do and much more to set in motion, as the battles ahead would likely be difficult and unforgiving. Markus felt in his heart was strong enough to face them, but also hoped Queen Zelina would remain well. For a few moments, he considered sending a message to Heofonia to ask for help, however he decided to trust Zelina and Wynveria.

* * *

As the sun rose, the Wynverian army gathered outside the castle. Amongst the others, Markus was nervous, even after he had met briefly with General Geoffrey Nersel, his superior while under the Wynverian Army. Markus had only spoken to the wizened old warrior briefly as there was much to do. He spent what little time he had getting to know the soldiers he was assigned to work with, but the moments passed in a tense blur. Markus, like everyone else, was steeling himself for the war.

Markus and his group obeyed as Zelina gave them final orders, alongside two tacticians who reviewed strategy with the generals and captains one last time. Once it was clear everyone knew the plan, Zelina decided to address the troops one final time.

"Today, for the first time in many years, Wynveria faces an invasion. This land that we love where our ancestors settled, a land once protected by wyverns until we inherited it, is now at risk. No matter our strength, no matter our bond, we cannot afford to underestimate these foes, lest we lose our land, our loved ones, and our lives. Today we fight a war to save our motherland, our brothers and sisters, fathers and mothers. Even in the face of death, know your bravery will be remembered by the Arbiter, by your Kingdom, and by Mother Aurah." Zelina stood firm. "However, we do not fight so that we will die, but so that we can all live free, so go and return, so we can celebrate a new generation of Wynverian legends!"

The deafening cheers were heard in the hall as all resounded with their queen's message. For a long time there were chants of victory until they departed far and away to intercept their foes. The army started by flying away, with Zelina seeing them off. She watched as many of those who could only march also advanced on the path that was ahead of them.

Markus was in the middle of the force he was assigned to, but after a few hours he had been asked to fly ahead and to act as a lookout, in case something was wrong. As a smaller flier, he would be less conspicuous and more likely to make it back to the group unnoticed while General Nersel's went in another direction.

Behind him, Markus could hear the beat of their wings sounding off thunderously, announcing the presence of a storm. Markus was sure their enemies would know that they were coming, but that was fine by him. After all, he knew they wanted their foes to know that they were on their way, to instill fear in their opposition. In that noise, no one would notice him zipping by, as their attention was on the obvious threat.

* * *

After three hours of flight following the trail of destroyed villages left in the invaders wake, it became obvious that there had been many attacks, and Markus felt confident they were catching up to their foes. As all of them watched the ground, Markus was made aware one of the Wynverian soldiers noticed something moving beneath them. Looking down, Markus saw a group of travelers, fleeing in the opposite direction of the trail of destruction. It looked as if they were refugees, judging by how women and children were among them and none of them wore clothing that matched the enemy force's description, but he was unsure. Unable to wait, the soldier with Markus asked for permission to speak to them and soon landed, with Markus and another Wynverian flying down to join him.

"Are you alright?" Markus asked the presumed survivors once he touched down.

"As well as we can be," one of the group's members, a Wynverian man, said. His arm was in a sling and his clothes were worn and torn. The rest of the group, mostly other Wynverians but mixed with a few haggard and mourning humans and Ellons, looked to be in a similar state, and an air of bleak depression haunted them. "Our home, Folrei Village, was attacked two days ago. They... they burned everything to the ground and killed everyone."

Markus and the soldiers were silent for some time, mourning with the survivors.

Soon, the man collected himself and managed to speak again. "You...You're from Arachon, yes?"

"We are." The taller Wynverian's voice was soft, but soon became firm. "Are there more survivors? Your group aside?"

"A handful, but we scattered when the invaders came. We're all trying to reach Arachon now."

"Then you should continue along this trail. Aid will come before you know it."

"We don't have time!" the leader shouted, desperation in his eyes. The man tried to stand tall, but it was obvious his spirit was broken. "Please, tell us you're here to help us."

The taller of the two soldiers with Markus stepped forward and nodded. "Yes, we are. Take me to your wounded and ill. Once we have them separated we can talk to our superiors about transporting them someplace safe. My comrades will speak with others to see if we can help them along next."

Nodding, the Wynverian refugee walked with the soldier among the people, leaving Markus and the other soldier there with a few others. Among the others, however, one man stood out to Markus, as if locking eyes with him.

Nowhere near as somber as the others, the man had a distinct air about him. While he was as tall as most Wynverians, he was different. He was muscular, but not as stocky as many of them. The man had cinnamon brown skin and dark, but glossy raven hair, short and covered by a fur hat. He was dressed in heavy furs like many Wynverian civilians wore, though he wore a light sash around his waist and golden bangles around his wrists. The man seemed to not be bothered by the cold, judging by his exposed right arm, one that bore a large birthmark, one shaped like four crescent moons; for a few moments Markus wondered if it was a tattoo, however it seemed natural. The man's birthmark seemed to glow slightly, especially when his steel gray eyes met Markus' sky-blue ones.

"Who are you?" asked Markus.

The man stood firm before speaking. "I am Ihsan vas Getael vas Aurman. I came from far away on a quest of my own, but it seems I came at the wrong time."

"Well, relief is here." Markus gestured to the Wynverians flying above.

"For some, but I cannot sit idly by," Ihsan said, folding his arms. "Not when others are disgracing this beautiful, but frigid, land and someone I care for may be endangered."

"Wait, aren't you going with the others?"

Ihsan shook his head. "Well, no. If it is allowed I would like to assist you. Most others here are peaceful folk, but I know quite a bit about magic, if you'll allow me along."

Markus frowned. "You're a mage?"

"Qalairn. We're born mages, if one looks at it in simple terms." To demonstrate, Ihsan waved his arm slightly. The whites of his eyes turned black, and then a sudden gust of wind to tear through the snow near them, causing a small flurry before Ihsan made it fade. "Impressed?"

Markus gave a half-hearted nod; he wasn't a fan of magic, but he wasn't in charge, and this was not a situation where he could be picky. "We could certainly use your help."

The soldier nearby agreed. "There's much I need to tell General Nersel, just to keep him informed of the situation." The soldier then looked to Markus. "Orders, sir?"

Markus stared back and nodded. "Relay the information about the refugees and Ihsan accompanying us to the general and return quickly once you do." Turning back to the taller, tanned stranger while the soldier transformed and flew off. "Ihsan, how far is Folrei?"

"Half a day's travel on foot, considerably shorter by flight," Ihsan said. "Will you be checking back for any survivors?"

"Most certainly," Markus replied firmly. "I think the general will want to hear from the lead refugee first, so we leave after he's on his way."

Ihsan nodded firmly as he waited with Markus.

Eventually, the soldier from before and others came to assist the refugees and take them to where a temporary camp was set. Once they were done, Markus, his two followers, and Ihsan followed the trail. After some time, they made it to the village's remains, the horrendous sights giving them pause. All that greeted Markus was charred hovels that were once houses and the foul scent of dead bodies wafting through the air. While the Heofonite and company solemnly traversed the area, trying to stomach the horrors.

The dragon corpses were unaffected by the fire, but still they were being eaten at by pestilence as flies surrounded them and vermin scurried around. The same rats scampered through the rust-colored puddles of blood where the smaller, charred bodies of others were, alongside bloodied weapons and scrapped armor. The scent of death was overwhelming and the look of the remains chilling. Markus tried to put it out of his mind but felt shaken to his core.

Markus had never expected that the realities of war to be so gruesome. While training and during his duties as a Guardian, he realized that there would be tragedies that he would face, but it did not compare to the bodies around him. He saw his Wynverian companions knelt before the bodies and started to pray to Aurah and the Wynverian Arbiter, while Ihsan bowed his head.

Still, Markus knew he had work to do, and composed himself, resolving to stop this from happening to others. He was a Guardian, and they were those he swore to protect. Solemnly, he closed his eyes and offered a prayer for those who had passed to Aurah as well.

It was then Markus heard a noise, which sounded like earth being moved. "Huh?" Carefully, Markus turned and saw Ihsan rummaging around though some wreckage until he found a shovel. Ihsan began digging, placing dirt aside. "Ihsan?"

"I'm giving the fallen proper burial. It is the least we can do for the dead."

Markus looked and saw the soldiers with him had already transformed, using their claws to dig great heaps of earth aside, although carefully. Realizing he was the last, Markus began to search for a shovel too. "I'll assist."

With resolve, Markus, Ihsan, and the Wynverian soldiers managed to lay the bodies to rest. For Markus in particular, he felt uneasy as he looked at the bodies, whether young or old all of them further saddened him. After dusk began to fall, the group decided to search for any other survivors. Finding none, they felt the air chill further as the sun set and night fell upon the desolate place. When their work was done, Markus decided to give an order. "Let's fly back to camp and report in."

Nodding, the Wynverians took flight, one of them carrying Ihsan before Markus followed solemnly.

* * *

The campsite looked like it had seen much use in one day, with several tents lined thick with furs pitched across the plateau while the remaining snow was well trod. Markus' group could feel the warmth of several campfires heating them up and melting the cold snow. Several soldiers stood at their stations, while those at ease warmed themselves by the fire. It was refreshing to be in the heat after a long day of cold air and snow chilling them. The scent of roasting meat and boiling stew was thick in the air. After many hours of travel with no food it only reminded Markus of his hunger pangs and made his mouth water. Offhandedly, he could hear some soldiers even laughing and exchanging tales of past battles and legends of long ago, but Markus and his group could not relax until their duties were done.

After reporting in, they met with a lieutenant who debriefed them, with Markus and his group giving their report and finding the survivors were being taken towards Arachon by another group. It made them all relax somewhat, though it was short lived as the lieutenant placed a hand on Markus' shoulder.

"Guardian, before you go, General Nersel wishes to speak to you."

"Of course," Markus said somewhat nervously. It wasn't long after when he went to the tent of General Nersel.

General Nersel was a war hardened and aged Wynverian, having short, steel gray hair and bright, jade green eyes. He looked to Markus for a time, trying to gauge his temperament. "Are you alright, Guardian?"

"I'm well, sir. My group and I merely finished our burials."

Nersel nodded. "Sadly, this may merely be the first of many times we will have to see bodies to rest. Regardless, I am going to order your group to serve as our rearguard. Our soldiers are more likely to meet combat in the front and coordinate more effectively while you watch behind us for unexpected strikes."

Markus nodded solidly, though he had a faraway look in his eyes as he remembered the many bodies he had seen that day.

The general paused a moment before he looked Markus in the eye. "Perhaps it is best if you take time to rest; you and your group have been hard at work today."

"Of course, General..." Tiredly, Markus waited until Nersel called in a guide to take Markus to an empty tent. Going within, Markus began to remove his armor before lying in bed, trying his best to rest peacefully. However, hunger kept him from slumber and he saw Ihsan and his other companions were not too far off.

Realizing he couldn't even recall his companions' names, he thought it best to socialize at least a moment, as well as eat. Going to Ihsan and the others, he waved to them. "Everyone alright?"

"Doing well, just familiarizing myself with everyone." Ihsan gestured to the rest of Markus' group, now more relaxed and out of their armor.

"He's a pretty good storyteller," the taller one said as she drank ale. The black-haired woman looked to Markus. "Did the general need anything?"

"No, we're just serving as rearguard for now." Markus sat down, though the other Wynverian, a red-haired young man with blue eyes handed him a large bowl of hearty stew. "Oh, is this for me?"

"We got it when we went to get grub." He started to eat some from his own bowl, smiling as he did. "Very good, too."

"Thank you," Markus said as he sat and consumed the hot soup, realizing how good it tasted; He hastily consumed more.

"Alya was right. She thought you'd love it," Ihsan chuckled.

"Hm?" Markus asked, confused on who Alya was.

The taller Wynverian smiled. "Turns out I was right. Better than the food in Heofonia, right?"

Markus' eyes widened as he realized the Wynverian woman in his group was Alya. He swallowed before nodding, trying to play the situation off. "Um, it's very good, much meatier." Markus ate more, trying to move the conversation along. "So, have we all introduced ourselves?"

"Yes. I've gotten acquainted with Regis and Alya, too," Ihsan said. "Still, I'm surprised. How does a blacksmith's apprentice and an adviser's daughter end up working with a Heofonite Guardian?"

Alya smiled. "It's an easy promotion job. My mother had me assigned, after all. She says it may help relations between our lands if I work with a Guardian and a promotion at least if I work with someone assigned personally to the queen."

"I wish I had connections like that." Regis shrugged. "I suppose I showed some promise. I was asked by my commanding officer, Captain Grey, to serve with this group. I just want the war to pass and to get back to reopen my family's forge."

"Why aren't you there now?" Markus asked as he finished his soup and contemplated getting seconds.

"We didn't have the money to sustain it. It's ironic; had the war come a year or so ago we might still be in business," Regis replied.

"There never really is a good time for war, but there is always a good time for stories. Perhaps one to lift your spirits?"

"What kind of story?" Markus asked, intrigued. "Since we're in Wynveria, why not one of the Arbiter?"

"Who is the Arbiter exactly?" Markus asked. "I heard of him in texts, but I don't think I actually read about him."

"He's the judge of Wynverian souls," Alya explained.

"All the more reason to tell," Ihsan said with a chuckle. "Years ago a Wynverian told me about the Arbiter and I was eager to learn more from the motherland of the legend."

"Why aren't they written down?"

"The Arbiter is supposed to appear differently to each person, and what is true for one may not be for another," Regis added. "Besides, not many people who go to the afterlife have time to jot notes down, and people who only go near death, well, they see lots of different things."

"Either way, I am happy I came here to collect tales of the Arbiter. I think a figure like he should be known by others. Now, may I share a tale I heard?"

"Sure," Alya replied as she reclined. "Regis and I will pipe up if you get it wrong."

"Doubtful. A master of legends never misses a detail!" Ihsan smiled and began his tale.

For a time, Markus, Alya, and Regis listened closely, hearing Ihsan tell his story about the Arbiter, with Markus learning more about the spiritual dragon and those he judged. After hearing the tale and finishing his meal, Markus began to feel more comfortable and slowly forgot the trials of the day before. After a few more stories and laughs shared by all, the group separated for the night and Markus slept. Hours passed in a deep, dark sleep, one that Markus was slow to rise from. Rubbing his eyes, he stumbled out of the tent after some time. He was startled, though, when he saw the entire camp around him was gone, save for his group, many of whom were packing away their things. "What happened?!"

"General Nersel insisted on leaving before dawn but told us where to reunite with his main forces," Alya said.

"Markus gave off a sigh before composing himself. He was a bit embarrassed that he was the least prepared of the group. "I'll have to ready up. In a bit we can conduct our search. My apologies."

Ihsan smiled. "No apologies needed. I must say, though, you slept rather hard. I assume you were quite tired."

"Good assumption, still, I'll be ready shortly. You all check in with the others," Markus instructed.

Complying, the three went to check on the other Wynverians who had yet to finish, assisting where necessary as Markus finished his own preparations.

Before taking flight, Markus' group went to gather their possessions, securing them before taking their time to follow the path before them. With the wind at their backs bolstering them, they were able to easily cover distance, following behind the rest of the army's trail. The rearguard looked around once they were on their path, making sure the main forces had not overlooked anything until they noticed a village off in the distance, one that looked to be ablaze.

"What is that place?" Markus asked.

Alya turned her head to look closer as she flew. "I think it's Galaren, one of our villages."

"Then we better head there, fast. With the others, Markus set off. Their journey to Galaren wasn't long, however they did notice that there was an odd, disconcerting silence when they touched down. Markus didn't know why, but the silence made him slightly nervous, despite several buildings still aflame. He looked around and saw that Galaren was destroyed, with all of the buildings in sight little more than rubble and burning buildings. It took some time for the others to organize, though they all gathered soon, returning to human form upon landing.

"Where could they have gone?" Ihsan asked.

Alya looked at the buildings, her hand on her hip as she kept it near her sword handle. "I'm not sure, but we didn't see any soldiers leaving from here."

"Maybe they never left." Markus began to look around, noticing that there were some boot imprints on the ground nearby. He pointed them out to everyone quietly before looking at Ihsan. "Be careful."

"I will, no worries." Ihsan gave a slight grin before walking ahead with Markus a few steps. "However, a preemptive strike would be advised, yes?"

Markus nodded, signaling the others to help. "If you can do something along those lines."

Regis and Alya readied their weapons, a mace and a sword respectively, while the others raised their guard. The two signaled that they were ready too before Ihsan winked. The Qalairn raised a hand and snapped his fingers. Suddenly, a small gale began to swell, focusing around the two, before it grew bigger and more intense. The group watched as the wind picked up, becoming a fierce tornado that blew away the stones and wood, causing cries of pain to be heard.

"That must be them," Alya said.

"Very possibly. Let's see." Ihsan intensified the focus of the wind, causing the howling whirlwind to focus on the area around the men in uniform, with dust and ash from the ground being swept up, pelting the confused soldiers. "Got them!"

"Not quite yet!" Markus pointed to a small group of soldiers who managed to rise up, while their allies were still bewildered. Turning to his forces, Markus roared. "Everyone, after them! Charge!"

"Attack!" one of the men roared as he and his allies charged, their weapons raised and their courage high.

Markus deftly avoided being skewered by a lance when he jumped into the fray, grabbing the shaft of the spear and pulling it away from his attacker. Retaliating swiftly, Markus struck the assailant in the face with his palm, knocking them unconscious.

While Markus engaged a few members of the group, others began to target Ihsan, drawing near to him and trying their best to attack. One man swung a large club, hoping to catch Ihsan unaware, only for Regis to knock the opponent back with a swing of his mace.

Once Ihsan was safe, the Qalairn was quick to activate his magic, using a spell to generate an orange burst of energy, which obliterated the weapons of his foes on contact before Ihsan kicked his assailant away.

While the battle initially went smoothly, the tide turned as several Wynverians fell. Even with their greater size and numbers, the enemies managed to wait patiently for openings when attacked and exploiting even the slightest missteps. As three of his men fell to the ground, Markus felt the threat of defeat draw nearer, growing sharp as he barely ducked an enemy's sword swing. The bright blade sang as it cut through the air Markus had stood in a moment earlier. Markus only hoped the superior strength he and the Wynverians possessed would turn the tide, along with Ihsan's potent magic.

"Everyone, move!" Ihsan bellowed before focusing his magic. There was suddenly a bright flash coming from his birthmark and his eyes darkened. There was a great gust forming, blowing around ash and smoke, taking everyone by surprise.

The enemies tried to attack when they realized Ihsan was the source of the growing gale, but the Wynverians managed to intercept any attacks aimed at Ihsan, until at last the Qalairn unleashed the gathered tempest, the blowing wind targeting the Elustrians and flooring them.

"That's some advanced magic," Markus marveled as he and the others disarmed and restrained their foes.

Ihsan humbly bowed before assisting in securing their foes. "We have quite a few captives."

"Yes, we do." Markus felt smug satisfaction as they struggled against their restraints, the Wynverian soldiers rounded up most, though some still tried to fight and resist. "You may as well stop, it's over."

A woman with red hair glared intensely at Markus as she struggled against two Wynverians who were hoisting her up. "We will *never* quit! Our mission is too important!"

"Why not tell us about that?" Markus asked, feigning kindness before motioning for his men to stop. "Tell me about it." The enemy soldiers grew silent and stone faced; none of them gave even the slightest response, least of all the woman Markus spoke to.

"It seems their silence speaks volumes," Ihsan stated. "Perhaps we should take them elsewhere?"

"Yes, they need to be detained and interrogated. Send a messenger out. For now, we prepare."

About an hour later, the interrogations were underway. The Elustrians had been separated into different areas, distanced from their fellows and each being spoken to by a single Wynverian soldier, save for Markus and his two guards. With each Elustrian alone, they could not rely upon solidarity or the support of their fellows. The interrogations largely proved fruitless, however. It didn't matter how long they were spoken to or if coercion was used, there was no credible information gained. A few Elustrians were taken back, obviously bloodied or injured by their guards.

Markus was uneasy with the show of force and simply hoped for compliance from their captives, but after three hours of interrogations his patience was thin. In particular, Markus was doing his best to deal with a young soldier who was holding his silence.

"You have to realize that if you don't cooperate this is all over for you. You might live if you give us some information."

The soldier remained silent, his brown eyes trained on Markus.

"The Wynverians aren't going to be too happy after all of this is over, understandably, but you have a chance to get out of this war and live," Markus said sympathetically. "If you do this, maybe you can save your friends too."

"I'd rather die for Raleigh than live a traitor. It would be an honor." The young man didn't avert his gaze from Markus. "You'll get nothing from me."

"Then I suppose I can do nothing for you." Markus stared at the two Wynverians with him. "Take him."

"Hold on a moment..." said a raspy, rough voice. Markus turned until he saw the owner of the voice, an approaching man. His thin body was partially covered by tattered rags he wore. The emaciated, gaunt man did not seem to be in pain, however, but possessed with determination walked forward. The most striking thing about the stranger was how the long shock of white hair hung from his head. While the mostly gray hairs were neat and had a sheen to them, his white hairs hung limply and fell to the side of his head, remaining unkempt. The stranger walked around barefoot, with wrappings to his ankles and wrists, on his waist was a large bag, which made a noise as it moved, one that sounded like rattling.

Markus felt a chill as the man walked up, with the stranger's jet-black eyes were focused, though, despite the bags from tiredness beneath them. "Who are you?" Markus asked. He noticed the restrained enemies seemed unnerved by the stranger, and somehow he couldn't quite blame them.

"Dante." The man walked nearer before looking at the captured young man intensely. He didn't react at all to the captive's repulsed expression, or the stares he received from the disturbed Wynverians. "I'm familiar with these men and I desire to assist."

"How do you know about them?" Markus asked. "I was approached by their master, a man called Raleigh. He asked if I would aid his side and I refused."

"A wise decision." Markus was still unsure what to make of the man. "How did you find us?"

Dante cast his gaze towards Markus. "I followed the Elustrians. Still, I can tell they are giving you difficulty."

"Yes...I need them to inform us of their intentions for the safety of Wynveria."

Dante was quiet for a time, his expression unchanging, and yet Markus felt as if Dante was giving the largest of grins. "I could assist, if Wynveria would reward my efforts."

Markus noticed the Elustrian seated nearby seemed to be fearful of Dante, his hairs all standing on end at the sight of him. Markus began to consider it, as well as what might be the best way to get information. Eventually, Markus made his decision. "If you can guarantee useful information, I'll personally make sure you're rewarded."

"Good." Dante stood, keeping his gaze on the enemy before he raised his hand in the direction of the captive. "This will only take a moment."

Markus wondered what was going on, when he saw that the captive was starting to pale. The Heofonite began to wonder if the man was that afraid of Dante, when he realized that the captive was starting to cough. At first it seemed like an odd coincidence, when he began to cough up blood.

"Where is Raleigh?" Dante asked.

"I won't tell," the young man coughed, only to let out even more blood.

"That's no answer," Dante said calmly. "Tell me."

The man tried to stay silent, but his veins were showing and he began to shake. "He's back in our homela-" The captive stopped mid-sentence, biting his tongue until he drew blood.

"No lies, either," Dante chided. "The truth."

Markus felt fear creep upon him as he heard the man groan and whimper, before at last speaking.

"He's with our main forces! They're making plans to recruit more allies in Wynveria."

"Thank you." Lowering his hand, Dante waited until the man's breathing calmed and he recovered. "Now, then, what else can you tell us?"

"Nothing! Erin would know!" The man looked at Markus. "The woman with the red hair, that's who knows our other plans."

"Then we question her next," Dante said before looking at Markus.

Markus instructed the Wynverians to take the man away and bring the woman called Erin in. The whole time, he was pensive, unsure of what had transpired. "Did...You curse him?"

"Not lethally."

"Then what happened?" Markus asked.

"A small hex for those unwilling to speak." Dante stood quietly for some time, seeing the concern on Markus' face. "If you cannot watch, I will get the information alone."

"N...No. This is war, and war has a cost; better the pain of one than death of many."

"Pragmatic."

Markus and Dante waited, until Erin was brought to them, her eyes widening when she saw Dante.

"You!" Erin gasped, taking a step back.

Dante nodded. "Me." He began to raise his hand, when Markus put his over it. "Hm?"

"Wait." The Guardian faced the woman. "Erin, was it? Speaking would be in your best interest."

"I'd rather die than tell you what I know!" Erin proclaimed defiantly.

"We'll see about that." Once more, Dante raised his hand as Markus looked on in quiet discomfort.

* * *

When the interrogations had ended, Markus had gathered his inner circle and introduced them to Dante. After explaining the deal that had been brokered, Markus also explained what they had learned.

"Does this Raleigh really intend to try to conquer Wynveria?" Ihsan asked.

Dante faced Ihsan. "The man told me as much himself. He made it clear he was a figure to be feared, though it was already quite apparent. With each country he visits, he adds to his army, leaving the countries he defeated with rulers who are loyal to him and his cause, all of them funding his campaign and sending their strongest with him."

"Why?" Markus asked, unable to fathom Raleigh's motivations. "What could he possibly gain from killing so many people? Taking over one country is already an incredible amount of power, so why take so many and not even rule them personally?"

Dante gave a dry, humorless laugh. "Some appetites cannot be satisfied, but his is not a hunger for rulership; The man seeks a challenge, not power."

"Which explains why he came to Wynveria," Regis said. "Queen Zelina must be his target, since she's the mightiest among us."

"Then I feel pity for the ruler of Wynveria," Dante said simply.

Markus glared at Dante. "If Raleigh thinks he can take over Wynveria, he better think again! Queen Zelina is too strong to die to him."

Dante matched Markus' glare. "So you say, but we will see." Dante looked to Markus. "Will you inform the Queen?"

"Of course. We better tell General Nersel first, though." Markus looked to Alya and Regis. "Will you two help Dante to find his rations? We've put off eating long enough and everyone must be hungry about now."

"You can count on us," Alya said before gesturing to Dante. "Follow me."

Shortly after, Dante left along with Regis and Alya, leaving Markus with Ihsan who seemed curious.

"Something wrong, Ihsan?" Markus asked.

"He has quite curious magic. When it flows through him, it's unlike anything I've seen."

"You could sense his magic?" Markus asked. "When?"

"Twice, presumably during interrogations. It wasn't far off so I could feel it easily. I have to say, a man like him could make for a useful ally."

"He could be, but I'm not sure I trust him," Markus muttered to Ihsan. "He claims to know Raleigh and the Elustrians know him. For all we know he could make a habit of treachery."

"One can never know, but the enemy of my enemy is my friend," Ihsan said. "Besides, isn't his business concluded once you relay the information?"

"True." Markus began to rub his temples; he still felt his stomach churning from seeing Dante's hexes up close. To call them unsettling would be a severe understatement. "We can at least keep an eye on him, should all else fail."

"Of course, my friend!" Ihsan nodded to his ally, confirming. "For now, we have captives to take in, right?"

"Right. Let's get to it." Markus rose. "We eat and then we make preparations to leave. We've got a long trip ahead."

* * *

After asking confirming with a messenger, they had found out that General Nersel had stationed himself and his men at Joyeuce Keep. It took them a few hours, considering they had to fly the captives in as well and they had to fly out of the range of the enemy. As it had turned out, Joyeuce was under siege already, but thankfully the group was able to go inside the keep without incident.

General Nersel was happy to hear that Markus' group had returned with no casualties, and with valuable captives and information. Soon, the others were given a moment's rest before they had to assist in making sure the keep did not fall during the siege.

Markus noticed the keep was heavily fortified after he had taken time to explore, and that the soldiers who had been combatting the invaders were constantly on alert. Surprisingly to Markus, the keep had large halls and, curiously, some of the ceilings were made of wood, resembling drawbridges. The curious architecture only held Markus' attention for a short time before Nersel spoke with him and asked him into his war room, along with Dante and Ihsan.

Once all three gathered, General Nersel gestured for them to sit. "I have to admit, taking those soldiers alive is quite the feat."

"I have our entire team to thank for this, as well as Dante and Ihsan for the help they provided."

"Yes, it was truly invaluable. Because of your actions and the intelligence that Dante and the captives gave us, we know much more about our enemy than we did previously." General Nersel sighed. "We've also been able to corroborate some rumors we gained from spies of our own."

"Such as what?" Ihsan asked.

"Such as that their leader is a man called Raleigh, the general of the Tyre Empire and its many provinces."

"'Many provinces'?" Markus asked.

"Yes." Dante turned to the others. "Tyre is a nation from Elustria, said to have been a poor, starving plot of land. It eventually managed to rally its people and overtook another country, and so on and so forth...Gradually growing into a large nation and calling its conquests provinces."

"You know from being there?" Markus asked. Dante nodded. "I had consultations with some of Raleigh's men. They're very loyal to him, and vice versa."

General Nersel looked out a nearby window to the army outside. "...Perhaps we could use that to our advantage."

"What do you mean?" Markus asked.

"If he would be foolhardy enough to try to storm this place, it means we can make a trap for him and his men. According to our intelligence, Raleigh himself won't be here for another five days, so that gives us more than enough time to prepare."

"Excellent." Markus smiled, glad to see things were coming together. "Please, let me know how I can help!"

"You can help by assisting in defending this keep. It will take all of us to make sure the Elustrian Army goes no further than where they are now."

"You have my word, General," Markus said before bowing. He then looked at his two companions. "What about you, Ihsan? Dante? Neither of you are formally part of the war, but we would appreciate your continued assistance."

Ihsan shook his head. "I must go. I was originally looking for my friend and I need to be sure she is well. Although I am glad I volunteered to help, this is where I must leave."

"Your friend?" Markus asked.

Ihsan nodded. "Noaveme. The matter is a bit personal, but I don't want her caught up in this war if possible."

"We understand. Then we'll send you off with a map and rations when this siege settles," Nersel said. "I would spare more if I could."

"Any hospitality is appreciated," Ihsan said warmly.

"It's the least we could do," Markus said with a smile, before looking to the gaunt man. "What about you, Dante?"

"My business is mine alone. I will, however, expect my reward when opportunity presents itself."

"Thanks," Markus replied flatly, somewhat bothered by Dante's bluntness. "Well, I'll be ready to help as soon as I can, General."

"Of course. That will be all for now, I will send for you when it is time." Nersel then bade each of them farewell before departing.

Ihsan was the next to stand, but he extended a hand to Markus. "It seems our road together ends soon."

"Sadly. Still, however short it was, I enjoyed your company. It means a lot to me that you stayed with me when I needed support the most. I won't forget you." Markus took Ihsan's hand.

"I know you won't." Ihsan gave a nod to his friend. "I just hope we can meet again, soon."

Dante scoffed, but for the first time that Markus or Ihsan had seen, the man smiled. "Such bonds. I do hope they last. Lives may end, but friendships can last an eternity." Without another word, Dante departed.

"Well, that was...Odd." Ihsan shrugged. "Nonetheless, perhaps some drinks to end the night? Regis and Alya are waiting."

"Of course," Markus said with a smile. "Just one, though."

"Heh, speak for yourself, friend." Ihsan said. "I could use a few to help end the night."

Markus laughed, but nodded as the two of them went to join their allies. By then, Markus was in much better spirits and hoped that all would end well in the war.

However, the next day would be filled with new struggles.

* * *

The approach of Elustria's reinforcements was seen from miles away. The invaders did not try to be stealthy or secretive. Rather, they sought to garner the attention of the Wynverian forces that would soon face them the hue of their armor evoking freshly spilled blood on the battlefield. As the fighting force drew near in great number, marching in unison, Wynverians took notice.

The warriors within the keep were organizing themselves. Battle would be upon them soon and they needed to be proactive, or else they would be defeated. While the warriors began gathering their weapons and falling into order, Markus stopped what he was doing to assist.

Markus had spent most of the morning helping prepare the fortifications, having heard the enemy was moving nearer. The work went smoothly, but the growing knot in his stomach was a sign of worry and despair. It didn't matter how bravely or fiercely the Wynverians fought, the Elustrians seemed endless, and the morale of those within the fortress was low, judging by how much dread the proud warriors carried with them. The despair was palpable and had only grown as word of the upcoming battle pervaded the fort.

As Markus hoisted another barrel of arrows to the wall, trying not to give in to the growing dismay, he spotted Ishan and a sentry coming towards him, looking grim. "What's happening?" he asked, sweat on his brow from his constant labor.

"Guardian Markus, the enemy forces will be upon us within the hour," the sentry said, his voice resolute but starting to crack. "Judging by their numbers...We most likely will not last through the night. By General Nersel's orders, you are to take word to Arachon and Her Majesty about these grave tidings. You leave immediately, so say your goodbyes."

"But wait, what about Ihsan, Regis, Alya and the rest of my men?" Markus asked, taken aback by the orders and not wanting to leave his companions. "We're a unit."

"The general needs them. You must understand and go!"

"He will shortly. I just need a moment to speak with him." Ihsan stared at the sentry who nodded before joining his fellow soldiers. "Markus, perhaps it's best that you leave now."

"What?! But what about you and the others? Or even Dante?" Markus asked. "I'm a Guardian, and my duty-"

"Your duty is to Wynveria, if you told me correctly," Ihsan said sternly. "Now's no time for heroics or trying to be noble for nobility's sake. I know you want to protect us but protect Wynveria first. Go, and we'll care for ourselves. You have the information General Nersel gave you?"

"Yes," Markus said, realizing Ihsan's words rang true.

"Good...Then trust we will see each other again, my friend, and here." Ihsan's eyes changed colors once more as he placed a hand on Markus' armor. It took a few moments, but there was a glow as a sigil appeared on Markus' armor. "A charm to give you a tailwind, to speed you along."

"Thank you," Markus said gratefully. Despite his distrust of magic, Ihsan's kindness and care had begun to change Markus' mind. "I'll make good use of it."

"I know you will. For now, go. Leave this place and the others' safety to me."

Despite his instincts, Markus obliged and decided to make his escape as soon as he could. Running as fast as he could, past the others, Markus made his way to the highest tower. Once there, he looked and saw the many Elustrians, gasping at their sheer numbers. As far as he could see, there were soldiers adorned in their crimson armor, faced down by a smaller contingent of Wynverians, many of whom were in their dragon forms.

Markus could see trap doors opening across the fort, letting out more transformed Wynverians, roaring mightily as they flew to the approaching army. He stared in awe and fear as the battle began in earnest but remembered his purpose. Steeling himself, he stood firm and jumped before taking flight, away from the army, from Joyeuce Keep, and towards Arachon and Zelina. All he could do was hope that he flew fast enough and that the others made it out alive.

However, his hopes were doomed from the start.

* * *

Once Markus was gone, Ihsan decided to look for Dante, fearing for the mysterious mage's safety. He searched extensively, asking who he could, but he found that Dante had already left, perhaps in the chaos of the impending battle. Deciding his next best course of action was to find General Nersel, Ihsan left to find him.

Unbeknownst to Ihsan, General Nersel stood at the top of one of the castle's towers, overlooking the scene of battle, along with a cadre of archers, including Regis. Nersel watched grimly as his men faced Raleigh's forces, the number of combatants in the enemy number truly staggering him.

His men had flown down in dragon form, spewing fire down on the field, however Raleigh's men were talented marksmen, shooting the Wynverians in their wings to send them crashing to the cruel ground below. Nersel had watched two dozen of his men go out and battle, nearly none of them coming out.

"The Elustrian army is fierce, to be sure," Regis said, a twinge of fear in his voice as he readied a bow.

Nersel nodded. "That they are, but ferocity dies in the face of a superior force, one way or another." Nersel then signaled his bowmen, while the next wave of Wynverians flew above the loosed volley. "On my command, shoot!" Soon, Nersel signaled, and a hail of arrows darkened the sky for a moment as hundreds of projectiles flew through the air.

However, the Elustrians were prepared. Operating as one, they braced, raising their shields around them to block the rain of arrows. The arrows managed to make their way through some openings in the enemy's defense. There were cries of pain and many fell dead, further destabilizing their guard as their men fell.

"Now, we rain fire upon them!" Nersel commanded as a dozen of the Wynverians gathered, Regis included, began to change, taking their dragon forms as they stood at the top of the keep's walls. They flew, going lower than anticipated, all while Raleigh's forces tried their best to lower their shields.

Soon, the flying Wynverians spewed their hot, burning breath upon their enemies. The arrows that had been dipped in pitch caught fire. The flames produced by dragons were already hotter than those of natural fires. While the shields were already growing almost too hot to hold, with the pitch the combined heat made the shields start to melt. Many succumbed to the burning hell their surroundings had become, falling in defeat or dropping their shields. Even for the more resilient, the lumps of burning metal soon grew too hot to bear and scores of Raleigh's men perished from the extreme temperatures, while many more struggled to flee, their armor almost burning them even after they escaped.

Nersel gave a satisfied grin. The fire would at least slow down Raleigh's forces and make them think twice, however, that was when he noticed something else, further off into the distance. What he saw made him blanch, the color draining from his face rapidly as dread took hold of him. "It can't be…"

Off in the distance, he could see several catapults, the war machines rolling closer to Joyeuce Keep. It had been inconceivable to Nersel that they could construct any or transport them without notice, much less move them up the mountains. As the stones flew through the air, his heart sank. The tide had certainly turned, but for the worse.

* * *

Ihsan and a handful of soldiers were on the run as the Elustrian army overran the fort. Nersel was nowhere in sight, but the Wynverians were fighting hard. Walls had been demolished, bodies from warriors on both sides littered the ground.

There was no interest in capture, surrender was ignored. There was only slaughter and chaos, as Regis and a few other unfortunate Wynverians discovered. Many Wynverians fought bravely, taking down their crimson clad enemies, but most of them joined their brethren and the droves of enemies on the ground as corpses.

Ihsan breathed heavily, his lungs burning as he ran towards the dungeon, trying not to watch the battle or listen to the roars and cries of war outside. He had never found Dante and suspected he was long dead or caught trying to escape. Ihsan's only leverage was the group of prisoners they held, which hopefully a commander in Raleigh's forces would trade for the safety of some of the people within the fort. If he could not run, Ihsan thought exchanging the lives of the Elustrians captured for his own and the survivors' might work.

"It utterly astounds me," Ihsan said tiredly as he stood outside the cells, speaking to himself as much as the captives.

"That your scaled friends fell before General Raleigh?" One of Raleigh's men taunted from behind the bars.

Ihsan shook his head as he caught his breath. "No, that they'd sacrifice more of their men to get back a small handful. It's tactically unsound, almost suicidal."

"Perhaps, but then again we all knew death would come for us the moment we donned our armor and joined the war," the same soldier said. "Even if our brothers die, we'll fight and die so they can continue to promote the glory of-"

"Yes, yes. You are fanatics. Lovely." Ihsan suddenly heard a sound, he raised a hand and summoned magic forth, only to see that it was Nersel, bleeding heavily from his side. "General!"

"Ah...Ihsan, was it?" The general coughed, holding his wound before rushing in, holding a bloodied saber, his armor deeply scratched and his face smeared with lingering dust. "Are you alright?"

"Fine enough. Where are your men?" Ihsan asked.

"Most are dead, some deserted....We only have a few, but I posted some men outside this room. I would say we can count less than thirty among us...These prisoners are our last hope to escape alive."

"Trading them was the plan...I hope we can manage it." Ihsan still prepared his magic, the symbol on his right shoulder glowing as his eyes went black. "Otherwise, this won't be fun."

"I'm sorry, was I missing when this was fun?" Nersel chucked darkly.

"I guess we both were." Ihsan smiled back, knowing it very well could be his last smile. That was when there were noises, grunts, cries of pain, and at last the approach of footsteps. At last, a whole horde of Raleigh's men were present, at least a dozen stormed the room, before at last Ihsan loosed his magic. "BEGONE!"

Suddenly, the glow on Ihsan's mark disappeared, and there was a blinding flash from his palm. There was an explosion of force and energy, something indescribable came forth, blasting the very wall and obliterating the men, Ihsan's breathing heavily again. The spellcaster was visibly sweating, dust coating the perspiration on his brow and over his body. Ihsan was still standing, though he shook a few times before regaining his bearings and steadying himself.

"Impressive, but pointless..." A confident male voice said, "You killed a few of our men, sadly, but given yourself away...Which is why our army does not employ mages." The man strode forward, still obscured by the dust cloud. "They're powerful, but such a liability when riled. For example, they could blast open an entire doorway, possibly disturbing a building's integrity."

"Enough babble," a young, female voice said. Then, suddenly, Ihsan felt the harsh, sharp pain as an arrow entered his arm and another his abdomen. He couldn't focus, much less stand. He looked over to see Nersel was already on the ground, bleeding out, the arrows piercing his arm and part of his chest.

From the dust walked out a man with rust colored hair, cut short and kept trim. He had an oddly warm smile, but it came with an air of smug self-assurance. His eyes were focused, like a tiger eyeing its prey hungrily. With a single dagger in hand, he pointed to Nersel's body. "It seems you finished off this one, I wonder what spoils he left for us..."

"Don't be a vulture, Tiernan. It really does not suit you."

"Shary, if you insist on not claiming spoils, someone else will. For example, I think I spy something now..." Tiernan drew closer to Nersel's body, seeing it was dead before picking up his blade. "Ah! A weapon of fine make, fresh from a battle. Perhaps I can find the sheathe for it?"

"Leave his body alone!" Ihsan managed to roar, despite his pain. He was panting, but there the was suddenly a crossbow aimed at his face. Looking up, he saw that it was a woman with long, braided black hair and mossy green eyes. Her clothing had some chainmail for protection, covering her chest beneath a coat she wore, but her arms and legs were covered by light, flexible armor. Her outfit was deep red, with bright silver trim, well-polished and battletested.

"Quiet, unless you want to join him." She then directed her attention to a soldier who drew near. "You, help break down the cells and free the men."

"Yes, Captain Auchmere." A soldier rushed to the cell, looking for a way around, when he heard a whistle.

"The departed general has keys on hand. Perhaps one of these will help." Tiernan tossed the keys to the underling.

"Thank you, Captain Raye."

"No problem...Aha!" Tiernan found the scabbard and turned his attention to Shary. "So, then, we should make sure the survivors are rounded up and given to our great leader."

Shary rolled her eyes before focusing them back on Ihsan. "And this one? He's half dead."

"Then send him the rest of the way. It may take him out of his misery."

Ihsan could only grimace as the woman stared him down, crossbow still leveled at him. "That it may..."

With little opportunity to escape, Ihsan grimaced, feeling defeat and the nearness of death.

* * *

Weeks later, Queen Zelina sat upon her throne, her fingers interlocked as she rested her head against them, feeling pensive. Her gaze was cast downward as she thought about the recent loss they had suffered. News had spread that Wynveria was in a full-blown invasion, and what was worse was that their foes were still making progress towards their Arachon.

Battle plans had been discussed, troops had been mobilized, and Zelina was dispensing more spies, yet there were rumors that more Errant Broods were siding with Raleigh, who decimated those who refused and rewarded greatly those who joined the Elustrians. In mere days, and armed with more knowledge of Wynveria, there had been reports of as many as two dozen villages attacked in the past few days, and most of them destroyed. There had been a large number of refugees trying to get inside Arachon, so much so that the great city was starting to become quite full, with almost all the inns and shelters filled to capacity.

Thoughts of worry entered Zelina's mind; Wynverians spent so much time trying to prove themselves as strong warriors, yet now another strong force came in and was causing them plenty of trouble. Her people's pride was on the line, but more importantly, their country and their lives. Every inch of the Queen wanted nothing more than to go find the warlord and put a stop to his warmongering ways, but she couldn't. Too much was at stake for her to go out at the moment, and she was waiting on news.

As Zelina continued to think, there was the sound of someone opening the door. Zelina saw that it was Delys and motioned for her to draw near. "Is there any news?"

"Some. Our friend, Markus, is back. He wants to give you some information when you have time, milady."

Zelina was surprised, but pleased. She had not expected him to return until the conflict was over, though she was very worried that he might meet his end on the battlefield. "Send him in immediately." Zelina could already feel herself begin to anticipate the worst. If Markus was back, what news could he possibly bring?

In due time, the Heofonite approached, his expression was one of relief. "Queen Zelina, I have news from the front lines!"

"What information do you have?" Ever since Markus had first returned with his letter about the Elustrians, she had mobilized her forces to combat them. Even so, the battles had been uphill, with heavy losses even when battles were won. Zelina noticed that since the battles had begun, Markus' own optimism was beginning to wane.

"The Elustrians near the valley villages have been routed, but many others have fallen to larger forces, with Raleigh leading them personally." Markus retained his grim expression before looking to Zelina quickly. "I've submitted a report with further details."

"I see." Zelina scowled as she recalled when Markus first returned and told her of Raleigh; When he had returned, she felt it was good to finally put a name to the threats that had been plaguing her and her land, but he remained a source of fear and concern ever since. "What other news do you have?"

"From the other battles against him and his forces on different fronts, so far we've managed to repel them more often than not, but a certain group of his is making steady progress toward Arachon. If it keeps up they will reach us here in no time."

Upon hearing the news, Zelina's eyes practically burned with horror and indignation. "Our forces should be more than ready. If this Raleigh seeks a challenge, he's a fool to challenge the Wynverians in their own domain."

"No doubt the advancing force is the group Raleigh is traveling with." Markus' expression remained firm and contemplative.

Zelina was silent, she gripped the armrest of her throne as she thought "No doubt, but if we defeat him it should hurt his army's morale."

"And improve our odds," Markus stated, his eyes focused and his will strengthening once more. "What should we do?"

"We make a plan. Once their leader is out of commission they'll become less stable, and maybe even give up this conquest entirely. Now, go gather my strategists. We'll work with them to come up with a plan of action."

Markus bowed. "As you command, Queen Zelina." The Heofonite turned to go to the door.

"Also, Markus."

"Yes?"

"I am pleased that you made it back safely again. I ask that in the coming conflicts you serve at my side, so I can call upon you for counsel."

"It is my duty and it would truly be an honor," Markus said sincerely.

"Good...Now, as you were."

Obeying, Markus bowed once more to the monarch before exiting. Once he closed the door, he went to gather the tacticians and brought them to Zelina for planning.

After the meeting had been adjourned, Zelina was still inside the throne room by herself, wondering if facing the foe directly was the way to go about this.

Despite their best efforts, Raleigh was still winning more battles than she felt comfortable with, and she could only face him on so many fronts for so long. She knew that they had enough people to fight the war and they could certainly block paths and still travel with their ability to fly, but she had to prioritize the defeat of their leader. Once Raleigh was defeated, it would simultaneously bolster her people's morale and crush that of the Elustrians.

Taking a calming breath, Zelina smiled, reaffirmed and certain that she and her allies would resolve the issue at hand. Zelina only hoped that a decisive win would keep the tide of war in her favor, and soon.

* * *

Markus felt a sense of nervousness and concern as he considered his upcoming report. It was difficult enough trying to help the Wynverians and feeling helpless as he struggled to only save a handful of lives, but it was another to covertly report to Heofonia without telling Zelina. As Markus looked at the crystal, he felt torn. He thought it would be simple for Heofonia to literally swoop in and aid the Wynverians, however he was told that Heofonia would not intercede as they waited for the conflict to unfold. Nonetheless, he was charged to give reports and to contact the scribe who was assigned to him. Markus only hoped she would take the information and make something useful of it. After making contact, he saw the crystal he had been given turn clear before revealing the face of a Heofonite with raven black hair and pale skin. He didn't recognize her, however he decided to speak first. "Hello? This is Markus."

The other Heofonite looked back to him, her expression bored. "Guardian Markus, this is Helah. I'll be your scribe for this update."

"Good. I'm reporting in from Wynveria."
"Wynveria? Not one of the principalities?" Helah became more attentive, paying attention to Markus.

"Yes," he replied, noticing the awed look on her face. "I-"

"I'm impressed. I've actually never been outside of Heofonia." Helah smiled somewhat, apparently lost in thought. "What's it like on the surface?"

Markus grew somber. "It's beautiful, normally, but not lately."

"Really? Maybe I can learn more, but for now what will I be recording for you today?" she asked as she produced a quill and parchment.

"I have a report on the war in Wynveria," Markus said to her grimly. "Recent sites of destruction, casualties, and other matters of great importance."

"A war?" Helah paused, surprise in her voice. Clearing her throat, she stood up straighter and looked at him. "My apologies."

"You didn't know, but maybe you can pass a message along? To the Sovereign? Someone who can provide aid?"

"I'll do my best," Helah replied, her voice firm. "For now, tell me all you can."

"Very well." Markus began to relay the recent events to Helah, telling her of everything he had said to Zelina and the plans Heofonites had for their counter attacks. He saw her write quickly, doing her best to jot everything down, but he noticed towards the end there was a look of concern on her face. "Helah? Is something wrong?"

"You mentioned the Elustrians are the opponents?" Helah asked, concerned.

"Yes. Why? Have you heard of them before today?"

"I'm a researcher. I know a bit about their history, but I've heard talk that Guardians were also sent to Elustria."

Markus felt confusion wash over him; he had never heard of contact between Elustria and Heofonia. "Sent to combat them?"

"No, to offer them an alliance."

Markus froze. "How long ago?"

"A few months ago. I transcribed a document that was to be delivered to a man named Raleigh there, the leader of their military forces."

"Helah, what was in that document?" Markus asked,

"An offer to be assigned a Guardian, but they declined according to reports I overheard," Helah explained to him.

"Makes sense they would. Warmongers like Raleigh and his subjects don't care for negotiations at all, just conquest," Markus asserted.

"Raleigh. Not his subjects," Helah replied harshly. "What do you mean? Elustria is our enemy." "Officially, they're only Wynveria's enemy, and you mean their army specifically. Being so quick to say another culture is one thing is the easiest way to blind yourself. Yes, their leader may be a warlord, but they are people of a flawed nation, the same as us."

"But...Heofonia isn't the same as every place else. We're trying to help spread peace and unite people."

"And you really think our people are the only ones who want that?" Helah asked him.

"N...no. After seeing Wynveria I think they want something similar, or to live in peace, but things are so different."

"Free, you mean?"

"Helah, we are free. We live by guidelines that keep Heofonia safe."

"So you say," Helah replied.

Markus looked at her, startled by how she sounded. "You don't approve of Heofonia's ways?"

Helah merely shook her head, visibly disappointed with Markus. "I believe I've said all I should, but Markus...Best of luck on your quest, and I hope this experience does open your eyes."

"If I survive it, I hope so too." Afterwards, Markus closed communication. Letting her words linger and thinking on them, he began to pack, wondering what he could do to help.

* * *

Zelina and Markus' journey was relatively quiet as they and the squadron Zelina travelled with flew into battle. While everyone was on guard, Zelina had confidence their scouts would alert them of any trouble. Instead, she decided to focus on making sure she was mentally prepared, not only to fight, but to lead her people and keep them from losing morale. She tried to remember the lessons from her youth, where she learned fear and dread could destroy an army faster than any mortal foe.

For a few more hours they flew, passing over mountains and towns, with other Wynverians flying off beneath them towards Arachon, or those without the ability to fly journeying in groups. Her people were scurrying like mice away from cats, but she would be damned if she wouldn't protect them.

After some time, the group made camp on a mountain top. It was cold there, snow blanketing the ground, though the Wynverians were used to rocky ground, and from so high it was unlikely that their enemies would come for them.

At the camp, Zelina was back to her human form, sitting within her tent. She had finished a war council earlier, and their plan of attack was set. The only issue was that with Joyeuce Keep captured, it meant that many of her own soldiers had fallen. She began to feel guilty that Nersel and so many others had died, but she knew she had to bury that guilt and protect all they had died for, honoring their sacrifice.

As she began to go over the intelligence that Nersel had gathered one more time, there was a knock on the post that had been set outside of Zelina's tent. "Yes?"

"Queen Zelina?" Markus' voice was calling to her. "May I enter?"

Zelina sighed before carefully putting away the notes and walking towards the exit. Once she was outside she stared down to Markus. "What is it you need?"

"Oh, sorry, Your Majesty. I was just coming by to see how you are."

"As well as I can be." Zelina noticed Markus was shivering, the cold bothering him as the outside winds blew. "And yourself?"

"The same. Still, I hope it isn't a bother, but I notice you and some of the other Wynverians speaking another language."

"Yes, it's Dragontongue."

"Wait...Dragontongue is a language?"

"Yes. All Wynverians can speak it with ease when we change shape, but speaking it in our human forms is more difficult if we don't practice." Zelina opened the tent flap. "You may come inside, it is a bit too chilly to speak out here, unless you want to hold the rest of the conversation with you freezing."

"Thank you, Your Majesty."

"It is no problem, Markus." Zelina let him in, expecting the conversation might take some time.

Once they were both inside, Zelina saw Markus breathe a sigh of relief. It made her chuckle a little before she sat down on a stool she had brought with her. "Sit anywhere you would like."

Markus found a cushion that looked comfortable enough and, looking at Zelina for permission, sat down, keeping his eyes on the Queen. "I'm surprised at how warm this tent is, especially with all the snow outside."

"Thankfully, we use charmed tents, but even so, everyone else has long gotten used to the cold. That being said, no reason to eschew comfort when we can have it."

"That's smart," Markus praised, before he saw Zelina was offering him a drink. "What's this?"

"Ale. Just a little something to lift the spirits," Zelina took a drink from the cup.

"I don't know if I should; In Heofonia we're taught not to drink anything alcoholic, save in moderation on special days."

"Well, whether you drink or not is up to you. Still, why don't you at least try before you assume you won't like it?" Zelina asked curiously.

"Because it can lead to dependence," Markus stated plainly.

"Some people are like that, yes, but to assume that of everyone shows very little faith."

"Maybe, but it is all I have known," Markus admitted. "Since I came to Wynveria, I'm starting to realize things are different here."

"Things are different no matter what part of the globe you go to." Zelina took another, deep drink of her cup. "The world is a wide place, and what's normal for one person is different for another. You have to learn not to box everything as bad or good without context."

"Maybe…" Markus took his cup and drank at last, expecting it to feel the drink burn, but instead he just tasted the savory beverage. "It's not so bad."

"That's correct, but it's also not what you think it is," Zelina chuckled.

Markus took a second to take the drink again before making a realization. "Wait…this isn't alcoholic?"

"I never said it was." Zelina smirked impishly. "Just playing on your expectations."

Markus was embarrassed he had been tricked, but knew that he would have found it humorous if anyone else had fallen victim to Zelina's joke. "Well played, then." Markus took another drink himself. "Perhaps you really will become an actress when this is all over."

"True, though I doubt I'll be able to put on any productions any time soon. After all, there will be a lot to rebuild once we oust Raleigh and his followers."

"Well, when we do I know you'll make Wynveria everyone can enjoy."

"Thank you for the vote of confidence, Markus." Zelina smiled, glad to know that her new ally believed in her as much as her people did.

"It's no problem. Maybe I should consider my own dreams, too."

"Do you have any?" Zelina asked.

"I'm living mine," Markus said. "Helping Heofonia, aiding Wynveria, it gives my life meaning."

"Your life has meaning already, Markus, though that sounds like a duty more than a dream."

Zelina watched as he began to ponder the statement.

"It kind of is, but I'm happy with it." Markus gave a small, but genuine smile.

"Well, you should be. You're doing a fine job. Regardless, let me tell you about my acting dreams, if you don't mind."

"I'd love to hear more."

After that, Zelina and Markus continued to talk until late into the night, the two of them forgetting the war for a brief time and remembering that they each had someone to rely on.

* * *

The flight continued the next day with the Wynverian forces finally catching sight of Raleigh's men. Markus had been sent ahead to act as a scout high above, using his smaller figure to keep the wary enemies from noticing him, as they expected dragons.

When Markus returned, he was quick to detail the situation. "The enemies are going through a mountain pass. There aren't many paths in the direction they've gone and there's only one way out. If we can block it, maybe we can trap them there."

"Perhaps, but what if it is a trap?" a captain in the Wynverian army asked after she turned to face Zelina.

"Then we'll have to make sure that we're ready for them," Zelina commented. "Our best bet is to separate them from their larger weapons and then pick off the remaining foes from afar. In the chaos, I doubt they'll be able to counter and we can thin out their numbers."

"How, Your Majesty?" the captain asked.

"We'll need a few boulders to start with. Captain Grey, have your men gather them immediately. Markus, I want you and ten others to go block the end of that pass where it is narrowest. Everyone else, prepare for battle. Am I understood?" The queen's expression was stern, but she was hopeful. If they acted quickly, the advantage would be on their side.

"Yes, Queen Zelina," all said obediently.

As soon as they were able, Zelina's forces readied themselves, gathering all they needed. They flew low to the ground in a roundabout way, so as to avoid being spotted by their foes. Eventually, the group was ready and the plan was set into motion. Later flying far above, where they could not be sighted by Raleigh's men, they watched. She made sure that everyone was in position to attack, all of them clear on their parts to play. Finally, Zelina stood atop the canyon wall, watching the Elustrians and waiting for the perfect moment to attack.

"On my signal, then..." Zelina stared down, waiting until she was sure the enemy's guard was down before she gave the order to strike.

It started with dozens of dragons taking flight with great boulders clutched between their claws, their wingbeat echoing through the air. As they appeared before their foes, blitzing them, the Wynverians spread out to assail as many Elustrians as possible before releasing the boulders. The plummeting rocks fell like meteors from the heavens, their shadows growing much like the fear of their enemies below.

Cries of pain and death joined the crash of the boulders as many of the foe where crushed beneath them, throwing their ranks into disarray. What was more was that the great weapons were utterly splintered and fractured as the ballistae and catapults lay decimated with their operators. Ahead, more boulders were strategically dropped in the confusion to make the canyon impassible in front of and behind the scarlet clad invaders.

In moments, the Elustrians realized that the path behind them was blocked off, and that was when, many Wynverians from a second group rained down fire, while the archers, on either side of the canyon fired down. The Wynverians who had dropped the boulders had already flown out of the way as those who breathed flame and the archers went after those who still lived. The sky darkened again from so many arrows for a few moments before the flames brought a final light to the eyes of the Elustrians.

From above, Zelina looked down, seeing her foes start to panic, the acrid scent of burnt flesh billowing up as the storm of fire heated the cold air. She saw a handful had even tried to jump down from the path to the crags below, hoping to survive somehow rather than be burnt or skewered by arrows. As tragic as the sight could be, Zelina felt no pity for the invaders. Instead, she watched the rest of the assault until she saw that a few were firing arrows back in vain. "Finish them!" she roared. Part of Zelina wanted to turn from the carnage, but her men were watching, and the foes below were her enemies. They had shown no sympathies to the men they slaughtered, the women they murdered, or the children who had lost all they had along with their brief lives.

Zelina clenched a fist, fury welling up within her as she thought of her people and those who had lost their lives and safety. It didn't take long for sympathy to fade from her heart and for her to internally hope that their gods would damn them to worse suffering when they died.

And with a few final, precise shots and a great blaze of fire, the Elustrians were decimated. Her forces regrouped and looked down at the defeated and the dead. She turned from the sight to see her people before her, many of them in dragon form still.

"We continue our search. Let's ensure no others are on their way."

Afterwards, the others started to take flight high into the air once more, keeping a watch on the mountain scape below. Before the queen of the Wynverians changed too, she saw Markus draw near. "What is the matter?"

"Do you think Raleigh was in that group?"

"I sincerely doubt it. Such fortune would be too much to expect, and even then we have many more Elustrians to deal with," Zelina said firmly. "We'll have to take this slowly, one by one, until all fall."

"Yes…Queen Zelina," Markus replied.

Zelina could see he was wavering for but a moment, but she knew he would follow her regardless. "Check for any survivors, after, we will regroup and learn where they seek to strike next."

The time after the battle was quite tense. Even though there were few survivors and the group had destroyed many of their war machines, the reality was the Elustrian invaders were still numerous, and the Wynverians would have much harder battles ahead in order to fully oust their enemies.

* * *

After many weeks, Zelina and her army were located in the Devail Plains. It was one of the more level fields, not too far off from the mountain range that led to Arachon. Zelina's forces had settled there, as the pass they were camped at was the most likely one that any invaders would take, bordering on the only one passable for large groups.

Situated in one of the tents, sitting upon a cushioned chair at her table, Zelina began to go over a map. The walls of the tent had several other maps placed for reference, while several reports had been separated into piles, regarding if they were relevant or irrelevant. The bare minimum for comfort and effectiveness was within Zelina's tent as she looked out the tent's opening, seeing the gently falling snow.

Zelina was reading the reports, making sure the Elustrians were indeed on a route towards Devail. Sure enough, the reports were consistent, and the vast majority of those taking alternate routes had been routed or captured.

Feeling smug once she had discovered that they were on the right track, Zelina tried not to grow too cocky. It was a good sign, but she knew the Elustrians could grow dangerous if backed into a corner. Still, she had to remain ready. Walking around her tent, Zelina found her sword and lifted it.

It was a family keepsake and one that had been used by ruler after ruler in Wynverian history. While most swords that old would be ceremonial, much care was taken in preserving the weapon's utility. She merely hoped it would carry her to victory in battle.

In the past few days, several Wynverian forces across the area had coordinated and defeated most of the enemies before them. It took time and there were a few losses, and while there had been several casualties, the battles greatly favored the Wynverians as compared to the Elustrians, who were tired from travel and far less familiar with the area. Some Wynverians were impressed by how bravely their enemies fought, but they took great pride in their victories over the Elustrians, who were being overrun. Zelina was looking over the reports from the day, as well as messages that had been sent to her. There was news that the Elustrians had been repelled on several fronts, but there was also news that there was an uprising in the Errant Broods. Zelina could only assume that that they wanted to use the confusion in order to raise themselves up and upend the current rule, regardless of who won the war.

The queen of the dragons could only hope that they would also try to defeat Raleigh's forces as well. She awaited to hear more while thinking about how to find Raleigh and end the Elustrians' assault, when she noticed one of the captains drawing near.

"Captain Grey," Zelina said, addressing the captain.

"My liege, it looks like we've caught sight of Raleigh at last." Captain Grey stood at ready, waiting for the queen's response. The snow-white haired woman kept her aquamarine eyes on the queen.

"Have we?" Zelina asked, the news sounding too good to be true; there was certainly excitement in her voice, however she could feel a certain tension as she realized the enemy leader was nearby and that the next few decisions would be critical. "How do you know it is him?"

"Based upon reports from scouts and refugees who claimed to have seen him in person," Captain Grey went on. "Your Majesty, the intelligence we have makes it reasonable to identify the man we have located as Raleigh."

"I see. What can you tell me?"

"Only that it appears as though he is moving as covertly as possible. It seems it is only him as well as a few other soldiers traveling in a small group away from the mountains," Captain Grey reported. "Without his long-range weapons, he is quite clearly at a disadvantage."

"And if we crush him here and now, that will be that." Zelina thought on it. After so many struggles, Raleigh was there now, without a large force to battle alongside him. It felt almost too good to be true, but if there was a chance to end the suffering of her people and secure peace in her land, she would not think twice about taking it, or the bloody general's life. "Then the sooner we are rid of him the better. Tell everyone they are to prepare for battle."

"Of course, Your Majesty." Bowing, Captain Grey took her leave before leaving Zelina alone once more. The queen of the dragons was slow to move at first. She could not believe that after all the time she had invested in the war that Raleigh would be foolish enough to travel alone. From all that she had heard of his reputation he was a seasoned warrior and tactician, so endangering himself would be ill-advised. Then again, Zelina considered that it was his pride as a warrior pushing him to do something foolish and outlandish. The possibility was there, but she still planned to proceed with caution.

Picking up her ancestral sword, Zelina made sure that her armor was secure. When all of her followers were assembled and ready, the entire group took flight, the Wynverians and sole Heofonite now high in the sky.

Much later, the Wynverian army had several scouts scouring the path that Raleigh had been sighted on before returning some time later. The army itself had been seen not far off, found when the Wynverians were combing the area looking for the Elustrians. Once Zelina was satisfied that no support or reinforcements were behind the main army, they began to take stock of situation. Zelina made sure to collect the reports and confer with her commanders before she was satisfied enough to approve their attack. "Two dozen of us will head off Raleigh while the rest move into position to surround him. Given the location, he has very little choice save to surrender or be executed."

"Queen Zelina, can we not simply all strike at once?" Markus asked. "If you all used your flames or struck in dragon form, he would be defeated, even if he had his army to back him up."

Captain Grey shook her head. "Our enemy deserves a chance to surrender or challenge our leader to honorable combat. It is simply the Wynverian way."

"Captain Grey is correct. We shall face Raleigh our way, and should he resist, he will fall to us just as felled so many of our people." Zelina stared intently at the two. "Guardian Markus, Captain Grey, you both will join my group. Captain Goransson, you will command the others." Once Zelina was sure her orders were taken, she took a calming breath before focusing fully on the task ahead. "We leave now."

Obediently, both followed Zelina when she transformed, along with three others as they flew high in the sky. Once they were all above Raleigh, the dragons and the sky native all descended around the imposing warrior.

"Such a gathering for one man…I am insulted you did not bring more."

"You say as the Queen of Dragons stands before you," Zelina replied, her voice booming as she remained in dragon form.

Raleigh merely smiled and stepped closer to her. "The God of Dragons and perhaps a thousand more would please me."

Zelina, not rising to the taunt, changed back to her human form. The Wynverian queen then walked towards the man, determination in her stance and defiance in her eyes. The man before her was the one who had brought death and suffering to her people, and Zelina, containing her fury as best she could, was intent on exacting the same anguish on the warmonger. Even though Zelina herself was quite tall, the man was still a hulking figure, taller than even her; the muscles beneath his scarlet armor large enough to make any Wynverian or strongman envious as he cast a wide shadow. She smiled back ruefully. "And why would we aim so hard to please a dead man?"

Raleigh smiled and began to laugh. "Ah, I see your people banter almost as well as they fight. I am glad you Wynverians have not betrayed my expectations. Worthy opponents are so rare in my home continent and I desired to see what the world had to offer me."

"We may have offered you a friendly challenge had you merely arrived and asked to do battle with us, but you came for war. Now we offer you the chance to surrender or perish." Zelina's eyes remained locked on his, a cold fury dwelling within them.

"Such kind words, but I do not desire kindness from those who are not my allies. To counter your offer, I make one of my own," Raleigh announced proudly.

"And what is that?" Zelina questioned, unamused.

"The opportunity to swear fealty to me." Raleigh stood tall, staring Zelina directly in her eyes. "Your people have been as strong and resilient as the land in which they were born. I offer you an opportunity to serve Elustria, to become a follower of my banner. Should you and your people accept, no more blood will be shed from Wynverian veins. We shall join and split the spoils and glory of battles and wars waged on this continent, building a stronger world in the wake of the defeated."

Zelina was taken aback when she saw the warlord actually offered her his hand. As far as she could tell, he was serious. She could only stare in shock at him and his grandiose offer before snarling. Violently batting his hand aside, she began to breathe heavily, trying to control her rage as her breath came out like steam, making her enemy raise a brow. "You dare to invade my land, have my people slaughtered by the dozen, and come to me to offer to serve UNDER your empire? The only service we will give is allowing what remains of your rotten corpse burial once I am done! You'll pay for every drop of blood lost and every life cut short by your delusional actions!"

Raleigh sighed, retracting his hand and staring at Zelina as if nothing had happened. "Tsk. A shame, after I showed your warriors such respect."

"Says a man who claims to be a warrior but slays villagers! I have no respect for your people or your goals, and if any of your damned people come back after I'm done with you, I'll go to your homeland and return the favor!" Zelina roared, almost literally. "Now, we shall end this war."

"My war has only begun, queen. This skirmish is nothing compared to the contests to come." Raleigh drew his blade, pointing it at Zelina.

"We shall see." Zelina drew her own sword and stared down her opponent. "Are you ready to face a dragon's full might?"

"So long as you are prepared for the fight of your life." Wasting no more time, Raleigh struck, slashing downwards at Zelina.

The queen of dragons used her blade to block quickly, holding back the powerful blow and trying to force her opponent away. The might of the two warriors was very nearly even, however Raleigh's weapon was bigger, his intent was fiercer, and he had gravity on his side. Zelina could only hold him back for so long before she moved aside and drew her weapon away, separating from the clash readying herself for the next strike. Rushing in, Zelina attacked with a volley of quick stabs.

Zelina struck again and again, watching closely and reacting as Raleigh fended off her strikes. Yet Zelina was begrudgingly impressed as Raleigh fended off her strikes as, even with such a large blade, Raleigh moved much faster and more deftly compared to what she had expected. Stabbing with great might, Zelina managed to upset Raleigh's footing by making him stagger before taking the opportunity to strike him with a punch while he was unbalanced.

The veteran warrior's head snapped to the side as Zelina's fist smashed into it. The queen's face flashed with a triumphant smile as she struck the first successful blow, only for it to fade when Raleigh turned his head back, smirking with a bloody mouth. She pulled back her arm to punch again, but he acted swiftly, moving a hand from his sword, grabbing her wrist and roaring before ramming his forehead into her face violently within the span of a couple seconds.

The blonde ruler recoiled as her nose bled. She fought through the pain, letting anger fuel her as she wrested her arm away. She saw Raleigh raising his blade and, with her sword arm unprepared to strike, she opted to act swiftly and kneed Raleigh in the legs, making him falter. Moving back more and composing herself, she took a deep breath and roared before moving in to attack again, swinging her sword.

The scarlet clad warrior smirked as he swung his own blade, blood dripping from his nose further stained his clothing red. "You fight well, young queen!" Raleigh said, praising her despite how violently he fought. "You surely are powerful, but can you keep up?"

"I'll leave your body in the snow, you blood-soaked bastard!" Zelina pressed forward with her blade again, putting as much force as she could manage into repelling Raleigh before knocking him flat. She stabbed downwards, aiming to impale her foe, growling as Raleigh rolled to avoid it, her blade breaking the earth where his head had been. She saw Raleigh rise a short distance away, though he had dropped his great sword. Moving quickly, she took the handle of Raleigh's great sword in one hand and tossed it aside, out of the warlord's reach before pointing her sword at him. "You're disarmed. Surrender is your only option."

"Were I lesser man, I would. However, no weapon defines my might!" Raleigh roared as he rushed Zelina.

The queen was surprised by the foolhardy action that her enemy was taking. Still, she waited until he was near enough for her to stab, lunging at him only for Raleigh to dodge to the side and grab her arm. Zelina winced as he got ahold of her wrist and twisted, disarming her too. She watched as sword fell at their feet and Raleigh gripped her arm tightly.

"This time we're both unarmed!" he shouted smugly.

"Are we?" Zelina glared as she began to change, her eyes becoming reptilian as she began growing much taller and expanding outwards as her body shifted and became draconic. She grew in size, becoming too massive to hold as she took on her dragon form, roaring loudly and releasing a plume of flame directly at Raleigh as she bore down with the forelimb he had released as she changed.

"Damn!" Raleigh cursed in shock as Zelina nearly incinerated him. He was only able to avoid death by diving aside, leaping as far as he could. Where he stood there was scorched ground and melting snow.

Zelina smirked and turned, using her tail to knock him away while he was down, sending the warrior sprawling through the dirt. Now with a full advantage, Zelina smirked. The battle was hers and she could finish Raleigh off. Opening her maw, she breathed out another great stream of orange fire, watching Raleigh run from it. When she saw he was rushing towards his sword, she leapt in front of him, just as his hand grasped the sword's handle, before she rammed him with her head.

There was a loud crack as Raleigh was hit, knocked several feet away with the chestplate of his armor fractured. He rose wearily, but his hand was on Zelina's sword. Picking it up, he stood and watched, his eyes dark and challenging Zelina to come near him.

Begrudgingly, the dragon found herself respecting the warrior's resolve. Even when he was at a disadvantage, he had no fear, just desire for victory. It was a spirit Wynverians themselves nurtured, but few embraced it as Raleigh had. Part of her wished that he had arrived in her land under more auspicious circumstances, but knowing the man's atrocities, she hated that the thought even crossed her mind. Lunging, Zelina intended to end their struggle with a single bite, however, Raleigh leapt forward as fast as he could, and Zelina felt a sharp pain in her chest.

Moments passed before it was fully evident that Raleigh had plunged Zelina's blade into her chest, aiming for the softer scales near her belly. He removed the blade and stabbed twice more, roaring viciously as he did, steaming hot dragon blood spraying him and the field of battle. Leaving the blade plunged inside Zelina on his final strike, he ducked under the stumbling dragon.

Part of Zelina felt unsteady, but she knew she could not falter, lest she push the sword even deeper into her body. If she changed back, she had no idea how much damage the blade could do, but she would have a hard time using her forelimbs to grasp the blade as a dragon. From the corner of her eyes, she saw the fearful expressions of her allies. Captain Grey's face was flushed with anger and disbelief, but Zelina's gaze lingered on the gaping, shocked expression on Markus' face. What startled her most, though, was the group approaching from behind her own forces. Eyes widening, she realized what was going on. "Trap! It's a trap!"

By then, however, roars of the Elustrians deafened the others to her cries. Arrows flew, axes were thrown, and bodies hit the cruel, hard ground. Zelina saw at least three of her people fall before the others realized what was happening.

In a rage, Zelina turned, looking for Raleigh. Her pain was forgotten as she felt her fury erupt, the flames in her mouth going from bright orange to light blue as she finally gave in to her deep, destructive instincts. Her search and anger, however, were short-lived when she saw Raleigh had his great sword back. Part of her tried to take flight and shake him off, but by then he was already attacking. There was a sudden, deep, overwhelming pain as the blade hacked into her back.

Her very muscles were split, and she could have sworn the blades reached her bone near her left shoulder, right near her wing. There was another, severe cut that made her nearly black out from pain, emitting a deep, echoing cry.

Suddenly, Zelina fell, her body giving out as she felt as if something vital was being drained from her, her consciousness flickering as she felt her spirit fade, as if something had been severed from her being. The deep anguish was only accentuated as Raleigh spoke during Zelina's suffering.

"Your life is over, queen of the dragons. Your kingdom is mine!" Raleigh gloated, raising his bloody sword high as he was overwhelmed with the rush of victory.

In that moment, all Zelina knew was pain. She had been defeated, her right as queen was usurped by a madman, and her spirit wounded as her life began to ebb away.

The true horror of war dawned on Markus in the moment that Zelina was brutalized before him, but the horror only grew as a deafening roar was heard, one formed from many voices shouting in unison.

Time felt still, almost slower than normal, but in those moments all he knew was that he had to act, or Zelina would die. He knew he was challenging a powerful warrior, but hardly cared. Markus knew he could take pain if it meant saving the queen's...no, his friend's life. Spreading his wings, he flew towards Raleigh. Darting in as fast as he could, he rammed into Raleigh. Markus watched as Raleigh was knocked flying, careening through the air before crashing into his own men, knocking them all into a heap.

Markus leaned down, desperately trying to rouse Zelina, fearing she had already died. "Zelina, you have to get up!"

There was a weak roar. Zelina was alive, but barely. Markus removed the sword from within her, even as blood still flowed from her wound, steaming as it hit the cold air. She slowly reverted back to her human form, just as she was losing awareness.

Markus knew she needed immediate attention, but he could barely get her up before he noticed Raleigh was soon standing and followed by his men while there was chaos all around.

"Heofonite, are you truly sure your attack was wise?" Raleigh asked darkly as he strode up to him, raising his blade.

"I won't let you anywhere near Zelina, you fiend!" Markus shouted, defiance ringing out in his voice.

Raleigh gave no response, save the raising of his sword. He walked forward deliberately, his pace measured, making Markus feel a sense of dread come over him, knowing Raleigh was to attack soon.

Markus was only saved by the appearance of someone rushing in and ramming into Raleigh's back with a shield. He watched the wounded warlord fall forward, winded by the strike.

It took Markus a second before he realized who it was. "Captain Grey!"

"Markus! Take the queen and leave now!" Grey shouted, drawing her sword and attacking Raleigh, only for him to dodge. "We will not lose her to these honorless monsters!"

"No one interrupted my match and I attained victory fairly!" Raleigh boasted as he rose and swung his own sword, his blade blocked by Grey's shield. "Now death is assured for you all!"

"Not if I have a say!" Grey shouted defiantly before looking to her ally. "Markus! Go!"

With no choice, Markus tried to lift Zelina, hearing her pained gasps. Bringing her up, he heard a groan and the dripping of her clothing, drenched with snow and blood.

Cradling her in his arms, Markus flew off frantically, hoping that he would be able to escape. Behind him, he heard much yelling before several archers fired at him. Markus could only try to fly faster, spurred on by Ihsan's wind seal that had made Markus' flight faster. In the back of his mind, even amidst the chaos, part of Markus was thankful for Ihsan's magic.

Markus heard the sounds of other Wynverians flying away, their wings beating heavily as he carried Zelina away. The sound of arrows zooming through the air. He flew as fast as he could, carrying Zelina with him as others tried to escape too, scattering about in the sky.

After some time, the fliers were away from the field of battle. Markus was frantically looking for a place where they could land. Zelina needed immediate attention and they needed a place to hide. Going back to the base felt like a good option, but in his panic, the Heofonite had flown in the opposite direction. To go back now would mean that he would have to take Zelina back through the battlefield, which was practically choosing death.

Faced with the options present and seeing how badly things had turned out, Markus felt a deep heaviness in his heart. What was going to be a resounding victory turned into a stunning loss, and even worse, Zelina might lose her life. Even though he could hear the wingbbeat of other Wynverians on retreat, what was loudest in Markus' ears was the beating of his heart and the fear that Zelina would not make it. As he felt her bleed, that fear grew stronger.

Mentally berating himself, Markus tried frantically to think of another option. That was when he saw the mountains in the distance. If he could fly there, he could lay low. There was a lot of land to cover and as he remembered it was out of the way from the path to Arachon. With no choice, he flew there, with the Wynverians following behind him.

* * *

When the sun rose, Markus found himself waking from his resting spot, a cavern wall a few feet away from Zelina. The injured ruler was laying on several cloths and a pile of dry cloaks, arranged like a makeshift bed. There was the sound of crackling fire as well, keeping the queen and those within the cavern warm. Several weapons were placed on the cave's wall, alongside the few supplies the group had.

Outside, Captain Grey and a few others could be seen keeping guard, watching the skies and the mountains below, none of them in dragon form. Markus walked to the cavern's entrance and looked outward, seeing the rising sun and its light glistening on the ivory white snow below them. On any other day, Markus would have found it beautiful, but somehow it was a reminder that time was running short for Zelina and Wynveria.

They had arrived on the mountain top after a few stops. Once Raleigh had defeated Zelina, they only had so much time to try to save her. The frigid air and grievous wound were already threatening her life, but they were able to stop the bleeding and warm her up on a hill far from the field of battle. However, knowing they couldn't stay without being followed, the Wynverians and Markus flew off with Zelina, going as far as they could, hiding in the mountains.

By the time she arrived, she was still in pain, but unconscious, breathing heavily. It had made everyone uneasy, with Markus barely able to sleep out of concern. He had insisted on being part of the group who watched over Zelina personally, a few hiding out on lower peaks in order to keep an eye on the path.

The whole of the group was dour, however, especially with the fact that Zelina had lost her right to rule and might die, dashing all hope of ousting the Elustrians.

From where they were, Raleigh's forces would be unable to reach them, at least unless they were willing to climb day and night and then figure out where they were. The army's remnants had bought themselves some breathing room but knew Zelina herself could be running out of time.

The queen laid unconscious within the cavern, breathing shallowly as she laid on her side, the wound on her back covered by bandages. She moved every so often, fitfully tossing, only to go still for a time. She was restless, but her agony kept her from rising, and exhaustion kept her from waking.

Markus felt a sense of worry grow as he watched over her. After a short while, a soldier who had been tasked with Zelina's care came over to check on her.

As she carefully examined Zelina, Markus spoke up. "Excuse me, miss?"

"Audny," the Wynverian said, presumably her name. "What is it, Guardian?" she asked shortly, looking at Zelina's wound and not facing the Heofonite.

"Is she going to be alright?" he asked, his voice wavering for a moment.

"...I'm not sure...Her bleeding has stopped, but she has a fever. We can barely give her the care she needs as it stands," the soldier said bluntly. "Right now we need more people with medical training to assist."

"Have others come?" Markus asked.

"Yes, a few others have joined us, but Captain Grey asked if any were healers and found none among them."

Markus gulped, the worry he felt swelling as the situation grew more and more grim.

"Don't get too worried. The queen is faring better, but we have to remain vigilant...Still, with others wounded we have to have everyone doing their part." Audny pointed outside the cavern. "Perhaps you can check in with the captain while I treat Her Majesty. The captain's waiting for the others to get back with food before we plan our next move. We need to keep Her Majesty nourished and find a way to help her heal faster, but there may be something you can do."

Markus nodded, but he could feel his failure to protect Zelina weighing on his shoulders. He could not let his charge...no, his friend, die. Shakily, Markus went towards the cavern's entrance, soon seeing Grey on the other side.

Markus saw that Captain Grey had been talking to two Wynverians who were in good health, both of them saluting before transforming and flying in separate directions. Captain Grey looked up at the two of them going away as fast as their wings would take them. It was then that Markus noticed the extent of her injuries.

The captain had a deep gash on her left cheek, hastily sewed shut, her left arm in a sling and several other wounds marked her body. Her expression was pensive and stern, the current situation keeping her on edge. Slowly, she turned her head towards Markus, giving him a short, gruff nod before facing him properly.

"Captain, are you alright?"

The captain tried to smile, only to wince from her wound. Rubbing her cheek lightly, she grunted before composing herself." I'm alright, but I'm far more worried about Queen Zelina. It looks as if she might not make it and with most of our people were slaughtered during the ambush, help may be a ways away." Captain Grey's tone was even, but Markus saw her looking to a group of Wynverians being tended to by another healer, many of them nursing broken arms or covered in bandages. Captain Grey took her gaze from them before looking back at Markus.

A few awkward moments passed before Markus spoke again, uncertainty in his voice. "Do you think the anyone from our group survived aside from us?"

"I would wager very few. The Elustrians didn't give anyone any opening to leave. We were overwhelmed so fast that if anyone is alive, they're probably in bad a shape," Captain Grey replied, bitterness in her voice. "We shouldn't have let our guard down as we did, but now this is where we are and there's little we can do."

"So now the Elustrians can just continue to attack the rest of the army?"

"The army, officially, will defer to Raleigh when news spreads of his victory. There will be those who resist, but they should be wary. I sent two of our people ahead to warn the rest of our trustworthy allies and have them on guard. It won't be long until the Elustrians head to Arachon, but the rest of the army we depend on can slow them at the absolute least."

"But with their numbers and familiarity with the land, the rest of the Wynverians could wipe out Raleigh's men."

"That's assuming they attack, but once news spreads they may be allowed to pass freely by those who acknowledge his victory. I'm sure that they will be in hiding until Raleigh heals. My main concern is the state of our people."

Captain Grey started to look down, disheartened. "I worry their morale will fall if they hear Queen Zelina fell in battle and lost her crown. We lost so many of our brothers and sisters, but to lose the queen too would be unbearable, as well as our kingdom to such a warmonger."

"But she hasn't fallen, so we can't give in to doubt yet," Markus said firmly. "We can still save her and fight Raleigh. I know she'll recover and we'll win this war."

"Markus...You know that it may not happen. Death is a reality of war, and none are exempt from that. The queen is hurt badly, and while we all will do what we can to save her, there's no guarantee. Even though Zelina has our loyalty, by rule of law...Raleigh has all but won Wynveria, and many will flock to him due to that fact."

Markus fell silent. He wanted to say something to fill the captain with hope, but nothing he said or felt could make it so. Bitterly, he accepted that fact. "For now, I can only hope Zelina lives, then."

"I hope so, too. Raleigh will likely want confirmation Zelina is dead, however. Our job is to protect her any way we can and to get as many of our people as possible to occupy Arachon." Captain Grey looked at Markus. "When the others arrive, we'll plan how to get back to Arachon and marshal a strike against Raleigh."

"But I have to ask, how will people know Raleigh won unless survivors talk about it?" Markus asked. "I can't see anyone willingly doing him any favors."

Captain Grey sighed. "It's not about him so much as the laws of the land. If one challenges and defeats the ruler in formal combat, they become the ruler. Even if he's an outsider, by the laws we keep he has right to the crown, and I know errants and a few Wynverian loyalists may spread the word to end the war faster."

Markus balked. "They would betray their leader?"

"Leaders come and go. The laws were put down by our ancestors, and any ruler has to be strong enough to overcome. This isn't the first time in Wynverian history an outsider ruled, but given Raleigh said his plan is more war, it feels like this will be worse in the long run...Which is why we have to be proactive, before we're reduced to more warriors and fodder in his schemes."

Markus stopped; It was important to follow the rules of the people, as he had learned in Heofonia, and Captain Grey was right. Even so, he couldn't entirely put his emotions and disgust aside, or his feelings of personal responsibility. "So how do we do that?"

"No doubt if he hasn't learned of his victory yet he will learn within a few days, so time is of the essence. I'm having those loyal to Zelina gather and rally. If we occupy the castle, we can fortify it before he arrives.

Him sitting upon the throne would be the final forfeiture to Zelina's rule, but if we stop him prior to official coronation, Zelina has right to challenge him for a rematch and her title."

"But what if we don't stop him?"

"Then the moment he is seated on the throne, Zelina loses any right to challenge him again. Others may try, but there is no one I trust with the crown more than her, and such upheaval would make our already weakened kingdom in a worse state."

"I understand." Markus placed a hand to his chin, thinking over all he was told. "So, Raleigh technically is the rightful ruler, but if we can stop him from being crowned, Zelina will still be the ruler?"

"That's right. As of now, we no longer are with Wynveria proper...We're part of Zelina's resistance."

Markus nodded. Part of him thought it odd that the official leader of such a resistance wasn't the founder, but he knew for the sake of what was in the kingdom's best interest, it hardly mattered. For better or for worse, he was with the Wynverians, and he had come to care for the country as if it was his home in

Heofonia. He wouldn't let his charge die, and he certainly wouldn't let Raleigh's atrocities go unpunished.

As night fell over the camp, Markus collapsed in his bunk, exhausted. His muscles ached from a day of frantic activity, helping out wherever he could; gathering firewood, helping pitch tents and check on supplies, joining the soldiers on guard duty and foraging for medicinal herbs to hopefully help Zelina, calling upon the lessons in care he had learned during training to be a Guardian. He was happy for the moments rest, even as the camp buzzed with activity. Wynverians were milling to and fro at Captain Grey's orders, leaving on patrol or returning, messengers setting out across all of Wynveria looking for allies and carrying tidings. The gamey smell of mountain goat stew wafted over the camp, tempting Markus almost as much as sleep, though more than anything, concern for Zelina gnawed at him.

Going to her side, he watched as one soldier placed several herbs into boiling water and let them soak before tending Zelina's wounds. Placing several cloths inside the water, they started to dab her wounds with it, with Zelina gasping at each one before her expression softened and she began to rest. Markus stood and walked near, opening his mouth to speak and ask how the treatment worked, but realized he would distract from her treatment. He knew Zelina needed to heal, so he decided to leave and pray for a swift recovery, going to sleep in a different cavern to give her space.

The next day, at dawn, Captain Grey gathered them for a meeting. It had been days since the battle, and with Zelina injured, Captain Grey's scouts had returned with representatives from Zelina's loyalists. There were about thirty gathered altogether, some of them having brought others with them. The snowy field had a calm, cold air, with none of the people there talking as Captain Grey stood before them.

"Before we begin, I would like to thank all of you for coming and bringing supplies and followers of your own. I know you all took a big risk coming here, but for the sake of both Zelina and Wynveria itself, you have done an immeasurable service." Captain Grey then gestured to the cavern where Zelina rested. "I know we're all worried about Queen Zelina, but we'll be moving her someplace more secure, and further from Raleigh."

Another female officer stepped up, speaking. "With her injuries, can we risk moving her?"

Captain Grey nodded. "Every day we're here in these mountains we risk a blizzard or her wounds getting infected. I believe it is riskier to remain than to leave."

"So how will we move her?" Markus asked, genuinely curiously

"We'll take her to a less dangerous area nearby, one where we can fortify our resources while we have her treated. Markus, you carry her while the rest of us fly in smaller groups to keep an eye out for threats and keep from being trailed."

"Before we do that...None of us had healers we could have brought in?" a male officer asked, more to the group than to Captain Grey.

"We have more than a few who can help her superficially, but first aid isn't enough, especially in the cold as we are, and since going to settlements carries too much risk, we'll have to seek out aid from outside of the royal forces. Am I clear?"

"Yes, Captain," all of the gathered responded in unison. As they stood there, together, united in their mission, there was a certain firm warmth. Their resolve uniting them as they thought not just of their ruthless enemy, but also of their queen and homeland.

There was a strong, unwavering look in Captain Grey's eyes as she looked at her allies with both pride and admiration. "Good. Then for those of you who cannot stay, we'll send messengers to keep everyone informed. Otherwise, we're seeking healers from the nearby villages to help us. Until they arrive we'll remain and work as a group to ensure the survival of not just our queen, but our nation!"

Thunderous applause and cries of praise broke out around Grey, all while Markus looked at the captain, impressed by her spirit and dedication. He could see the determination within her, and her desire for a better future. It made him think of how he felt about his own homeland and how it often drove him on.

Captain Grey looked to everyone, speaking louder, letting herself grow more emotional. "We'll do everything we can for the queen, and if she should pass, we'll fight tooth and nail to save this kingdom in her memory."

Another soldier stood and agreed. "Until our last breaths."

"With our bodies and our own souls!" one more shouted, joined by cries of agreement by his fellows.

Before long, all of them, including Markus, stood up and agreed. Their determination helping them all to become more courageous.

"Then we leave tonight. Everyone be ready." With nothing more to be said, the camp was soon packed up and the group prepared to go on.

That night passed quickly, as soon everyone left. Measures were taken to hide that they had been there. Even if the Elustrians wouldn't arrive for some time, it was considered better to be safe than sorry.

After Markus made sure the queen was settled at their new camp, he noticed her blood was still staining the cloth and that she seemed more feverish. Looking at her, he silently promised himself that he would do anything he could to make her well again.

* * *

Markus was gathering firewood the next morning, careful to grab the drier pieces while he was near the few trees that had already fallen. While he did this, gathering lumber, he noticed two shadows flying overhead. At first he thought they were allied Wynverians, but they seemed to be meandering, searching. He thought about reaching out to them, when he considered if they were allied with Raleigh. Deciding to be cautious, he flew back to the camp and seek out the captain.

Once he arrived and explained to her what he had seen. Markus waited while the rebellion leader began to ponder the situation before coming to a conclusion.

"We should be diligent. Even if these are our own people, there is no guarantee they haven't been followed," Grey said.

"So what will we do?" Markus asked, awaiting instruction.

"Meet them away from camp and make it seem like we're approaching from another direction." The captain then faced Markus and looked towards where Zelina was. "Go find two others to accompany us and make sure Audny keeps close watch on the queen once we leave."

"Yes, Captain." Markus deferred to the Wynverian's expertise, hoping that it would help them navigate the potential danger.

As the figures flew closer to the hideout, Markus and the Captain, followed by two others, decided to direct their attention elsewhere. Markus flew with Grey, who spoke to the Wynverians, and it was agreed upon that the Wynverians would go to a clearing and then transform, hailing down the two from above.

Once the group had traveled to a plateau devoid of trees, the Wynverians transformed and roared loudly. Markus had to cover his ears, though it didn't keep his body and armor from rattling from the sheer volume.

It didn't take long for the unknown dragons to notice the group, landing down opposite of them in the clearing. The two Wynverians transformed. One was a man, the other a woman, both clad in Wynverian uniform. They stood attentively, though they seemed to also be on edge as they watched Grey's subordinates transform back to their human states.

Grey spoke first, her tone commanding and calm. "What are your ranks and names, soldiers?"

"First Lieutenant Xandri and Sergeant Valise," the man said. "We came in response to a cry for help. We were told the queen may have perished."

"Is there anything we can do, ma'am?" the woman asked, her eyes on the captain, as well as the others.

"Yes. Tell me, what station did you come from?" Grey asked.

"Enavi's outpost, ma'am," the man said. "One of your men made it to us and told us everything. Our Captain sent us ahead to scout."

For a moment, Captain Grey's expression turned serious, her eyes studying them as the captain became lost in thought. A few moments passed before Captain Grey gave a smile. There was a loud sigh as she smiled. "By Mother Aurah's benevolence! I can't believe you both made it safely from Enavi. I'm sure the captain sent you as fast as she could."

"Only her best," the woman said with a warm smile. "So, is the queen alright?"

"She's recovering well. Tell me, which are you?" Grey asked the woman.

"Sergeant Valise, ma'am," the female Wynverian replied.

Captain Grey nodded before stepping forward, placing a hand on her hip. "Can you tell me how many others Captain Moncrieff sent?"

The man, Xandri, took a step forward and spoke. "Half a dozen more are combing the mountains. If you'd like, we can find them and have them meet you at your hideaway, ma'am."

Captain Grey shook her head. "No need. I'll lead you there." Captain Grey motioned for the two to walk ahead before moving her hand to her hip, near her weapons. Once Xandri and Valise were close, she reached for a dagger at her side and quickly brought it to Valise's neck. "Move and I slit your throat. Everyone! Detain the other!"

Immediately, Markus went with Grey's subordinates as they surrounded Xandri, all while Valise panicked.

"C-captain?! Have you lost your mind?" Valise asked, her eyes frantically searching the area and seeing that her partner had no way to escape.

"That's funny. Anyone who was actually from Enavi would know that Captain Moncrieff passed two years ago... Now, who are you?"

The woman gulped nervously as Grey pressed her knife against her throat. "Valise... Carodd."

"And your partner?"

"Xandri Justar."

"Captain, why do their names matter?" Markus asked warily, not taking his eye off Xandri.

"Don't you know, Guardian?" one of the other soldiers asked. "The Carodd and Justar are Errant Broods."

"And now it seems they're collaborating with Raleigh." Grey stared down Valise. "Why?"

"The invader promised our families prestige again. Far better than what Zelina has offered us," Valise replied, indignant, but with a twinge of fear. "He's already reached out to us and at least half a dozen other families she has dishonored."

"The dishonor is yours, especially since you would kill others of your own homeland to become a warmonger's lapdog."

"War and glory have always mattered to our people!" Xandri shouted, his hands still raised in surrender, but speaking with bravado. "You talk as if we did not conquer and defeat one another to create the Wynveria we have. We drove out the Wyverns native to this place in order to build this nation in the first place!"

"You seem to forget we didn't eradicate the dragons that lived here before our people!" Captain Grey shouted back. "We made room we could for our people and we did fight for supremacy, but we always respected the dragons and one another's tribes. Our name as a people and this land's name were chosen to respect those dragons and this land's history, one we forged together. A man like Raleigh will only eradicate the past and build his own future, with no regards to the people who helped him build. Even a fool like you should see that."

"All we see is opportunity. Eventually, either we or the Elustrians will find you and end Zelina's life," Valise said. "Make it easy, surrender...You may yet live."

"We might..." Grey admitted, "But you certainly won't!" Swiftly, she slashed the captured Wynverian's throat, feeling hot blood come from her neck and spray the white, snowy ground, melting much of it.

Within moments, the two soldiers drew their swords and stabbed Xandri, however, the enemy Wynverian did not die, not right away. Instead, he transformed, roaring.

The men tried to pull their swords from his body and stab again, but they were stuck and Xandri had already changed. Roaring, he bit down on one soldier's body, rending his chainmail as if it was nothing and perforating his ribs. The vicious dragon shook the other Wynverian several times before tossing his body towards Captain Grey and the now-dead Valise.

The other soldier who had stabbed Xandri finally managed to pull his sword loose from Xandri's scales, but by then Xandri pressed his foreleg down on the man, crushing him. There was a loud scream as the dying Wynverian cried for help, his flailing arms flinging the bloody sword mere feet from Markus.

Markus was left aghast by the brutality he saw, for a moment he felt fear grip him before he managed to seize control of himself. Two of his allies were dead again, the captain, himself, and Zelina would soon follow if he did not act. The Heofonite would not let that come to pass. Picking up the sword, he glared at the dragon, hatred, anger, and even raw spite now fueling him, but beneath it all, his desire to protect those on his side who remained. Xandri hatefully glared back at Markus before spewing forth a cloud of fire.

The billowing plume of flames would have razed Markus, had he not flown up instinctively. Flying high, he gave off his first and truest war cry before bringing the sword down and going into a full dive, with both all his strength and all the additional power gravity would lend him.

The result was a loud, sickening crack as Markus' sword cleaved open the dragon's head, scales and bone in all as it was embedded into the dragon's body. Markus clutched the handle of the embedded sword, not letting go in case his foe still lived. When he felt the dragon's death throes, he pushed down further until Xandri was completely inert, and a pool of scalding hot, steaming blood pooled around his boots.

For a while, Markus stood there, the reality of his actions not fully setting in. Life and death had approached him, and Markus had chosen life…Leaving Xandri to be taken by death. For a moment it haunted him, until he remembered those Xandri killed were still around him, and that many more would have died had he not acted. Finally, he took a deep breath, just as he heard a voice. "Markus, are you alright?" Captain Grey asked, holding her broken arm gingerly.

"I will be when Queen Zelina is." Markus finally let go of the sword and turned to the captain. "How are the other two?"

"Dead. We need to give them a proper burial…As proper as we can."

"Yes, Captain. As for the errants?"

"Leave them. We have to bury our own, as well as move camps once more."

Finally, it sunk in that Markus had taken a life. "Right…" Markus tried to comfort himself by reminding himself that he had killed a murderer, and had taken his life for the right reasons, but even that did not did not make the sudden heaviness in his heart fade.

* * *

The same night, the Wynverians and Markus hastily moved their camp to avoid detection from other errants. Flying low under the cover of night, they made efforts to avoid patrols of other dragons, keeping lone scouts ahead to make sure the path was clear as they progressed. Eventually, they landed lower down the mountains where it was warmer and easier to conceal themselves. Fires warmed the area further while Captain Grey sat near one, speaking with Markus in private. The talk was tense, especially when Grey proposed limiting contact with allies as well. However, she had one bit of good news.

"I dispatched someone to look for a safe place to bring her for medical attention," Grey said to Markus. She sounded optimistic, however not blindly so.

"Hopefully we'll hear back within the next day. If not…We may very well have to risk it."

"A chance is better than no chance at all," Markus said warmly. "We'll do what we need to in order to keep her safe, right, Captain?"

Captain Grey nodded. "Yes, we certainly will. Even if she should pass, then the Arbiter will judge her fairly and we will continue to champion her cause."

For a moment, the Heofonite began to remember his nights working alongside Ihsan and the others, hearing tales of the Arbiter, though his memories of the lore were not precise. He had been more concerned with escaping the hardship of war through time with his friends rather than learning at the time, though he regrated not learning to some extent. "He's also a god, right? The Arbiter, I mean."

"Not quite. More of a forefather and a spirit, much like his mother, Aurah. The Arbiter was the first Wynverian and one of greatest of our kind," Grey said with reverence. His duty is to judge the souls of the Wynverians who came after him and grant them passage to Aurah's kingdom, should they prove worthy."

"Thank you for reminding me. I believe he will help Zelina, but I thought that the Arbiter was only a myth."

"To be fair, your people's seclusion led many to think you were a myth too. Sometimes you have to believe in what you can't see."

Markus nodded. He wasn't sure he believed in another land's gods, but all he really wanted was to make sure that Zelina would fully recover. In fact, both he and Captain Grey were approached by a guard.

"Queen Zelina is awake, and wishes to see you both!" the guard exclaimed. "Come, quickly!"

With haste, the two followed, making their way past everyone going about their duties around the camp. At last, they reached Zelina, who sat up and stared at them both, her expression firm and as strong as it could be.

"Queen Zelina, you're awake!" Markus cheered, going nearer to the wounded monarch.

"Yes...Well, awake enough to actually move," she replied, her voice a bit raspy and her skin pale. She tried to rise further but winced.

"At least you're well enough to communicate with us," Grey said, kneeling.

Zelina grimaced. "Well is one word for it...Ow."

Markus came nearer, raising his arms to assist Zelina. "Don't try to move so much. Your wound-"

"Yes, I can feel it," Zelina sighed weakly and in annoyance. "Blast that warmonger...I'll have to repay him with interest for this."

Still concerned for Zelina's condition, Grey spoke to her queen with reverence. "I feel far more confident he'll get his just desserts knowing you'll be able to lead us again."

The queen looked at Grey before speaking with sincerity. "I hear you led well in my absence. I owe you far more than I can repay. I'll need to reward both you and Markus for your services. Still, I can't believe I lost to Raleigh..."

Markus looked at her closely, sympathy in his voice. "He planned an ambush during your duel. It wasn't your fault, Zelina."

"No, it is," Zelina insisted, gripping her sheets and gritting her teeth. Her hot, steaming breath was visible in the room as she grew angry. "I could have just had him killed. I should have, but I had to make a show of things."

"You shouldn't blame yourself for things you cannot change," Markus replied. "You still have time to stop him once you recover."

"Markus, even if I do recover, it will be months before I'm fully up to speed," Zelina replied somberly. "I don't know if I'll fully recover, either. The wound is near my spine and no one will tell me how deep it goes."

Captain Grey shook her head. "None of us are qualified, but a proper medical practitioner can tell us. I have faith that it won't be severe."

"As do I," Markus said, measured in his sureness.

Zelina sighed once more before giving a faint smile to them both. "Markus, Grey, your optimism is a treat... I am glad I got to see you both in agreement, at least. I'll remember it while I can. Still, it certainly doesn't feel like I'll be able to do much of anything soon."

"Queen Zelina..." Markus could hardly hold back the tears welling up in his eyes.

The queen gestured to the tent's entrance. "Please, Markus... Get the others. I need to address them while I am awake."

Nodding, Markus left and obeyed, feeling worry for the queen. That night, while Zelina slept, the sound of pained, shallow breaths and crackling fire echoing in the cavern filled Markus' ears. It was the dead of night and the fire within the cave was all that kept him warm. Listening to the fire and Zelina's breathing, Markus stared at his friend and superior, seeing her alternate between a shallow rest and agony.

Despite the pain she felt, Zelina was the best she had been since she had been wounded against Raleigh. Even with the queen of the dragons more stable, Markus was still pensive and worried for her health. Wishing the queen a hushed goodbye, Markus spread his wings and braced himself before flying off into the tempestuous storm of snow outside. As her words echoed in his mind he went to take some time to clear his thoughts. Even if the thought of losing his friend hurt him, he had to be steel his mind, to be there to defend her until the end.

The next few days were dour for all in the camp, with Markus' change in demeanor evident. The Heofonite grew less lively and more hesitant. Though most in the camp merely thought it was the strain of the war or homesickness bothering him, Zelina and Grey worried it was something more serious. However, the queen was met with crushing news of her own. All the healers that had been sought were either overrun caring for wounded refugees or lacked the resources to assist. It had been days and days of scouring, but in the end it became apparent that no one would be able to come and treat Zelina.

Zelina could feel tension during the meeting of the Wynverians. All were gathered around their queen for what was to be a solemn occasion, many of them being as silent as possible while others who could not contain themselves tried to hide traces of worry and concern on their faces. Even so, it was all too obvious to see. Captain Grey's eyes were red, something one could see even with her head cast down as she tried to hide her sadness at how dejected Zelina was. Likewise, Markus was beside himself with sorrow, his body trembling now and again as he was overcome with sadness.

The queen could only glance aside at them before speaking, feeling a pit in her stomach as she swallowed. At first, she merely wanted to know of their situation. It hadn't taken long yesterday for Captain Gray to tell Zelina what had transpired since her injury. After a short time, going over the information one last time in her mind, Zelina spoke. "Everyone here, all who stand by me after my defeat...I owe you thanks. Thanks not just as your preferred ruler, not as who you swear loyalty to, but as a person. Even as death looms near for me, along with the Arbiter's judgment, I swear to fight with you, to repay the deep kindness you have all shown me. From here on, I will continue our campaign at your side for as long as I can, for all our sakes as well as Wynveria's!"

As Zelina paused, she listened to cheers and calls of adulation, her people agreeing with her message and showing their faith in her. As firm as she remained, she felt warmth in her heart that made her feel a bit stronger still. Soon, Zelina directed her attention to Captain Grey, motioning for her to draw near. Once she had, Zelina spoke again. "In the event that I pass, I wish for you to have command of these forces, Grey, at the very least until this war is resolved...You are to join the rest of our forces that remain loyal to our cause and lead them against

Raleigh. His death is our highest priority, and afterwards, either negotiate the surrender of the Elustrians or wipe them out. His army runs united by him, and should he fall, so will they eventually...But I cannot allow the same to happen for us. I may die, but I will not have Wynveria fall with me. I implore all of you to fight for a greater cause than just me, one that we all believe in. A united Wynveria, one not torn by war, but together in strength and principle."

Zelina saw Grey was trying to stay strong, her expression stony, save for the occasional tremble. Her tone came out strong after she cleared her throat. "Consider it done, my queen." Grey faced everyone, no doubt taking in the true measure of her new responsibility, though she turned back to Zelina. "If I may, though, we could very well have a competent healer for you. We just need to send out more scouts, perhaps a bit further?" she said, her voice filled with hope.

Zelina's eyes widened, her ally's desire to see her recovery made Zelina feel better, before she recalled the lingering, undeniable sense she would perish soon. As much as she wanted to live for her people, and herself, there was a nagging sense her time was near. "I know, but I rather plan for the worst case and hope for the best...At this point we have to accept what has come to pass."

"Who says you must come when death calls?" came a male voice, raspy and guttural, breaking out among the crowd.

Everyone turned, seeing two figures approach. The shorter one was wearing tattered rags, his hair long and lanky, while the one next to him stood tall, wearing similar robes and a fur hat upon his head.

"Intruders!" shouted one of the Wynverians, calling the others to arms, raising a spear before his fellows also prepared for battle.

"Yes, ones to not be trifled with," the shorter figure said before walking nearer still, with his companion flanking him.

"Wait..." Markus looked closely, pushing the crowd aside and going past the armed Wynverians as he drew closer. "Dante? Ihsan?! You're both alive!"

"Yes," Dante said before he walked closer, adjusting his ragged robes and looking at Markus blankly, all while Ihsan remained stiff. "I managed to escape, thankfully."

"How?" Captain Grey asked suspiciously, also drawing near.

Dante glanced at her a moment before casting his gaze to Zelina. "Not your concern. The queen's life is, however."

Zelina stared at him, wondering who the stranger was and how Markus knew him. "You're a healer of some kind?"

Dante nodded briefly before he stared Zelina in the eyes, drawing nearer. "Of a kind. I can bring you back from the brink of death to full health." His gaze was as if he could see through Zelina, past her firm expression and to her true state of being. "I can tell you feel it looming near."

Zelina was silent, but rose and spoke to him, challenging his assertion. "And how do we know you aren't some mere charlatan? Or worse, a spy for Raleigh's forces?"

At this point, Markus stepped up, gaining Zelina's attention. "I traveled alongside him briefly," Markus interrupted. "I've seen him use magic firsthand against Raleigh's followers, and Ihsan too." Markus then turned, his happiness evident as he saw Ihsan was well. "How are you?"

The usual warmth and jovial nature of Ihsan was nowhere to be seen. He stood still, casting his gaze to Markus, but said nothing as he stared.

"Ihsan?" Markus asked. "Are you alright?"

"He was tortured by the Elustrians," Dante said. "I saved him, but he was subjected to treatment that robbed him of his voice...And much more."

Markus looked more closely and saw that Ihsan's stare was utterly blank. The way he was stiff, lifeless...He wasn't even breathing. Markus reached out, touching Ihsan's arm, but he felt no body heat, and it was only a second later when he was pushed back by Ihsan. "That's not him."

"Of course it is," Dante replied. "You can tell it's his body, plain as day."

"It is his body...You killed him!" Markus accused, going to Dante and grabbed his cloak and lifted him by its scruff.

Dante stared at Markus, almost bored, his tone not changing. "No, I didn't. He was dead and I brought him back, then I simply made use of his natural talents."

"So you're a necromancer, and a selfish one at that! I thought I could trust you!" Markus roared.

Dante waved an arm as Ihsan's body raised an arm and summoned magic, a bright light emitting from his hand. "You can trust you will die if you don't unhand me...After all, I came to assist."

Markus refused to move, but it was then that Grey stepped in. "You plan to turn Zelina into a revenant? That mockery of life won't help any of us."

Dante tilted his head to Grey, almost sneering. "My skills can also preserve life. Don't dismiss what you can't understand. I can have her flesh mend and regenerate more thoroughly than any healer's medicine could dream, for a price."

Zelina could hear the confidence in his voice, but was wary. A necromancer was nothing to trifle with and she could tell Markus was tense. Calmly, she ordered him to put Dante down before talking. "And that price is?"

Dante revealed a small grin as he was let down and unhanded. "Land. I desire land of my own in this country where none can trespass. I also desire Raleigh's blade, once it falls into Wynveria's possession and lifetime access to the royal tombs of Wynveria."

"Why would you want that? To keep desecrating the dead?" Markus spat, disgusted. Around him, the listening Wynverians began to murmur among themselves, some with disbelief at Dante's skills, others with disdain for his demands, sharing Markus' outrage.

Dante raised a hand, dismissing Markus' statement. "Concern yourself with the living. Let me worry about the departed...and keeping Queen Zelina from joining them."

"So those three things are all you ask?" Zelina inquired after weighing his statements.

Dante nodded. "They are."

Zelina gave a sigh, realizing she couldn't bargain too much. If she could be healed and face Raleigh again, she would pay such a price. After a few moments, steeling herself and hoping it would work, she spoke tersely. "Then I suppose I have no choice. I accept your offer."

"Queen Zelina, you can't be serious!" Markus shouted, his fist clenched as he cast a rueful glare at Dante.

"Markus, I know your feelings all too well, but do not second guess me," Zelina said sternly, reminding him of her authority. "If we need to make a deal with this man to stop an army, so be it. At worst, only I suffer instead of our people and those past our borders...Besides, I trust you all will know what to do if he reneges on his agreement."

Markus nodded, gritting his teeth as he stepped back. "Yes, Queen Zelina."

"Good, thank you." Zelina gave Markus a nod before she turned to Dante. "I agree to your terms. You have my word."

"I must ask for more than your word," Slowly, Dante reached into his cloak and pulled out a jagged, short knife. The edge was pristine, kept in fine condition and the black metal of the weapon shone with an eerie light, even in the dim cavern. Slowly, he dragged the tip of the knife over his palm until blood was drawn. "Do the same and take my hand, then we may begin."

At that moment, Grey stepped forward, echoing Markus' concern by whispering in Zelina's ear discreetly. "My Queen, I ask humbly, are you sure this is what you desire?" Captain Grey looked at Dante warily. "We can take our chances to look for a proper healer."

"But every moment we waste is a moment Raleigh draws closer to Arachon. I will take every advantage I can to reclaim my kingdom....No matter the risks to myself." Wasting no time, Zelina then extended her arm, revealing her hand for Dante. "Consider our pact made."

Nodding slowly, Dante slowly cut Zelina's palm.

The queen watched her blood flow out slowly, but once it was over she merely took the stranger's hand and shook. Slowly, however, she felt her consciousness fade as she began to enter what felt like a deep, stifling sleep.

As Zelina fell asleep, Markus watched Dante like a hawk, making sure that he wasn't up to anything. The gaunt man merely guided Zelina's body down to the ground, his cut had healed over after he released her and looked down at her. Still gripped by anger and distrust, Markus glared at Dante, who dismissed his look of disdain.

"Healing her will take some time," Dante said blandly as he looked to Ihsan, who handed him a bag.

"Can we assist?" Markus asked tersely, barely hiding his anger.

"No, disturb neither Ihsan nor myself. Any interruptions may risk Zelina's life," Dante replied as he went about his business.

"Is that a threat?" Grey asked, a slight edge to her throat.

Dante sighed. "It's the truth. Your threats mean little...It benefits us all if your queen lives. Now begone so I can help her."

Grey nodded, acknowledging his statement. "Alright. Do your best, necromancer."

"I will, now clear out a space where I can work," Dante commanded.

With no more words to exchange between them, the mage was left with the queen while Markus and the Wynverians left, with Markus trying to put his faith in Dante, despite his lies and deception. While Markus couldn't do it fully, he could trust that Dante's own self interests ran concurrent with Zelina's.

In the back of his mind, Markus began to wonder just exactly who Dante was. While it was true he helped before, he had always looked for his best interests. There was no loyalty in Dante beyond himself, and him returning with Ihsan's body and desecrating it. The more he thought about it, the more sick he felt about the whole thing and how he had a hand in Dante's involvement in the Wynverian war. While he worried, he hoped and prayed Zelina would survive. After that, they would figure out what to do with Dante. Unable to trust that Dante would act in everyone's best interests, he decided to take matters into his own hands for insurance.

* * *

That night, while looking at the cavern where Ihsan stood, with Dante and Zelina within, Markus felt his resolve grow more firm. He sat inside his tent, feeling nervous as he thought about how Dante had resurrected Ihsan.

Ihsan, or his body, stood guard at the entrance, looking solemn, staring into the distance at nothing. Markus saw that the Qalairn was unmoving, almost like a statue. It was even alien to imagine Ihsan saying nothing, with it being a stark contrast to his old, jovial self.

Markus was consumed with guilt as he saw the reanimated remains of his old friend. He was worried about what had happened at Joyeuce Keep after he had left. He wondered how Dante escaped and if he had a hand in Ihsan's demise. He would never know for sure, but he couldn't stomach the thought of Ihsan going unavenged.

As he continued to stare, Markus felt the frigid air enter his tent and noticed that Ihsan wasn't showing any kind of sensitivity to the cold; he didn't shiver or try to move for warmth. It only further made Ihsan feel like a dead body standing in a once kind man's place.

The Heofonite felt sorrow, as he wanted to give thanks to Ihsan for giving him the wind charm. It had helped Markus often, but he would never have the chance. The spell was the last gift of the now departed Ihsan. Seeing the empty body made Markus worry that Dante planned to do something similar with Zelina, whether or not he failed when it came to healing her wound and saving her from death. That was when he looked back to his crystal again.

He knew if all went right then he and Wynveria would get help to turn the tide of battle from Heofonia, but he was unsure if his request would be approved. The communion crystal he had was a direct line of communication with Heofonia, the same he used to make reports. A very small part of Markus felt as if his request might be denied, even though he was sure Heofonia had Wynveria's best interests at heart. Still, he knew nothing could be lost for trying.

Once ready, Markus reached for his communion crystal. Lifting it up, he saw it emanate a pale, blue light, just enough for the glow to illuminate his face and brighten up his tent somewhat.

Gathering himself, Markus tiredly breathed, puffs of hot air escaping his lips as he folded his wings and tried to warm up. He shivered somewhat from the draft coming in until he saw the face reflected within his crystal, standing stock still when he knew who it was. "Sovereign, sir!"

"Hello, Markus. I hope you are well," the Sovereign said in a friendly, but firm manner.

"I have been better, but thank you." Markus smiled; surely the Sovereign could help without anyone or anything hindering him. "I was expecting a scribe, sir."

"After I was appraised of your situation I thought it prudent to talk to you personally. It seems time is of the essence."

"My sentiments exactly, sir. I have something to ask of you, but first I'll make my report."

The Sovereign smiled. "Your enthusiasm is reassuring. Well, then, I must ask...Is it true the man known as Lord Raleigh and Queen Zelina did battle?"

"Yes, it was a personal duel," Markus said, ruefully.

"And was the queen defeated?" The Sovereign asked.

Markus nodded, though his tone remained grievous. "I'm afraid so. She's critically wounded. Her back was slashed by Raleigh's blade, but she's recovering now."

"So she is alive, but beaten? If so, by Wynverian law, Raleigh has become rightful king of Wynveria."

Markus thought about it. "By the letter of the law, yes, but she wasn't defeated fairly. His men attacked and distracted her."

"Did they directly attack her, though?" The Sovereign asked, his gray eyes sharp as he looked at Markus.

"No, Lord Sovereign."

"Then for all intents and purposes, by their laws, he is the King of Wynveria. I must admit it will likely harm the morale of the Wynverians clashing against him...To lose one's homeland in such a tragic way."

"But they don't have to!" Markus tried to bargain. "If you can send a healer to fix Zelina's wound immediately, or perhaps more soldiers to assist, she'll be grateful enough to ally with us and together we can reclaim the throne so she can rule."

The Sovereign shook his head. "Markus, I am glad to see your heart is in the right place, however caring for her is no longer your duty."

Markus stared at the crystal in disbelief, the brown haired Sovereign's expression firm. "What?"

"As King Raleigh is now the rightful ruler and you are a Guardian, your duty is to the protection of Wyneria's ruler. As the former queen is no longer the ruler, you are to leave and offer him your assistance."

"But he's our enemy!"

"He cannot be the enemy of Wynveria as he is, for all intents and purposes, the nation's ruler. Furthermore, he is willing to be an ally to Heofonia. When our last messenger made contact with him, he was left a crystal attuned to contact us. Two days ago he stated that he had overtaken Wynveria and wanted to discuss furthering our alliance. With your confirmation, we can move forward."

"Sir, you're asking me to betray the actual people of Wynveria. Those who live here, a woman who nearly died to protect this entire land. You want me to throw that aside?!" Markus asked, tears welling in his eyes as his hero and master stared at him firmly.

"Markus, I understand you feel attached to Zelina and the others, but see this as a chance to ensure their safety or otherwise keep them alive. King Raleigh may consider the request if you serve well. As to your other point, I am merely asking you to keep doing as you have been. I know you and that you served the former queen well. Please, do the same with King Raleigh and we can discuss your future in Heofonia."

Markus wanted to speak, but no matter how he tried, his voice cracked or failed him; everything had gone mad, his hero, the world, his very purpose. Markus merely stood there until the Sovereign wished him farewell and concluded their dialogue.

Markus felt numb, not from the cold, but from fear and shock. He fell to his knees, sobbing until a tear fell from his eye, slowly freezing as he continued to cry, unsure of what to do.

* * *

The day after Dante arrived, Markus was present when scouts informed Captain Grey that no healers who could help had been found, with all of them busy treating wounded survivors, both among civilians and soldiers. While the scouts reported most would live with proper care, none of the patients would make it if the healers were taken from their patients. Knowing that Zelina would not stand for saving her life by sacrificing others, and that Dante was already at work, it meant little to Captain Grey. The only promising news from the trip at first was that a fair number of Wynverians who had fled were found and would be willing to fight again.

At first Markus wanted to lash out at them for their cowardice and for deserting in the first place, but he could not blame them. When he had frozen in full blown war, he could not blame others for their own fears. He could not let his own pain make him into a hypocrite.

"There's more, captain," one scout said. "We located Raleigh's base of operations. He set up a large camp where he's settled for the moment, and we can confirm he was present."

"We were also able to set up a secure perimeter in the area. So far as we can tell, his forces have no clue where we are," the other scout added.

"Excellent, that's promising." Captain Grey instructed the scouts to send word out once more. "Instruct everyone that under Queen Zelina's orders, an eye is to be kept on Raleigh's allies. Any unfamiliar Wynverians or members of Errant Broods that hinder you should be struck down," Grey relayed to them firmly. "Have this message passed to all who will hear, and when you return the queen should be well and the rest of us will set off to plan our victory over Raleigh and the Elustrians."

"Yes, Captain!"

Then, after that, Captain Grey looked to Markus. "Markus, I need you to go ahead with these two. They could use your help and you're a swift flier."

Markus looked down, unable to stare Grey in the eye as he spoke. "Captain, I can't. I have orders from Heofonia."

"You do? Whatever they are, can't you do them before you depart?" Grey asked.

Markus sighed. Part of him felt guilt gnawing at him. "Captain...I'm not sure I can comply. I want to do as you ask, but my orders from when I called were to leave the camp immediately for another destination."

There was a short silence as Grey looked at Markus. For a while her expression was unreadable, until she turned her head towards her subordinates. "Men, go. You don't want to be here for what I have to say to this upstart."

Immediately, the two Wynverian sentries retreated hastily, all while Markus stood, waiting for Grey to speak. He saw a foreboding seriousness on her face. It was during those moments that he realized how much colder the air was on the mountain since Dante had arrived, and the pressure he felt, especially with Grey's disapproving gaze, made the few seconds stretch like hours. At last, Grey spoke, softer than the Heofonite expected. "Markus…I understand you care for this land and your homeland, but it seems you're at an impasse."

"I am, but I can't leave all of you, much less Zelina to Dante," Markus replied dejectedly.

"Yes. The queen is someone we in Wynveria care for. She's our pride and joy, but there's a harsh reality we've come to accept from millennia as a warrior people. Our loved ones die, be they kings, queens, our parents, siblings, sons, daughters, or even those we care for as friends, but their legacies and causes can live on. If Dante fails, we'll carry on her memory, and know that we will look after her and Wynveria's good, even if you cannot."

"That part about loss…are you speaking from experience?" Markus asked, genuinely, looking to the captain's eyes.

"Yes, on more than one front…Queen Zelina also bore witness to the death of her father and grandparents, all as rulers of Wynveria who fought to keep their crown and bled to the last drop for this country. All of us understand sacrifice and all of us bear its weight."

"I understand, but I'm a Heofonite, not a Wynverian…My homeland is beckoning me."

"Yes, but as a servant of my homeland I understand you as a servant of your own. You're letting your feelings affect your judgment, but at times you have to decide if following your orders matters as much as your personal motivations."

"You mean my training as a Guardian to protect another land's people?" Markus asked.

"No. Your feelings as a person to be there for your friends. Queen Zelina, the allies you made here, and myself."

Markus paused, touched and unsure of what to say.

"I'll admit, I may be misreading the situation. You could simply see us as foreign strangers you were assigned to, but after all of the laughs we've shared, the loss we've endured, and the genuine concern I've seen from you...You have grown to care about the nation's people, not just as an abstract."

"But...That's what makes this so difficult," Markus said, his indecision growing worse.

"I am sure, but I can tell for certain Queen Zelina, like myself, considers you not just a guard, but a friend...And as a friend I ask you to do what you feel is right." Grey gave a small smile. "If that means leaving, none of us will hold it against you."

"And if I consider my current course to be that?" Markus asked, unsure of her resolve.

"Then far be it from me to stop you." Grey stared at Markus softly before placing her hand on Markus' shoulder.

Shortly after, Markus thought on it. As much as he was taught he had to follow Heofonia's orders, here he was given freedom of choice. He could tell Grey was sincere in respecting his decision, and it solidified in his heart that betraying them would be wrong. He thought about what he could do and eventually spoke. "Captain...I'll need to leave, but I will be back."

"You've changed your mind?" Grey asked, surprised by his sudden change of heart.

Markus nodded, feeling more confident. "Yes. I can't do anything for any of you here, but if my plan is right, leaving for a short time will help save Wynveria and Zelina, and I'll do my part to make that come to pass."

Grey nodded. "I'm quite happy to hear that. So, are you going to go ahead to prepare now?"

"Yes. Before I go, can I ask you something?" Markus asked her, somewhat sheepishly.

"Ask away."

Markus cleared his throat, realizing the situation was somewhat awkward. "It's something that's been on my mind for awhile now. I never thought there was a good time to ask, but I suppose now is as good a time as any. What is your first name?"

"Deidrah."

"Captain...No, Deidrah Grey, I thank you for talking with me," Markus began, extending a hand, "person to person."

Captain Grey smirked before extending her own hand. "You've come a long ways in my eyes, Markus. Whenever you finish your business and return, with all of us together, this should make our victory assured."

"I wholeheartedly believe that, Captain." Markus continued to smile, even as they ceased to shake hands.

"Then let us work towards it. There's much I must do before the Queen wakes up, and I know you will prepare to depart. Why not go pack your things before I see you off?"

"Right, Captain. I'll do so now," Markus said warmly.

* * *

Raleigh's encampment was a strange place for Markus, especially since he had come stripped of armor, wearing naught but woolly clothes and other, furred garments to keep him warm in the cold. The conquerors of Wynveria were in a camp made of many tents, with the outer edge of the camp guarded heavily. The interior of the camp, Markus saw, was filled with the sounds of merriment; Men and women drank, danced, and told stories around the fire. A good number were in high spirits, and even the most hardened among them cracked a smile. The sight of Wynveria's enemies...no, his enemies, in such a state of glee sickened Markus, but he remembered they were merely human, celebrating what they saw as a victory for their people. He tried to tamp down the bile within himself as he was led to a great tent, one that was even more heavily guarded. Twin guards stood in front of the door, grizzled and stern. As Markus approached, they crossed their spears, preventing him from passing.

"Who have you brought?" one of the guards asked, taking a look at Markus' wings. "A Heofonite?"

Markus nodded. "I am. I'm the Guardian sent to meet you."

The first guard's twin looked at the man escorting Markus. "Is this true?"

Markus' guide nodded. "It is indeed, it seems the clouddwellers sent an errand boy to talk to Lord Raleigh."

The other guard stared at Markus' escort. "Show some respect. This is a Guardian, their own warriors; He's no mere messenger. Otherwise, Lord Raleigh would have no use for him."

"Peacekeepers," Markus corrected tersely, saying it to the guard who defended his station.

The guard said nothing, however, instead still staring at the guard with intensity.

Markus' escort nodded fearfully before looking at Markus. "Ah, beg pardon! Regardless, he is to see Lord Raleigh, if possible."

The twins looked at each other before one went inside to alert Raleigh. It took a few minutes, but the twin who went inside rejoined the others. "He is to come inside."

The man who guided Markus nodded before gesturing for him to go in.

Markus obliged, but was surprised when the guards blocked their comrade.

"Just the Guardian. You return to your post," one twin said. "Now."

The man grumbled before leaving, while both guards gave Markus a glance before closing the tent behind him.

Gulping, Markus stepped forward, still he had to stand firm and appear relaxed, the duty he was tasked with and the information he wanted. Going inside, Markus found the tent warm enough, with the sight of several sheathed weapons and chests of spoils being the first thing to greet him. He stared at all the loot, but also saw the path straight ahead led to another, larger room. As he passed through, he noticed there was an area where a small fire had been set, a hole above allowing smoke to escape. Walking within, he found himself at a large dining table made of wood. It seemed to be old and weathered, but was seemed to have been originally of fine make. A single white cloth was draped over the table, unstained and as white as the snow outside. On the table was a bowl of fruit and a single loaf of what looked to be baked bread, while nearby was a single, leather-bound book.

Markus wondered what the book contained, however before he could touch it, a familiar voice rang out.

"I was told Heofonia would be in contact, but I did not expect them so soon..." Raleigh strode into the room, a welcoming, inviting smile on his face. "Much less that of the warrior from before."

"R..." Markus caught himself, struggling to make the words come from his lips. "Lord Raleigh..."

Raleigh stood proudly and offered a hand, looking down at Markus with an avuncular friendliness. "I do not believe I have heard your name, young warrior."

Markus stared, dumbfounded. This was the same man he had opposed on the field of battle not long ago, having crossed paths with him directly. "Guardian Markus Astrann of Heofonia." Markus realized Raleigh's hand was still extended. A couple moments passed before he made himself take it. To Markus' surprise, Raleigh clasped it firmly, but with a familiarity one would give an old friend.

"Ah, now I know who quite literally knocked me off of my feet," Raleigh said before chuckling. "I admit I was tired after the duel with Queen Zelina, but I must give you credit, it was a strong strike. You showed much courage and loyalty."

"I...Merely did what I thought was right," Markus replied honestly, but he was shocked to see that Raleigh seemed earnest; there wasn't even the vaguest hint of malice or a grudge.

Releasing Markus' hand, Raleigh nodded. "Well, I hope I can depend on such strength and valor in the coming days, Guardian Markus. Your Sovereign told me much about your order, and at the same time so little, but when I saw you and experienced that strength, I felt it was truly worth investigating."

"That's...Very high praise," Markus said, stating the fact without pleasure. He watched as Raleigh started to laugh, obviously relaxed around Markus.

Raleigh gave a nod before speaking, his voice showing his curiosity and some excitement. "Ah, the cloudborn. Truly your people are a mystery...For the longest time I believed you were little more than legends made by the old, until your people sent a messenger. Even then, I was unsure what to make of you, but I certainly believe your people's strength very real after you attacked me." Raleigh gave a smile, as if chuckling at his own comment, and then looking Markus over. "I must say, you hit rather hard for someone with so little muscle."

"...Thank you?" Markus replied, unsure whether or not it was appropriate compliment; Raleigh obviously valued one's capability as a warrior, but Markus didn't hold such talents in the same esteem.

"You are very welcome. However, I hope you will forgive my prior ignorance. Warriors, wherever they hail from, always have my respect." Raleigh then looked to the loaf of bread on the table before taking it in his hand gingerly. "Have you yet eaten?"

Markus shook his head, but watched as Raleigh offered the bread to him.

"An appetizer until our meal is ready. Tonight is the night of a feast. You can also help yourself to the fruit."

Markus considered refusing, but he knew it would make his task that much harder. Markus reached out and took a piece, while Raleigh kept another part. Biting the broken bread he held, Markus hated to admit that it did taste good, especially after days of the bland rations he had in Zelina's camp.

"So, I am told you are here to serve me and Heofonia," Raleigh stated plainly as he inspected his morsel of food before eating it rather quickly.

Markus nodded, trying his best to smile without it looking too forced. "That is correct. Whatever you may need, as the rightful ruler of Wynveria, I am obligated to do for you."

Raleigh grinned before swallowing the rest of his bread and looking at the rest of the food on the table before facing Markus. "Excellent. Then let's start with something simple...Does Zelina still live?"

Markus stared, unsure of what to do.

Raleigh smiled genially. "Come now, you can trust me." The man's smile merely made Markus more uneasy, especially as Raleigh began to eat the bread, still smirking.

"She is alive," Markus said, the vaguest hints of smugness in his voice and a faint, but noticeable smile.

"Good," Raleigh replied earnestly as he continued eating. "I was hoping that might be the case."

"You were?" Markus asked.

"Yes. She truly was an impressive warrior and she had a lot of spirit...Not necessarily a rare find, but something about her was captivating." Raleigh cast his gaze to Markus. "I'm sure you know what I am speaking of. That presence of hers...Royal or no, she is something special."

Markus nodded, genuinely agreeing. "She is." "To rob the world of that, and a talented combatant of her caliber, would be sad...I can think of other purposes for her."

Markus took a moment to take in Raleigh's words, his skin crawling as he considered what Raleigh might be implying. He stared at the man as he ate an apple next, without a moment's hesitation; crumbs of bread scattered on the table as Raleigh continued to feed himself voraciously. "What are you saying?"

"I'm considering a solution that would make everyone happy. I am the new King of Wynveria, but who is to say she has to leave the royal court?" Callously, after eating quite quickly, Raleigh threw his cored apple aside before going on to a bushel of grapes, eating them with gusto too before discarding the bared stem. He consumed ravenously, not even for flavor or hunger, but as if to test his great appetite. "If she survives, she would serve a vital purpose as my betrothed. Those she and her people deemed as errant have joined us, but the greater masses still refuse me, even after word has spread of my rightful conquest. Marriage to Wynverian royalty, or former royalty, may quiet their complaints."

"And then what? You add Wynveria to your conquests?" Markus asked, his eyes flickering to the food remains for a moment before going back to Raleigh, as he noticed him reach for more still.

"Truthfully, it IS conquered; the people just don't wish to accept it. I want to make Wynveria more, though. An equal in these lands to the greatest nations in Elustria, as well as benefit my purposes and Heofonia."

Markus looked at Raleigh closely, the man grabbing a bushel of grapes and eating them. "How?"

"My bibliognost and other researchers have studied your people and told me of principalities Heofonia has made on the surface. Ones that refugees go to and further Heofonia's own influence. I would be willing to lend a few squadrons under my power to assist in those efforts as well as provide the principalities with new refugees...From non-guarded lands, of course." Raleigh chuckled as he greedily consumed more grapes, stripping the bushel bare of its fruit. "My power grows, your power grows, Wynveria remains intact, and all are happy."

"It sounds too simple."

"It needn't be complex; it merely needs to work." Raleigh grinned before casting the stripped stem aside. "Think on it, Markus, you could retain your position and become a part of this world's greatest empire. You could be pivotal in Heofonia's efforts to make a better world."

Markus thought on it. Raleigh's offer sounded reasonable; it saved Wynveria, strengthened Heofonia, and kept Zelina alive, but...somehow it felt wrong. Markus knew he had a decision to make, and only one answer would help him fulfill his true purpose. "I...Accept."

"Glad you see it my way, young warrior."

"Peacekeeper," Markus insisted, though unlike his men, Raleigh laughed.

"A more polite word for the same position. Who keeps the peace but those with power? Who extends a hand of peace except he who can ball it into a fist of war? Your nation may not be nearly so...Proactive as ours, but you have spilled blood, you are a warrior, and there is certainly no shame in it."

Markus wanted to object, but he held his tongue. He was unsure what bothered him more, that Raleigh spoke with such confidence and conviction in his opinion or that Markus found himself begrudgingly seeing the logic in such a mindset. "Again, you give such exceeding praise."

"Because I am proud to have a man of valor fighting alongside me." Raleigh smiled as he stood from the table. "I know Heofonia will be pleased too." Raleigh looked at Markus, waiting to see his reaction, when a soldier entered the room. Casting his glance to the new arrival, Raleigh spoke with warmth, still in a pleasant mood. "Is it time for our surprise?"

"Yes sir, the feast is ready. The men are eager to hear your speech and meet our new compatriot," the soldier said with genuine enthusiasm, which only grew when he saw Raleigh's expression.

"Thank you for letting us know and inform the others that I will be by shortly," Raleigh said, his tone gentle and welcoming before he turned to Markus.

Markus looked up to the warlord, who stood with a self-assured grin. The way Raleigh stared at Markus had a strange manner. Markus could see approval in the man's eyes as he looked, as well as a small bit of pride. Markus couldn't help but appreciate it, given how sincere the man's thanks seemed to be.

"Markus, the information you've given me will help save lives for not just us, but Wynveria. I know you've come to be fond of the Wynverians, just as I have. Together, along with the others, we'll be able to prevent needless bloodshed."

The Guardian wanted to rebuke the man for his words, no, for his hypocrisy about blood being spilled needlessly, but he also felt Raleigh meant what he said. "Those words are too kind."

"No, they are earned. Still, I hope you have learned something valuable from our talk. I feel we, Elustria, Heofonia, and Wynveria, will have much to benefit in the coming days, but for now, we feast. My men will be by shortly to guide you to the feast, but for now, I must go."

"Yes, of course." Markus waited until Raleigh left the room to begin to look around more. Rising from his chair and going around the room, Markus searched for maps, documents, anything he thought might be useful; He discovered, unfortunately, that there was next to nothing helpful at the table. Realizing it was a little much to hope for and that being caught rummaging around would look suspicious, Markus stopped and sat back down. Telling himself to be patient, he made note to try to search again later if an opportunity arose.

After a brief tour to acquaint himself with the common areas of the camp, Markus was taken to the meal hall. Once there he was among the Elustrians, all of them sitting together and sharing a large meal, with several large roasts, hearty stews, and a plethora of fruit and vegetables prepared for the warriors. The Heofonite had seen larger rations among the Wynverians, though he rarely saw so many tables of people talking so loudly and drinking deeply. While the two camps had different manners of expression, he could certainly feel how both had camaraderie in the atmosphere, a general sense the men trusted and valued one another.

Soon, Markus was seated two chairs down from Raleigh. Patiently, he waited until others arrived, knowing the meal would commence when Raleigh made an announcement. Even if he was eager to move along his spying and see if Raleigh let anything slip during his speech, Markus also felt pangs of hunger. Even if he hadn't been hungry, the warm, fragrant food would have still made his mouth water. A hot meal was always welcome, especially in someplace as cold as Wynveria.

As he eyed a bowl of stew, Markus heard the sound of laughter and saw a man dressed in polished armor approach, a grin on his face as he approached.

"Hail, Lord Raleigh. I hope you'll excuse my tardiness. I had business to tend to, all on your behalf."

"Of course you did, old friend," Raleigh replied jokingly, looking to the shorter man and laughing. "Go on, sit at my side. There is a space between myself and our newest ally prepared for you."

"Oh?" the man turned to Markus and extended a hand. "The long awaited Heofonite. I'm happy to see you alive and well, but most of all, on our side. I am Captain Tiernan Raye."

Markus looked at the man, taking note of his short and trim, reddish-brown hair. He had a welcoming smile, though dripping with smugness. Slowly, Markus extended a hand and shook. "Markus Astrann."

Raleigh gestured to Tiernan. "Captain Tiernan is one of my most trusted allies, and one of my two commanders."

"Why, thank you," Tiernan replied, a wide grin on his face before he thought on something. "Speaking of, where is Shary? She went her own way after we returned."

"She had orders to tend to business for me. I'll give you the details after dinner...Unfortunately, she won't be able to join us for the feast or the announcement." "Of course. Speaking of orders, I was sure to relieve the new prisoners of their goods, for the war chest, of course," Tiernan said as he took a seat next to Raleigh.

The leader of the forces laughed. "And I'm sure you didn't keep any of it for your own pockets."

"Not without asking you, of course," Tiernan replied. "I may enjoy my trinkets and trophies, but our group comes first. Still, it should keep our allies fed, armed, and marching forward. Besides, from time to time we get such lovely spoils." The man then gestured to a sword on his hip, one that Markus felt he recognized.

He looked at it for a few moments before he realized where he had seen it before. "That sword, it belonged to General Nersel."

"Oh, so that's the old owner's name. Good to know," Tiernan said, his tone almost disinterested. "I take it you met the man?"

"Yes, during the time I served with Wynveria," Markus said tensely. "How did you come to have it?"

"Let's just say it ceased to have an owner and I liberated it from where it once was. This weapon is of rather fine make, after all," Tiernan said. "A shame to bury it with a corpse."

"An ally of mine wielded that sword. Show some respect!" Markus demanded, his hand balling into a fist.

Raleigh stared on, intrigued by the exchange, but remaining quiet.

Tiernan smirked. "I respect his taste, but yes, it is poor to speak ill of the dead. Please excuse my callous commentary. Perhaps you would like the blade instead?" Tiernan began to remove the sheath from his sword belt. "After all, maybe this matters more to you."

Markus considered reaching out for the weapon, finding the idea of Tiernan keeping it repugnant, but he realized that in keeping his cover, he had to forgo his prior ties. "No...I may not like how you obtained it, but it is yours. Just wield it in a way that would honor him."

"Had I known the man, I would, but I can only do myself proud with this...No offense, young Markus," Tiernan said dismissively.

"None taken," Markus lied, trying to remain convincing despite him starting to glare.

Raleigh cleared his throat. "As entertaining as it was to see you two talk, that will do. I need to address the men."

"Yes, of course," Tiernan replied obligingly before sitting.

Rising, Raleigh stood and spoke. "Men, women, my friends! We have been met by a wave of good news and great events. Having all but conquered Wynveria, we also have managed to cement an alliance with Heofonia, the land of those who shine as bright as the sun!" Raleigh paused long enough to hear his followers cheer. He let the praise last a few moments before raising a hand. Once the soldiers saw, they quieted down and Raleigh spoke again. "Now, we will end our campaign in Wynveria soon. Adding them to Elustria's territories and beginning our assimilation of this land in earnest, with those who share blood with the noble, fierce dragons of the past. As their brethren they rejected have now added to our grand might, together, all of us will bring this continent to glory!"

The thunderous cheers of approval and adoration from the men to Raleigh almost made Markus have to plug his ears. He watched as, once again, Raleigh raised a hand, his devotees slowly silencing themselves again to hear their lord's words.

"However, I know that glory alone won't be enough to keep our people going. I promise, in addition to accolades, there will be wealth and riches to reward you, land to build a future upon. With these, you will seize the destiny you have earned as not only warriors, but as heroes."

Markus watched as Raleigh finally relaxed, letting the last cheers go on for some time, smiling as he saw the eagerness of his men and how pleased they were by his words. Despite himself, Markus could understand why everyone was swayed by Raleigh's words; What bothered him most deeply at that moment, more than having to pretend, more than seeing Tiernan brazenly carry Nersel's weapon, was realizing that Raleigh had no intentions of stopping his plan to spread war across the lands. For the moment, he decided to join in the clapping before sneaking away to see about the prisoners.

There was an hour or two of festivities after Raleigh's speech, with many of those gathered getting drunk or engaging in games of chance after having eaten their fill. Markus had also waited until Raleigh departed for the night, the leader taking brief moments to greet the men who had addressed him before he retired. Not far off, Markus also saw Tiernan playing cards with men, eager to collect coins and trinkets, properly distracted.

Markus realized it was his opportunity to slip away unnoticed. He considered what he could do, when he remembered what Tiernan had said about prisoners. Considering finding whoever Captain Shary Auchmere was, he decided to ask around. After awhile, though, he saw a woman enter the area.

She was flanked on either side by two tall men, her hair jet black and braided, while she looked around with dark, moss green eyes. She wore crimson armor much like many members of Raleigh's forces, but the sterling silver on her chainmail and other pieces of armor stood out in particular. Dismissing the men at her side quickly, she saw Markus at the table and approached.

Somehow, seeing her made him feel like she was staring through him, looking not at the Heofonite, but trying to take stock of his character. Finally, she drew near, speaking firmly.

"Are you the Heofonite everyone's been speaking of?"

"I believe I'm the only Heofonite here, period." Markus extended a hand, though she merely looked at it, with no interest in taking it. Slowly, he lowered his hand and cleared his throat. "Markus Astrann, Heofonite Guardian."

"Captain Auchmere," she replied in a plain manner.

"Are you the one they call Shary?" Markus asked. "Yes, and I am here for you." Shary stated. "Lord Raleigh saw fit to task me with showing you about the camp."

"He did? That's considerate," Markus said. He was trying to hide his glee, glad that an opportunity to learn more about the camp and maybe save survivors had presented itself. "I thank you."

"You're thanking me for no reason," Shary said coldly. "It's only practical a soldier should get acquainted with the camp's layout."

"Very well," Markus replied, further bothered by the woman's gruff manner. "Any reason we're still waiting then?"

Shary rolled her eyes before motioning for him to follow. "Just try not to walk too slowly; There are still duties to tend to."

Markus went behind her, listening as she spoke, guiding him around the camp. "I've been shown to Lord Raleigh's tent, as well as this mess area, but not much else."

"Then I suppose we'll start with a few simple places, the treasury is where we store any valuables or money we might need in order to continue our efforts. Tiernan is in charge of that area," Shary explained.

"He seems like a fitting choice," Markus commented, looking at the tent, seeing that it was guarded by eight men.

"He does his job ably," Shary said, though it hardly sounded like praise.

"Sounds like you don't like him. Isn't he your comrade?" Markus asked, hoping to gain more information.

"He is, but he's ruled by his desire for money, not need. It sickens me when so many fight to merely eek an existence when people like him greedily want more," Shary said, barely hiding her anger, her tone wavering a bit. "He's still a capable warrior, but his motives sicken me." Shary took a few seconds to gather herself before letting out a small sigh. "The next area is my purview, the prison area. It's on the way to the strategist's tent, so it's no problem to find our way there."

Markus walked behind to Shary, the two of them nearing an area of the camp segregated from the rest, far from everything else, including gates that would allow one to exit the camp. "Are we going in?"

"Yes. We just placed a few prisoners inside and it's best to show you how we deal with them." Shary folded her arms. Before motioning him ahead. "This is likely where we'll send any survivors or those Lord Raleigh wants held. I'm sure you can do well with convincing them to comply or convincing them to join our side."

Markus feigned a smile. "Yes, for their own good."

"Indeed." It was shortly after that they fully approached, and Markus noticed that the tent was under guard. It took a few moments for the guards in front to notice Shary and stand at attention, starting to look at her closely.

"Have you done as I've asked?" Shary inquired.

One guard gave a salute before speaking up.

"Captain Auchmere, the new prisoners are inside and secured."

"Excellent. Then I would like you all to wait here. I have to show our Heofonite friend how we handle our prisoners."

Markus was hesitant, but knew he needed to follow. Walking ahead, trailing behind Shary, he found himself inside a fairly large tent that was under watch. Taking stock of the area, he was greeted by a lantern-lit area of dim light, with a number of Wynverians shackled inside cages, with their chains dragging on the cold ground and their faces ones of dejection and contempt. Kept in sackcloth attire, riddled with dirt and blood, the gauntness of their eyes and how sallow their skin looked made Markus' skin crawl and his heartbeat slow as he tried to process what he saw. It was in that moment, seeing the captives, that Markus fully realized that peace with Elustria would not be possible with Raleigh in charge. Whether or not the warlord cared for his allies, it was apparent how those he considered his foes would suffer. Markus' abject horror was stunted, however, by Shary speaking up.

"As you can see, the prisoners are kept here. We typically hold them for questioning or otherwise if negotiations are needed. I believe you questioned our people before, correct?" Shary asked him.

"Of course I have," Markus replied honestly. "Then this will be no strange event for you. We won't be starting tonight, but this will be part of your tasks. Hopefully you can convince them to willingly give over the information."

"I will do my best," Markus lied, feeling guilt as the words left his lips.

"Good. Lives will hang in the balance. Both theirs and that of our own people," Shary said, watching him closely. "Would you like to keep looking here?"

"...Yes," Markus replied, sensing an opportunity. While he said nothing more, he began to walk around, the guards and Shary watching him as he began to look over both the cages and the entries and exits to the tent. As he took it in, glancing ever now and again, he saw the guards each had a set of keys, no doubt to the cages and shackles. Likewise, he noticed the prisoners totaled twenty in all, among both the new arrivals and those who seemed to have been there for some time. Once he returned to Shary, Markus spoke up. "For a moment I thought there might be someone here I recognize; Zelina's army is vast."

"Worry not, Markus, it will grow smaller by the day as we do our work." After that, Shary led Markus back outside to continue the tour.

After that, Shary pointed to another tent a fair distance away. "We won't be walking that way, but our arms are kept there and seen to so that we can keep everything well maintained. Of course, true warriors keep their own personal weapons on hand." After speaking, Shary gestured to her crossbow. It was well cared for, with the metal polished and the wood finely crafted.

Markus took note of the fact, thinking that it was most likely where his own armor was being kept as well. Shortly after, Shary had appraised Markus of the entire camp, making sure that he knew where to go if he required anything. "Thank you again for showing me around."

Shary looked at Markus. "You're welcome. Now that you know, we expect you to be an asset here. Lord Raleigh thinks you might be good for us beyond your duties...I hope I can see what he does soon."

"He really does trust me?" Markus asked, startled.

"Yes. I cannot say I agree, but I just want to see Lord Raleigh and my allies succeed, and you can count yourself among them now that you are with us."

Markus could feel the sincerity of her words and began to wonder how one could be so loyal to Raleigh. No matter how motivational a speaker or how caring a leader Raleigh was, nothing could excuse the atrocities and carnage his actions brought about. Being a captain in his employ, Markus was sure she knew of his brutality, but even so she sounded loyal to him. Realizing he had to respond, Markus spoke up. "Thank you. I would love to talk more, but for now I must rest."

"If you must. Sleep as well as you can. We have a few hard days ahead of us yet before we can consider this campaign finished." Clapping a hand on his shoulder, Shary went her way after. "Sleep well, Markus of Heofonia."

"Thank you," Markus said. Making his way to the barracks, Markus had been told a tent was prepared for him. While he went in, he decided to wait an hour or two, until everyone was either asleep or the guards were more lax. Finally, when he was sure, he exited his tent and flew high. He couldn't flap his wings much, but he took time to glide before landing near the weaponry tent.

Once there, he saw a guard and waited until others left, likely on a shift change. By his count from before, he was left with only the one guard, and Markus only had so much time to act. When he was sure the guard was alone, Markus swooped down swiftly, delivering a hard, crushing kick to the man's back, knocking him down and leaving him unconscious. Making sure no one saw, Markus took the downed man inside the tent. Within, Markus saw his armor, along with other materials in the tent. Donning his armor, Markus felt happy to have his possessions back. Shortly after, he went around the room, looking for something to keep the downed guard from getting up and warning others. Finding rope inside the tent, he bound the unconscious man before thinking of his next move. "Now to get the prisoners."

When he was outside again, Markus took off and flapping his wings. He could feel a refreshing gust of wind as he took flight, the wind seal on his armor giving him a tail wind. Markus had almost forgotten how much easier the wind had made his flight, given he had been using it for so long he forgot what it was like to be without it. Still, Markus was only able to enjoy the flight a few moments before he swooped down, landing atop a guard's tower, peering down at the prisoners' tent.

As he watched, patiently, he waited until he saw a number of the guards leave, waiting until it was vulnerable. The night dragged on, but Markus remained vigilant, until he saw that there was only one guard left at the prison tent. With the element of surprise on his side, Markus jumped before spreading his wings to let him glide.

Landing with a light thud mere feet from the prison guard, Markus struck fast to keep him from noticing or alerting others. Delivering a hard punch to the man's jaw, Markus felt his attack lift the man from the ground, the bewildered guard's feet coming from the ground before he hit the floor, unconscious.

When Markus saw the Elustrian guard was out cold, he quickly dragged the man into the tent and looked around. Seeing all of the other guards were no longer present, he then relieved the man of his keys. "This should help..." Looking around the dimly lit tent, Markus eventually found an empty cell. Taking a bit of time to find the right key, Markus opened the cell and put the guard in before shutting it. Breathing a sigh of relief, Markus held the cell key before turning to the imprisoned Wynverians, seeing one turn to him. "Hang in there, I'll get you all out."

"It's no use, we won't make it far," a brown-haired prisoner said. He looked at Markus, moving his unkempt hair aside and grabbing the bars. "You need to escape before they find out you came..."

"Why are you giving up? You're still alive, you can get out of this with your freedom and your life."

"Raleigh has slain our queen. There's no point in stopping him now. Even if we can, the nation will be lost in finding a new ruler."

"Not if everyone works together. It might be hard, but this is a land I know you love and you Wynverians are a noble people. Nothing Raleigh and the Elustrians ever do can compare to your talents if everyone in Wynveria unites as one force," Markus implored. "Besides, I know the queen is still alive."

"Raleigh and his men have been talking non-stop about Queen Zelina being dead."

"Trust me. I was at her side not long ago. She'll heal, but she needs us at her side if she wants to keep Raleigh off the throne."

One by one, the captives began to rise, looking amongst themselves. They were hurt, tired, beaten, but Markus was sure they could persevere. Finally, he heard another speak.

"The Guardian's speaking the truth, and I've seen firsthand how loyally he's fought for our queen."

Turning to the source of the voice, Markus gasped as he saw the familiar face of Alya, his old companion from before. "Alya, you're alive?"

"I'm just as surprised you're alive," she said. Alya had shorter hair than before and two scars on her cheek. "Others told me you were here when I slept, but I thought it was another Heofonite."

"You worked with him?" the brown-haired prisoner asked Alya.

"Yes, though our paths parted. I barely escaped the fort when the Elustrians attacked, but I was captured anyhow."

"When?" Markus asked.

"When I was helping villagers nearby evacuate to safety. General Nersel had tasked me with it when the situation turned too bleak..." Alya said. "I'd like to think he was trying to spare me, though it wasn't long after when that greedy bastard came in, waving around General Nersel's sword."

"Tiernan..." Markus grunted, clenching his fist. "I'm sorry I wasn't there, Alya, but I'm here now. For all of you." There was passion in Markus' voice, but all were not swayed. A few quiet, tense moments passed before the first prisoner spoke.

"...Can we trust him?" the brown-haired prisoner asked.

"I believe so, after all, he's here to free us. With or without him, though, I'll fight. Queen Zelina needs all of us, and even if it's just for her memory, I will fight," Alya said, her voice firm and resolute.

"As will I," another woman with a darker complexion said. "As long as there's hope, I'll keep fighting. My duty to Wynveria won't end with me in a cage."

"Or mine," another young Wynverian spoke up. He was likely little more than a recruit, but there was a fire in his eyes, one that Markus admired.

Turning, Markus looked at the first prisoner. "What is your name?"

"I am Ericsen," he revealed.

"Ericsen, all of us will keep fighting on. Even if you feel you've given enough, you'll still be set free, but I must ask...If it's for a better world, won't you fight with us, with Queen Zelina, just a little more?"

Ericsen looked at all of them before nodding. "I...Want to keep fighting, at least so the Elustrians won't hurt anyone else."

"Then all of us will be at your side," Markus said, before opening Ericsen's cage.

Uneasily, at first, Ericsen stepped outside, but he stood tall, walking with Markus as he then let out Alya, then another, and another, until all twenty of the Wynverians were free.

Standing together with them, Markus saw that despite their wounds and tiredness, their wills were unbroken and each was ready. Feeling put at ease, he spoke to them.

"If we're going to keep fighting this war, we'll need weapons; I think the Elustrians won't mind us borrowing some of theirs."

"They would be nice, but you forget, we're Wynverians," Alya said. "Even when we're unarmed, we're never weaponless."

No sooner had the words escaped Alya's mouth than she and the others began to spread out, each of them looking at one another. Smirking with a mixture of vindictive glee and joy at the prospect of freedom, each and every one of them transformed, growing bigger and taking on their dragonic forms.

Markus watched in awe, seeing them change in unison, realizing that twenty dragons, no matter how wounded, would be more than a match for Raleigh's camp. As space ran out in the tent, one after another, the dragons emerged.

The many Elustrians who were still around were taken off guard at first, before one screamed.

"THE PRISONERS ARE ESCAPING!"

However, the cries mattered little when several of the Wynverians went on to roar loudly, drowning out the cries and drawing the attention of the Elustrians.

Alarms sounded, but by then the Wynverians were already flying off, breathing pillars of incandescent flames. Their fire razed the warriors who dared stand against them, while several of the Wynverians flew off, albeit more weakly than normal. Hunger, pain, and tiredness were taking their toll on the Wynverians, but they were still able to flight high and far out of range.

As Markus flew among them, though, he felt something whiz past his face. Turning, he saw Shary up front, along with several spearmen. Along with the sentries upon the wall shooting arrows. Seeing Shary, he locked eyes with her, feeling his blood practically chill as he saw the gaze of pure hatred in her eyes. Markus saw her reloading her crossbow and firing again, the second shot hitting Markus, but his armor was strong enough to withstand the impact.

Focusing himself, he flew higher and faster, evading several more shots. Looking to see who else was injured Markus noticed some of the escapees were harmed, some of the arrows sinking into their scales or javelins that pierced them. Even so, they all flew on, out of range before they could take any major injuries. Soon after, they were far off, all of them fleeing Raleigh's base for safety.

They flew for the better part of an hour, but tiredness, undernourishment, and wounds were taking their toll. Between their new injuries and the cold of the snowy climate, all of them soon had to land, walking to avoid potentially falling and crashing to their deaths. Even then, though, their sojourn to freedom did not end.

It took all of the night and part of the next morning, but sure enough, they did manage to reach a village that was safe and out of the way of Raleigh's path. Relief washed over Markus as he learned the village had people and physicians willing to care for the wounded. Feeling exhausted himself, he decided to rest as long as he could before making it back to Queen Zelina and the others. He was sure that Raleigh would send someone after him and the others, so they couldn't linger long either way. All he could do was hope that his efforts made a difference.

* * *

Back at Raleigh's camp, the warlord found himself gripped with fury and disappointment. He had let in the Heofonite, thinking that he would be loyal to his land's orders, but it was evident that Markus was a rogue agent, or had been swayed to stay with the Wynverians. Whatever the case, the Guardian had gone from being admired by Raleigh to being reviled, and his treachery would be met with death.

As he watched the others begin to pack for their advancement, salvaging what they could from the burnt tents, he saw Tiernan and Shary approach. "Everything's proceeding as planned?"

"Aside from the fiasco our winged enemy caused, everything is still in order. The most important documents and plans were saved, as were majority of the weapons," Tiernan said.

"Good, then all that remains is to make Markus pay for his treachery," Raleigh said as he stared at the ashen earth around him. "In the meantime, I believe it is time I claim the throne. Even if her followers don't acknowledge me, I will have the true right of the land and the help of the Heofonites, along with those already on our side. The rest will either follow me in glory or follow the fallen to their graves."

"My lord, do you really want trust the Heofonites to help? After what that lying Guardian of theirs did?" Shary asked.

"I will use all resources I have, Shary. Besides, I imagine they will be just as eager to make an example of their disloyal underling as I am. It is a shame. I thought he held promise, but if he won't live as our ally, he'll die as our enemy."

"Just as many others have. So, what do we do now, my lord?" Tiernan asked.

"That is simple. You will accompany me as we make our way to Arachon, while Shary will track Markus and the escapees." He looked at Shary. "Captain, take whoever you desire and make sure you make them suffer. The time for taking prisoners has come to a close."

"And Markus?" Shary asked, sounding eager.

"I leave that to your discretion." Raleigh smiled as he placed a hand on Shary's shoulder warmly, watching her smile too. "I look forward to hearing your report when you return."

"Thank you, Lord Raleigh. I won't disappoint."

"You never do," Raleigh said to Shary, pride evident in his voice. He had almost forgotten his anger entirely, seeing what a truly loyal soldier looked like. He was sure that Shary could bring Markus down, just as he was sure that Wynveria was his in all but ceremony. Watching Shary depart to gather her men, Raleigh beckoned Tiernan and left as well, eager to continue his crusade.

* * *

Three days after Markus had arrived at the village and made sure everyone was seen to, news had come of how Zelina was still being treated by Dante. Markus had received the news from a Wynverian scout, one who had arrived on rounds.

Markus had told him what he knew of Raleigh's plans, as well as asked him to send people to help the village before he left. However, before Markus could depart, the scout spoke to him.

"Guardian. Before you head out, I want to warn you to be careful. We've heard Raleigh's men were seen near the area not long ago and a few of my fellow scouts failed to report in. I'll be looking for them too, but I wanted to ask if you would also keep an eye out. If Raleigh's men capture them..."

"It would be terrible," Markus concluded, remembering how he had found the others.

"Agreed," the messenger said. "I'll do my best to pass along your news to Queen Zelina when she wakes and the others, please remain vigilant."

Markus gave a nod before he watched the messenger fly off. Taking time to himself, Markus decided it was best to head out as soon as possible. He went to check on Alya and the others, seeing that they were recovering well. "Are you feeling better?

Alya rose slowly. She had been tended to by the village healer and while she was assigned to bedrest, she could hardly remain still. "Mostly. I'd love to get back to helping, but I'm told I need at least a few days more rest."

"It's best you take it," Markus said. "I know we'll do better against Raleigh and his group if we're all as rested as we can be."

"Yeah, true," Alya said. "The others are healing up too, but I wanted to ask when we plan on heading out."

"That's up to you, since I'm leaving you in charge." Markus said.

"Wait...You're leaving us?" asked Ericsen, having risen from his bed slightly, only to wince.

Markus had almost forgotten that he wasn't talking in private, while a few other Wynverians took notice. "I can't stay; Queen Zelina needs someone to watch over her and I feel like I have to be that someone. Captain Grey and the others are so busy keeping the army functioning, but someone has to stay at her side."

Alya nodded, though she couldn't help but tease him. "Hm...If I didn't know better, it sounds like you care about the queen, more than just as a bodyguard."

"I do. She's my friend," he said earnestly. "Besides, with all that's been sacrificed, I won't let her end up dead too, not if I can help somehow."

"So what do you expect us to do?" Ericsen asked.

"Wait until you've recovered and join us. The queen needs you all, but you all need to be your best.

For now, I need to go," Markus affirmed, both to himself and the others.

"Very well. We wish you safe travels," Alya said before she waved goodbye to Markus.

Wishing them well, Markus also left, ready to make his way back to Zelina and hope that all would be well. As he left, he went to gather things for his trip, though the village was very low on rations considering how many people needed to eat, including the former captives. Markus had managed to get a day or two's worth of rations from a few charitable citizens, along with some fishing line in case he wanted to try to fish to gather more food. Regardless, Markus wasn't picky and took it with appreciation before taking flight. Flying across Wynveria, Markus knew it would take some time, but he was prepared to move mountains and cross the heavens to help save Wynveria.

Traversing Wynveria without being detected was one of the most tense tasks of Markus' life, but also one of the most important. Walking through the country, warily avoiding Raleigh's patrols, his mind was focused on getting back to Queen Zelina and the others who needed him. While he knew flying would make things far easier, he knew that Raleigh's people were watching the skies during their patrols, and it would be far too easy for them to guess Markus' path as he was being hunted. With sweat on his brow, his hands calloused from climbing, and his legs sore from constant walking, he had to continue.

Nearing the mountain range, Markus spotted a squadron of Wynverians in dragon form, openly flying Raleigh's colors. Knowing he couldn't outfight or outfly the enemy, Markus slipped into the thick woods around the base of the mountain.

Beneath the shadow of the trees, the Heofonite breathed a sigh of relief as the massive silhouettes of the enemies passed him, though they circled the area. Skulking through the woods, Markus could feel the faint crunch of snow and the snapping of twigs beneath his feet. Looking, he saw an endless number of gold and brown fallen leaves on the ground, with many more still attached to the trees. Even as many leaves fell to the ground, accompanied by snowflakes countless evergreens kept many of the trees coated in green, with frost covering everything within range.

For some time, Markus went ahead uninterrupted, until he noticed footprints in the snow. Stopping, he looked around, remaining vigilant. Seeing no signs of anyone in the immediate vicinity, he decided to follow the tracks cautiously, going until he noticed a few red spots in the blanket of white, growing more sizable as he went closer in.

Growing nervous, Markus reached for the knife he had at his belt. He gripped the handle of the dagger tightly when he heard a low, pained cry. It startled him as his eyes darted around, looking for a source; at first, Markus thought it was a creature of some kind before he heard weak sobs. He felt a growing a sense of dread as he realized the blood belonged to a person, one who might still be alive.

However, as he got closer he heard a loud, agonized yell. He could have sworn it belonged some sort of animal, but he knew better. Fear and an oppressive heaviness in the air shrouded him, yet Markus went further into the woods, knowing that there was someone suffering, but unaware of where or why, or if he would be next.

Markus could tell he was growing closer and closer, but the nearer he got, the quieter it was. The realization that whoever it was may have died sunk in, with Markus looking frantically for clues, the blood trail was still visible, but growing fainter, and there were no hint of other prints, be they from a person or animal. Anxiousness and fear made breathing more difficult, and he worried about his own wellbeing as much as that of the stranger.

Following the trail past a copse of trees, Markus gasped, seeing the blood pool around one tree, a body pinned to it by several bolts. With one in his stomach, blood spilling out of the wound and running down until it pooled at the tree's roots, with the blood steaming even while a knife was stuck in his throat. Horrified, Markus barely registered there was another pair of bolts in each shoulder, the Wynverian dying in agony, the cold turning his flesh blue.

Rushing over, Markus tried to cover the neck wound, ignoring the boiling heat of the escaping blood as best he could, and spoke. "Who did this to you?"

The Wynverian tried to answer, but could only stare behind Markus, trying desperately to speak, but only bleeding more.

Confused and bewildered, Markus only focused on the dying man, until he heard a voice.

"Looks like we netted ourselves a traitor."

Wide-eyed, Markus turned, to see Shary, flanked by two other Elustrians, each ready to strike.

Time was crucial as Markus knew he needed to escape the trap. By then the two men had already cut off Markus' exits, rushing towards Markus quickly to capture him. While he was loathe to do it, Markus left the dying Wynverian's side to make his escape, lest he suffer a similar fate.

He only needed a moment to make his decision. Though he took no pleasure in it, he abandoned the Wynverian man and rushed away. The crossbow wielder fired at Markus, but he dodged, narrowly avoiding being shot in the shoulder as he ran. He had to get to his bag and then fly off as fast as he could manage. Almost as quickly, Shary had fired a shot from her crossbow, the bolt nicking his arm, but the glancing wound did nothing to slow Markus down.

Making sure his gear was secure, Markus took flight, putting distance between himself and his pursuers. Even as he flapped his wings to gain altitude, he didn't get far before he felt an agonizing pain in his right wing, followed by his body crashing into the snow coated ground.

Markus screamed as a barbed arrow shot through his wing. He began to falter, unable to maintain flight, until he crashed to the ground. Markus was in agony from crashing down, but as best as he could he ignored the pain and got up, stumbling at first until he was able to run, clear out of sight and deeper into the woods.

* * *

Minutes passed and night fell as Markus was barely able to gain a moment's rest. His lungs burned, his breathing ragged from running, but he had to stay focused. There was precious little time before they caught him again.

At that moment, however, Markus needed to focus on himself; he would not be able to help anyone else if he was dead. Once he was sure the wound was clean, Markus' next concern was a hiding place. In the dark he couldn't find one easily, but he eventually found a thicket of trees. Once his eyes had adjusted, Markus hid behind them, taking a second to collect himself and rest. He knew sitting around was a risk, but going on in an aimless panic would get him killed much faster. Taking some fallen snow and pressing it against his wound, Markus let out a small sigh. The tension remained, keeping Markus wary, when he heard the sound of footsteps.

"Are you sure he's here?" a male voice asked. They'd already caught up, Markus realized, with a feeling of dread. He could feel his heartbeat thumping, but he had to remain calm, they hadn't found him yet...

"The blood and trampled trail led this way. It disappeared, though," another male voice said. "Do you think he flew?"

"No, Shary hit his wing. If he could, he couldn't have gotten too far away."

Markus listened as the two continued to talk to one another, peeking out to see where they were. The two Elustrians were standing back-to-back, looking around. "Shame she didn't kill him along with our little decoy. At least the winged boy would've gone faster than that poor sap of a dragon."

"Yeah. Kid's probably frozen to death by now, wherever he is. Let's just find the body and get out of this weather."

With both of them unaware of his presence, Markus knew it was his only opportunity to attack. Moving as quietly as he could, he turned, hoping to take them by surprise. He knew for certain if he struck fast before they saw him, he'd finish them off.

Blitzing them quickly, Markus attacked one, grabbing him quickly and suddenly, tackling him to the ground before drawing his knife. Quickly, Markus stabbed his foe twice in succession, piercing the man's chainmail armor and causing him to cry out.

The other Elustrian grabbed Markus, only to be shoved away several feet, his eyes wide with disbelief as Markus continued his savage attack.

By then, Markus had little choice. He raised the knife high and turned his head before bringing it down, a sickening gurgle and the splash of blood marking the end of the grim deed. By then, however, the other Elustrian was scrambling to his feet.

Sparing no time, Markus left the Elustrian he had killed and rushed to the other. Markus watched him start to turn as he approached, but it did little good as he was knocked down again when Markus came upon him, kicking him and bearing down. The Heofonite stood over the man as he reached for his sword, only to stomp down on his sword hand, hearing a crunch as bones broke, followed by an agonized scream. Picking him up, Markus glared at the man. "Where is Shary?"

"I won't give up the captain, especially to the Wynverians' pet pigeon."

Markus felt the urge to throttle the man, but resisted; he needed to be alive to talk. "If you don't you die."

"And I welcome death if it is between that and betraying my ally." The Elustrian gave a dark, but pained smile.

Markus wasted no more words on the man. For a few moments he had considered letting the man live, but he knew it would come back to bite him. Raising the blood covered knife one last time, Markus glowered at his enemy

The man, defiant in the face of demise, smiled. "May Lord Raleigh lead my people to glory, and you to a painful death."

Markus brought the blade down again, ridding the world of his enemy. While part of him wanted to loot their bodies for weapons, they all held the banner of the Elustrians, and the idea of using them disgusted him. Throwing away the armaments, Markus left their bodies to rot before departing looking for Shary.

After hours of traveling in the woods, Markus began to feel the aching in his wing grow more intense. He was bleeding slowly, but it was adding up. He felt fatigued and tired, and against an enemy who could strike at any moment he couldn't take that chance. Keeping aware for even the slightest of noises, he froze when he heard loud rustling, focusing on the source. When he looked he saw it was animals, but he wondered what had made them scurry off.

When he looked closely, he saw that they were running from something. That was when he saw a shine of metal before jumping behind a tree. "Come out. I know you're out here!"

"And I know you're at death's door. Do yourself a favor, Heofonite. Give up."

"Why should I?" Markus shouted while looking for a way to escape without her noticing.

"You're freezing, bleeding, tired, and all alone. At this point I can at least give you a mercy kill. I don't mind doing people favors from time to time."

Markus scoffed despite the desperation of the moment. "Sounds like a strange way to define a favor."

"Trust me, if you're an enemy of my master, you're not going to get any mercy if you live."

Markus wanted to make a retort, but talking would give away his position. He needed to find a way to close the distance or bring Shary out so he could attack her. Suddenly, he had an idea. He knew there were risks, but if it worked, it would all be in his favor. "Of course. A coward like him will just stab me in the back."

"Watch your mouth!" Shary barked.

The Heofonite grinned. He did a quick glance around to make sure Shary wasn't around him directly. "Or what? Your balding oaf of a leader will send his talentless goons after me?"

"Talentless, eh? This coming from some interloper who let his master die."

Markus was about to shout back that Zelina was alive, but he held his tongue; He was gaining the upper hand and had to maintain it. "Maybe, but better a glorious martyr than a bloodstained lunatic." Markus felt a tad guilty that he was enjoying the exchange of insults. "Honestly, what deluded fools follow a warmonger who loses his men in droves?"

"Are you serious?! Our forces have decimated your dragons. These Wynverians aren't even a tenth as dangerous as the stories make them out to be." Shary's voice was louder.

Markus could hear her clearly behind his hiding place. Peeking up, he saw her, moving frantically, aiming her crossbow. Slowly, he crept nearer, watching as she continued her tirade.

"Before this is all over, I'll make sure I cut your damn wings off your back myself, you wounded buzzard."

Once she was fully turned around, Markus decided to make his move. Leaping out, he managed to get the drop on her, grabbing her from behind in attempt to restrain her. Grabbing both arms, he started to squeeze. What startled him, however, was Shary was fast to react. She shot down at Markus' left foot with her crossbow. When he moved it back, she rammed her heel into his knee. It made him stumble from the pain and soon, Shary was free, though she had dropped her crossbow while trying to get loose.

Markus managed to gather himself just in time to see Shary reach out for her weapon. Instantly, he kicked it away into some bushes before he reached out to grab her again, but Shary was too fast. By then, Markus felt her kick him in the chest, pushing him back as she ran off to get her weapon. The Heofonite only needed a few moments to catch his breath before he chased after her, their battle beginning in earnest.

* * *

Save for the chants of the mage known as Dante, all was quiet in the cavern where Zelina was hidden. While Markus had his own trials, another struggle was going on, Zelina's struggle to stay alive. Even with the necromancer's help, Zelina felt her life ebbing away, tethered to the world, but tenuously even so. The gaunt man who muttered his spells and cast unknown incantations was filling Zelina with arcane magics. As much as the queen appreciated the help, the foreign energies still made her uneasy even as they helped keep her alive and awake.

It was a hazy awareness, one where she fell in and out, her thoughts could only be composed for moments before it fell into an unclear mass of senses. She was cold and getting colder. Her pain, once sharp and terrible, was now becoming duller and fading...Along with all else. As Dante's own words became quieter, she felt as if a fog or mist was covering her vision at times. Whether her eyes were open or closed, she felt as if she was seeing nothing at some moments, and another world altogether at others. She was unsure of what she saw, but there was the strange, foreboding sense that it was very much real.

Zelina couldn't tell if her wounds bothered her less because he was healing her or because she was finally dying. She knew that Dante's magic had eased her pain some, with her wounds closing and pain ebbing, but she had also seen him struggle at times and the wounds reopen when his focus waned. As much as Dante was doing, the most dire injuries continued to persist.

Eventually, she began to hear voices talking, ones that didn't belong to Dante. They began as whispers. She strained to hear what they were saying, but couldn't from where she was, she had to chase after them. The queen could feel herself moving. It wasn't of her own accord, but Zelina was gliding towards the source of the voices. The distance grew shorter and shorter, though she couldn't see where she was going. Soon, unclear whispers became chanting.

Zelina felt herself fly towards the chanting, after a while she saw there was finally light. In front of her was a mountain, glowing bright blue with an ethereal light, the voices growing louder and clearer. She gasped as she realized what it was, the home of Aurah, the mother of all Wynverians. Aside from being where Aurah originated from, though, the Astral Mountain was also the resting place for the souls of departed Wynverians.

She stared on at the lush, verdant greenery. The grass glowed bright, with flecks of light constantly moving. Weaving in and out of the being were several glowing orbs. The fog that once obscured Zelina's sight was far off in the distance, and above pure white snow fell lightly, gently coating the light. Soon, the chanting before became a quiet song in background, one that put Zelina at ease. As she breathed, Zelina felt as if her lungs were filled with fresh air. In the deepest irony, it was the most alive she ever felt.

"I can't believe it. I didn't think that the Astral Mountain existed," Zelina said solemnly. Seeing it brought her joy; Although Zelina had been thought of the land, she always assumed it was a metaphor or a story. Now, seeing it before her, she felt herself marvel at it and walking ahead, until she heard a voice.

"Few actually do until they arrive here," came a calm, deep voice, echoing from all sides.

Zelina turned around, trying to figure out who was speaking to her. "Who is there?"

"I am the Arbiter."

Zelina froze, her eyes widening in shock; The Arbiter was, next to Aurah, the most mythical and powerful figure in Wynverian Spiritualism. He judged all the souls of the Wynverians, deciding whether or not they would pass on to the Astral Mountain or wander forever as listless spirits within the Wintertide.

Suddenly, she felt nervous as she realized she was before the one who would judge her life. "Arbiter…"

"Queen Zelina. It is time for your judgment." The Arbiter's voice sounded closer, still resounding, but with an added gentleness. "You have passed from your mortal being into your eternal one. Now is the time to decide if you will persist within the Astral Mountain, or face the Wintertide."

"I…I understand." Zelina was crestfallen; she was dead and her life had been taken from her. She felt disappointed that Raleigh had killed her, and that Dante's spells failed, but she accepted her fate. "How do I begin?"

The Arbiter appeared in the form of a colossal dragon, dwarfing Zelina herself; the whole of her body not even the size of a single claw. Slowly, his glowing, starry eyes met hers and there was suddenly and an understanding between them. Zelina did not need to tell the Arbiter about her past; he could see it directly as she had seen her own life.

"You have worked very hard, young queen," the Arbiter said solemnly. "I see no reason why you should not take a well-deserved rest. I have seen every event in your life as you have seen it," the Arbiter explained, lowering his head to get a better look at Zelina. "All you have suffered in this war shows the depths of your dedication."

"Then you know about what is going on in Wynveria? Even now?" Zelina questioned as she stared back up at the giant dragon.

"Yes. I am sad to see the kingdom is in such a state." The Arbiter's gaze seemed sympathetic. "Unfortunately, I can only observe and hope few others share your fate."

"Isn't there anything you can do to help?" Zelina pleaded.

The Arbiter shook his head solemnly. "I can only judge and see what has happened to those who have already passed. The future and affairs of your old world are in the hands of the living. If it is any comfort, however, the vast majority of those who died in service to you felt admiration for you and your rule."

"And the others?" Zelina questioned, feeling apprehensive. She began to consider just how many of the innocent citizens and Wynverian soldiers had died since Raleigh invaded. She considered the thousands who the Arbiter must have met, and those who could be dying even now.

"They are hoping someone ends Raleigh's threat. Regardless, you cannot dwell on matters beyond your control. You can only rest."

The queen wanted to accept his words, but something within her very being kept her from being able to rest. "I understand, however…I cannot rest."

"Hm?" The Arbiter stared at her more closely.

Zelina stared up at the Arbiter, her gaze firm and strong as she stepped forward. "I need to go back to help I...I can't let any more of my people die in this war."

The Arbiter looked to her, perplexed. "Others yet live who can protect the realm; You have earned your rest, take it."

"I understand, but I have a duty to protect them as best I can. I need to go back and help them, even if it means more suffering for me."

The Arbiter became solemn. "I am afraid that returning is not possible. If you reject the opportunity to take your rightful place in the Astral Mountain, you may be lost in the Wintertide. To exist as a wandering spirit, surrounded by cold. The spiritual pain would pale compared to you having to exist without rest, to see the world you left, but never again be part of it, or your true destiny."

"Death is not her destiny, not this day," came the solemn voice of Dante.

Zelina turned, seeing Dante, albeit a vague outline of him, but visible nonetheless. "Dante?" She approached, with the Arbiter following closely.

"Impressive. Almost no people outside of Wynverians have ever made it to this plane. Even among necromancers, I will say you have managed quite the feat."

Zelina noticed the Arbiter's tone was neither warm, nor fierce. She did feel what felt like a strange ripple of energy, and noticed Dante's outline become foggier for a moment, likely a reminder for the spellcaster to tread carefully. "Dante, why have you come here?"

The dark arcanist gestured to Zelina. "I came to make sure your soul was not taken."

"Her time has come," The Arbiter repeated. "She has been judged worthy to remain, or to face the Wintertide. Either choice is her own, but her fate is sealed."

Dante merely shook his head. "Not by you, Arbiter. The blade Raleigh carries is cursed. It will absorb the soul of whoever dies to its edge; The wound lingers even upon her soul."

Zelina remembered that the wound from the sword was what had caused her to die initially. "Then...Why am I here?"

"Because if your soul passes into the next world and is incomplete, a piece of you will linger in the world. It could be used to steal what remains of your soul, ensuring you have no peace at all." Dante stared directly at Zelina. "You haven't much time left to decide; Once your body has been dead long enough, it won't be habitable."

"All the more reason for you to pass before your soul is taken by that weapon," the Arbiter reaffirmed.

"This may be your chance to escape a fate worse than even the Wintertide. I can protect you from its power."

Zelina, however, had a different realization. "But what about the Wynverians who died to that sword? Surely you've seen them perish by it, even if through the eyes of another. All those souls are trapped within it with no escape. They cannot come to you, or their rightful home. If Raleigh survives, that sword may take the lives of not just more Wynverians, but also those of other people."

"...I understand. Your argument is strong, but I cannot send you back, young queen," the Arbiter said. Although his tone was firm, Zelina couldn't help but feel as if she heard a hint of regret in his words.

Realizing that emotion would not sway him, Zelina decided on another course of action. Stepping forward and staring into his eyes, she spoke with confidence. "Then Arbiter, as others have challenged me...I challenge you."

The Arbiter of Souls looked at her curiously. "You are challenging me for a chance to return to life? You realize you only have one attempt? And that I cannot merely let you win?"

Zelina nodded. "I am aware, but I have no other options. For the sake of our people and others, I propose a single duel between you and me. Should I win, Dante will return me to my body," Zelina explained.

"And you are certain?" the Arbiter asked, as if offering her one last chance to back down.

For the briefest of moments, Zelina considered it. She was large compared to Dante and he was even larger still compared to her. Where she could swallow a human whole if she desired, the Arbiter of Souls could crush her with a single claw. Still, her purpose would not leave her. Against all odds, she would pursue her goal. "Of course."

"Then let us duel!" the Arbiter shouted, his voice echoing as he let his power flow into the realm.

"Gladly!" Zelina roared before she soared towards the primordial dragon, her wings flapping as she flew through the atmosphere above.

Forcefully, the Arbiter of Souls swung to bat Zelina away with the back of his forelimb, only for her to dive under it and swoop around, spraying him with intense flames. The great dragon was staggered for a moment, before he opened his mouth and began to breathe in, his body swelling.

The vortex of the giant dragon's breath was intense, as Zelina nearly succumbed to being pulled in. She managed to fly free, feeling fear grip her as she realized she was nearly eaten.

The queen was taken from her thoughts, however, when she saw a bright, blue light emanate from the larger dragon's mouth. The great dragon let off a beam, emanating more like a ray from the sun than a fiery plume. Ducking low, letting her body fall rapidly, Zelina managed to avoid the Arbiter's beam, flying past his head toward the nape of his scaly neck. Steeling herself, she began to bite and claw, the attacks doing very little to harm him due to the thickness of his scales. Still, not one to give up, Zelina was familiar with less armored portions of a dragon's body. With her predatory eyes glancing around, she knew the fastest way to the front of the Arbiter's neck would be in a direct arc.

The great dragon bucked, smashing his massive body into Zelina and making her roll back on his spine, dazed as the colossal being took to the skies. The next thing she knew, Zelina leapt off of the Arbiter, swooping under him to attack him where he was weakest. Gliding near his underbelly, Zelina struck, clawing the Arbiter, though to little avail.

"Using your smaller size to your advantage. Clever…if not futile," the Arbiter mused.

Zelina responded by biting at the underside of the Arbiter's neck, piercing his scales and wounding him. Ultimately, it amounted to little more than a scratch, but it proved he could be wounded and, perhaps, even beaten. While Zelina managed a few scratches, none of them went deep, and served only to annoy the Arbiter. She knew she needed to focus her efforts where she could do the most damage, flying towards his neck, she prepared to attack, but the Arbiter wasn't going to make it easy. The queen's attack failed as the Arbiter flew upwards, his wings creating huge blasts of wind, knocking her away. Desperately, Zelina tried to rise, only for the Arbiter's colossal forelimb to smash into her, sending the queen plummeting into the ground below like a meteor, rupturing and collapsing the ground from the impact.

On the ground, Zelina faltered, grunting as she felt her body ache and radiate agony. As much pain as she was in, Zelina's will would not wane. Instead, she managed to rise, ignoring her injuries and looking up as the Arbiter of Souls was diving down for her, mouth open.

Reflexively, Zelina flew away, launching into the sky and narrowly avoiding the Arbiter's snapping jaws, which closed with a mighty snap behind her. Before the Arbiter could recover, Zelina drew in close and unleashed a stream of searing blue flames at his eyes.

The Arbiter let loose an echoing bellow of pain as Zelina's breath scored home, blinding the great dragon for a moment. Seeing her chance, Zelina wheeled into the Arbiter's blind spot and launched herself towards him with all the force she could summon. Finally, she crashed into the Arbiter's jaw, feeling the impact dislocate his jaw and, for the first time, sending him reeling. As she flew back to gain distance, she saw the Arbiter struggle and roar, a fang falling from his maw.

Zelina felt satisfaction when the Arbiter realized how hurt he was, though by that time he was enraged. Quickly, she tried to breathe fire at him again, but it was to no avail as the massive, elder dragon managed to swat her down with one of his forelimbs before pinning her in place.

Gasping, Zelina tried to find a way free of the crushing weight but could think of none. For all her fighting she had only given minor wounds to the great dragon, while her entire body was aching...Yet even so, she was not discouraged.

"Give up, Zelina. You have lost!" The Arbiter shouted, despite the injury to his jaw.

"N...No." Zelina groaned, opening her eyes. She could not look up. Instead she saw Dante, standing near where the fang of the Arbiter had fallen. His figure grew more and more clear by the moment, just as Zelina's will grew stronger. "I will not surrender!"

"Even if the cost is to perish yourself? To suffer a death of the soul in addition to that of the body? Even the Wintertide would seem merciful in comparison..." The Arbiter stated with a low growl.

"I...will not let my people suffer...If it is between that and dying twice over, it is no choice at all." Zelina's defiance was absolute, the dragon queen adamant in pursuing her goal. Even though she could not move, she would not yield.

"…Very well." The Arbiter finally lifted his limb, now letting Zelina up, his wounds disappearing.

Hesitantly, the queen rose, now unharmed too. "Hm?"

"You may return to life but only for a week. I will give you that long before I call your soul back once more," the Arbiter explained. "In that time, you must free the souls of those slain in this war. You and the intruder will both be held responsible for this."

"A week?" Zelina asked, shocked. Part of her couldn't believe the opportunity, but she was eager to accept; it was a chance many never received. "Thank you, it is far more than I feel I earned."

"It is what your valor has gotten you. For such a young Wynverian you hold promise. I believe you have done our people proud with your performance today."

"Your words are more than I could ask for."

The Arbiter nodded. "I am glad you accept it so graciously. Whether or not you end your war is up to you, but you have your task. Do not fail, for there will be no third chance."

"Yes, Arbiter!" Zelina replied, just before turning to Dante. "Can you return us to the physical world?"

The spirit seer nodded. "Come and I will do so now."

Feeling her spirit renewed, despite her aches and pains, Zelina left the realm of the Arbiter now more determined than ever to do what she needed. With so little time she would have to act fast and hope her allies would aid in the efforts.

Soon after she made contact with Dante, Zelina felt warmth, followed by a white flash of light. Then, without delay, she felt herself back in her own body.

Slowly, she opened her eyes and rose. Zelina felt different; she was no longer in pain, but also could feel her connection to the Astral Mountain, the sense of relaxation and calm the dimension gave her lingering subtly. As she looked around, she realized she was back in the cavern. The fire nearby that had helped keep her warm was little more than embers and glowing wood, emitting light smoke.

Groaning a bit, Zelina sat up, thankful her pains were mostly gone. She touched her back, realizing her wound had healed before she breathed a sigh of relief and looked to Dante, who had a slight smile on his face.

"Congratulations. You've defeated death," he said with the slightest bit of amusement in his voice.

"Bargained with it is more accurate," Zelina replied, though she could not help but smile too for the moment.

* * *

Meanwhile, as Zelina enjoyed her return to the land of the living, Markus found himself not far from death's door. The wounded Heofonite was pinned down and hunted through the pine forests by the Elustrian captain, Shary, who had tracked him and the Wynverians he had rescued from Raleigh's camp, just as they felt safe. Although currently only Markus' life was on the line, he knew his death would only lead to the deaths of the Wynverians he had helped free.

Diving into cover behind a great pine tree, Markus narrowly avoided the huntress' shot, hearing her crossbow bolt thud into the wood. Peering out of his hiding place, Markus caught a glimpse of her before he crept through the undergrowth. Every now and again he would peer out to keep track of her, but he couldn't strike. While Markus was sure he could defeat her up close, her accuracy was fearsome, as were her reflexes; being too hasty to attack would seal his fate.

As she stalked him, it filled Markus with fear when he saw her smile. It was a cruel grin as her lips opened, revealing her chalk white teeth. He could tell she was satisfied by the challenge, but Markus was terrified by the prospect. There was no denying that he was prey, and that the predator was eager.

Confident she had lost sight of him, Markus tried to recall anything she'd said or done back at the camp, to think of a weakness he could exploit, when he had an idea. "You know," Markus grunted, "you put a lot of stock into your leader…Why?" he asked, his voice echoing among the trees.

Markus could see Shary looking for him, unsure of his location. "Raleigh has always been a man worth following."

"Why?" Markus hoped riling her would give him an opening.

"It is not just that he is a great warrior or a brilliant tactician...Yet he's always risen above. He never forgot his allies, much less stopped trying to be better. He felt every fallen ally spoke to his shortcomings as a leader. He celebrated the lives of his fellow warriors, just as much as he mourned their deaths...Even the ones caused by you and the Wynverians."

Markus could hear the passion in her words, the way she said them with genuine devotion. Markus had seen for himself that Raleigh respected his soldiers just as Zelina cared for her subjects. Putting it out of his mind, he remembered he had to shake Shary's confidence so she would make a mistake; Focusing on her pride, he had an idea. "Which is why he sent someone who fights from the shadows and at range? He didn't respect us enough to send a real warrior."

"As if anyone actually believes ranged weaponry is cowardly," Shary scoffed. "Raleigh never once ridiculed me for choosing long range weaponry. He was...Proud of me and encouraged me to be my best, to fight in a way that I felt was best."

Markus peeked out from behind his hiding place, observing Shary. He noticed her expression soften as she recounted the tale from her past. He said nothing at first, waiting to see if she would continue. As she fixed another bolt to her crossbow, Markus could tell she was distracted, but not quite enough.

"After all I went through until I met him, I never expected such kindness."

"Why's that?" Markus shouted hastily, trying to distract her; he could tell she was emotional, and he took the opportunity to take out his old fishing line. Tying it to a nearby bush, he tried to pull the string until it was taut, hiding as best he could.

"As if you care. All I will say is that while I know Raleigh has ended many hundreds of thousands of lives...he saved mine. That's what I cling to." Markus could hear Shary drawing closer, no doubt catching where his voice came from. It took a few moments before she was finally in range, as he held the fishing line tight before he felt her leg against it, before she finally tripped and stumbled.

Markus, knowing he would not get another chance, rushed at her, getting up and running towards her.

Swiftly, Shary turned and raised her crossbow, surprise flickered across her face as she saw his hand grab the bottom of her crossbow. On instinct, Shary pulled the trigger, an arrow grazing Markus' face, leaving a cut as the bolt glanced across his skin, a trail of scarlet following it.

The Heofonite managed to forge on, grabbing Shary along with her crossbow and slamming her into a nearby tree forcefully. He heard the air escape her lungs before he wrested the crossbow from her and crushed it, feeling the wood splinter and metal snap as he exercised his might.

"Gah…Damn it…" she grunted, out of breath. "I should have killed you at Lord Raleigh's camp when I had the chance."

Markus said nothing. In the grips of tiredness and wanting things to end, he slammed her against the tree again, the force of the blow knocking her out as her head banged against the wood. Once he was sure she was out cold, he let her body slump to the ground before he took a moment to catch his breath.

With his injuries, Markus felt like flying was beyond him. Regardless, he had to make it to the Wynverian camp and reunite with Zelina's army. As he went through the possessions Shary had on hand, Markus discovered rope in her pouch along with shackles. Clamping them around her wrists and tying her to a tree, he went to search the bodies of the other two. Once he had taken anything he deemed useful, he went to the place where the dead Wynverian was pinned to the tree.

Markus could see his body had grown cold and lifeless, his blood staining the bark and the ground beneath. Solemnly, Markus pulled his body from the tree and took him aside, laying his corpse to a small clearing. Laying him there, Markus knew he couldn't bury the body. Instead, he made a small cairn, gathering a few stones and sticks to make it more distinct.

Leaning down, Markus placed a hand on the body's forehead. "I'll make sure your sacrifice isn't in vain." Afterwards, he remained silent for a time, until he went to collect Shary and head towards the camp, hoping the prisoner would make for a good bargaining chip.

* * *

Zelina's recovery from her near death was nothing short of miraculous, in no small part due to Dante's efforts. The queen of the dragons stood strong and tall again after what felt like a lifetime. She was beginning to feel as if it was a dream of some kind, but the joy on the faces of her allies and the soldiers felt all too real. Yet, she couldn't help but notice one face in particular was missing. "Captain Grey?"

"Yes, my queen?" Grey asked, all too thrilled to have Zelina back to full health. The miracle of the moment had brought relief to all at the camp, despite the dire situation.

"Do we know of Markus' whereabouts?" Zelina asked in concern. "From what I hear, he's been gone the better part of a week."

The captain's expression became more serious. "He claimed to have needed to leave for a personal reason, but that was some time ago. At this time none of us know where he is."

Zelina's brow furrowed as she began to wonder what it could have been. "We'll need to send out a search when the scouts return. For now I have a war council to tend to."

Captain Grey nodded in affirmation. "Very well. I'll inform the scouts that we want word on when Markus returns or if he is sighted."

Zelina nodded. "Join me once you've finished informing them."

Afterwards, the two of them went about their work, with Zelina in her council, going over strategy. Captain Grey joined her half an hour later. Once Grey had arrived, discussions of how to care for those too wounded to battle once they moved out, however, a scout quickly came in.

"My queen, apologies, but we've found the Guardian!" he exclaimed.

"You have?" Zelina gasped, surprised. "Take us to him, immediately." Hastily, Zelina then rushed outed with the captain, the two of them going through camp with the scout, when they saw other scouts were surrounded by a crowd. "Hm? What's wrong?"

"I'm not sure, my queen," Captain Grey replied quickly. "We'll find out now." Parting the crowd, Grey led Zelina towards the front, the two of them saw Markus being carried by a pair of scouts, along with a woman in Elustrian armor, bound behind them.

"Markus!" Zelina shouted, horrified to see he was in grave condition. The young man was barely conscious, caked in blood and covered in wounds. He was breathing heavily while his hair was matted with dirt. Stepping forward, Zelina took ahold of him, helping him stand. "What happened to you?"

Weakly, he stared ahead, until he noticed, Zelina. "Queen Zelina...You're back." He gave a smile. "I'm relieved."

"Save your words, Markus." Zelina looked to the scouts. "Take him to the healers immediately, make sure he's tended to."

"And the prisoner, Your Majesty?" one asked.

Zelina cast her gaze to the woman, noticing the hatred in her eyes. "We'll deal with her soon."

Zelina had to watch as Markus was taken off to be tended to. The queen of the dragons wanted to go as well, but she knew her people still needed her focused. Turning to them, she spoke. "We haven't the time to stand about. Everyone, back to your duties! Bind this prisoner and store her until we can properly decide her fate."

Quickly, the gathered Wynverians returned to their duties, readying weapons and gathering supplies and preparing for their counterattack against the Elustrian forces. The two guards Zelina had addressed grabbed the Elustrian and dragged her away, but the captive's gaze never left Zelina. By the day's end, the Wynverian army was ready, and Zelina was relieved to hear Markus' condition had stabilized and the Guardian's life was not in danger.

After a full day, Zelina was appraised of who Shary was by allies who arrived from the village and was unhappy when she had heard that no progress had been made in getting Shary to speak. Despite multiple attempts and different approaches, Shary refused to say a word.

Zelina had considered questioning Shary herself, but deigned to instead leave that to others while the plans for Zelina's counterattack against Raleigh were finalized. The coordination took days, but by the time they passed, Zelina had confidence in their victory.

That night, as Zelina walked back to her quarters, she felt a pair of eyes lingering on her as she traveled, until she turned. She saw Dante standing nearby, Ihsan's remnant standing behind him. "To what do I owe this visit?"

"I am departing. You do recall the terms of our agreement, yes?" Dante asked.

"I do, though that's contingent upon my victory. The sword, land, and access to the tombs will be granted to you," Zelina reassured him. "So, where will you go?"

"Where I must," Dante replied before he stepped nearer, Ihsan's body following suit. "Trust I won't be far when time to collect comes."

"I was hoping for a more specific answer, since you'll be traipsing through my country," Zelina retorted officiously, reminding him of her authority. "It is my right as queen."

"Was," Dante said flatly, studying her closely. "You did lose your crown to Raleigh, and unless you act soon you may yet lose your life...or more."

Zelina paused at his comment, noticing the necromancer's underling was too close for her liking. Stepping forward and staring down, the queen spoke firmly. "And yet you still require favors of me, and my blessing to leave this place whole."

"True. Though I have done you yet another favor."
"Ones that help serve your own cause. No need to phrase it as charity," Zelina replied tersely. "I have healed Markus."

Zelina's eyes grew wide with surprise. "You did?"

Dante nodded, motioning for his thrall to step back. "His wounds were less severe than yours, so it was no concern. Consider it a final gift until I come to take my toll. He will be able to serve you by tomorrow."

"Thank you, Dante," Zelina said, remaining on guard, despite her gratitude.

"Your victory is all the thanks I need, *Queen Zelina*," Dante then turned, motioning for Ihsan's remnant to leave with him. "Just remember my due when the time comes."

Zelina watched as Dante and the body of Ihsan left, the two departing out of camp and down the mountain path.

While Dante's departure filled her with a sense of foreboding, she was grateful that Markus was fully healed. After a few minutes, she went to the cavern he was placed in and found him laying down, but conscious, his wounds gone. "Markus, glad to have you among us again."

"I'm glad to be back," he grunted as he sat up, wincing in pain. "How was I healed?"

"Dante's handiwork."

Zelina saw Markus scowl a moment. "I suppose I should be thankful I'm healed...Sore, but healed." Markus stood up and spread his wings with a wince, testing them. Once he was satisfied he looked to Zelina and smiled. "More importantly, though, I'm just thankful that you're up. Are you fully healed?"

"Well, honestly, I..." Zelina briefly considered telling him about her deal with the Arbiter, but decided not to; one way or another she would end the conflict, and she didn't want to worry him. "Feel much better. Thank you for asking."

Markus' hand traveled to his leg near where he had been injured; Not even a scar remained. "No problem. It looks like Dante did a fine job with my wing and leg. Fully healed."

Zelina was pensive as she thought of the scar remaining on her back. "Good, then we can get back to stopping Raleigh."

"Do you have Shary, the woman I brought in?" Markus asked, concerned.

"Yes, the others informed me of her name and her importance when they arrived."

Markus nodded. "I fought her and a few trackers. I barely survived, but they killed at least one Wynverian that I know of."

"All the more reason for us to leave soon. I have Captain Grey overseeing the preparations and we'll be leaving tomorrow morning."

Markus gave a wry chuckle. "Well, I guess we really are getting back into the thick of it."

"Yes, but we will end it, one way or another." Zelina offered her hand to Markus. "Still, I would be delighted if my assigned Guardian would assist me."

Taking her hand, he stood and gave a warm, genuine smile. "I'd be a poor Guardian and a poorer friend if I disagreed... But..."

"But?" Zelina asked.

"I think I'll need a proper weapon. My recent misadventure taught me about how necessary it is to have a suitable weapon and the utility knife I had wasn't enough."

"Well enough for you to survive with, at least, but we'll find you something more fitting. We should have plenty for you to choose from tomorrow. For now, please rest."

Markus bowed to Zelina. "I shall, but I humbly request you do the same. We both will need our strength."

Zelina gave a small sigh, chuckling at how, even as he just healed, Markus remained concerned for her. "It's a promise. Good night, Markus."

"Good night, Queen Zelina."

It was the next morning when the army gathered, everyone standing together, ordered and unified by their shared goal and the arduous task ahead of them. Zelina watched and helped conduct operations as her people soon armed themselves and dressed for battle. The fires of their camp burned hot in the cold mountain air. It soon dimmed as the sun rose and as the fuel ran short, but every one of them was prepared to leave and support their nation's cause.

The efforts of the Wynverian army to rally their forces had borne fruit. After Zelina was first wounded, Captain Grey and others had gradually been calling for aid. While some came slowly, they all marshaled on that day in greater number than expected. In particular, Zelina was surprised to see some Errant Broods had also opted to join their side instead of supporting Raleigh's takeover.

Seeing everyone there filled Zelina with a sense of gravity she had never felt before. Though she had seen larger crowds during times such as her coronation or challenges, she noticed it felt different. What they were doing, facing Raleigh, was potentially her final act, but failure also meant an end to the country they loved as they knew it.

Zelina had never had a task with the level of purpose she felt there and then, but she felt certainty well up inside her as she stood before her people and spoke, an internal strength driving her on.

"We are each only given one life, and we are lucky if we are able to use it well. It is a precious thing, finite, even when it feels it stretches on forever...However, we have lost much of that resource in our history, and even more since the arrival of the Elustrians. War and its wages are part of the lives any society leads, but there are costs I refuse to pay. The loss of our nation, our freedom, being forced to fight for fighting's sake and wounding those who did us no harm...Those are prices too high for anyone of integrity to pay. Today, though, we will rally to prevent that. Not just for our sakes, not just for Wynveria, but those who could not stop Raleigh's warmongering ways, and those who suffered under his delusions of grandeur. Today, we fight for a better world, and to save the lives all involved have yet to live!"

After that, Zelina had heard many cheers, with everyone crying out in agreement and fervor. It didn't matter if they were a soldier or a volunteer, a member of the broods or born of high families, all of them shared in her vision and purpose.

Raising a hand to silence them, Zelina went on. "We know that he is on the way to Arachon to claim his throne, reports have flooded of the bulk of his forces making their way there, with him sighted on the front lines, but before long, he will find himself not on the throne, but defeated in the dirt, put there by our efforts!"

Again, cheers rang out, all of them chanting the queen's name. "ZELINA! ZELINA! ZELINA!"

"Now, we fly!" she roared above them all, feeling their roused spirits raise her own. "NOW, WE END THIS WAR!"

Zelina led the charge after, with everyone flying off in one, large group. There was no way to mask the flight of the army and those who were giving them aide, but none troubled them. If anything, Zelina wanted her enemies to see her and her allies were undaunted after the previous battle.

Long before Arachon was on the horizon, they saw the smoke blackening the sky, coming from Arachon, only furthering the grim sense of foreboding that was welling up within Zelina.

The skies began to burn black and orange, the black, billowing gas mixing with clouds, making the crown jewel of Wynveria become a hellish shadow of the one she knew.

Flying as fast as their wings would allow, taking only the barest amount of time to keep themselves rested and reach Arachon, they could soon see the great civilization in the distance, as well as well as the trail of carnage Raleigh's forces had caused.

Zelina and her group saw the Elustrians had broken the outer walls, seeing that countless Wynverians were on the ground, slain and bleeding out, their blood pooling and steaming as the fires raged.

Far into the city, past the besieged wall and on the path to the castle. Countless buildings were reduced to rubble, with Wynverians facing off against the crimson-clad Elustrians and their allied errants, who wore red as well to denote them as allies of Raleigh.

With the battle raging, Zelina could see her people were losing en masse.

"Everyone, stop them at all costs!" Zelina roared, rage taking her as she flew in, spewing intense flames and razing the Elustrians without the bulk of their forces even noticing. However, Zelina did see Raleigh far ahead, turning in time to see her, a host of slain foes at his feet while he stood among his men.

Far above in the sky, Captain Grey and a few others flew above where arrows could reach and breathed out billows of smoke instead of fire. The Wynverian defenders noticed these signals as their own, coordinating a strike from two sides against their foes.

Soon, the Wynverians were attacking together, using their overwhelming might and aerial superiority to overwhelm the overconfident Elustrians, ending their lives.

Zelina smiled sensing their morale rise as they went into the battle. She noticed Markus nearby and shouted an order. "Markus, assist in saving the injured where you can! Let us handle the Elustrians!"

Nodding, Markus replied above the roars and raging fire. "Of course, my queen!"

Flying high up with her own forces, Zelina roared and swooped down, razing the troops, her fire breath star-white as her followers joined in. Those among the Elustrians who weren't burnt alive were soon torn apart by the dragons' claws and fangs. As the troops on the ground were attacked, many of Zelina's allies surrounded the errants above who defected to the Elustrians' side, with three or four crowding any one of them, attacking their wings forcing them to crash to the ground and ruined buildings below.

The chaos around the Elustrians alerted them to Zelina's army, with them scrambling to attack back. As they rallied and mounted a resistance, Zelina's forces pushed back the Elustrians, slaughtering them and forcing the army to take notice of their presence.

As scores of the Elustrians fell after they fought back, Zelina could feel victory approach, but remained cautious, knowing that the counterstrike was still early. Despite the overwhelming assault, the Elustrians soon gathered together, starting to push Zelina and her allies back, shields locked together and their ranks holding firm. Zelina was once again impressed by the might of the Elustrians. While she held no love for the invader's cause, their dedication to battle and ability to rally under pressure made her envious of their union.

The queen, however, decided to show them the union of the Wynverians. Breathing in, she released a loud, cascading roar, renewed white flames emitting from her maw as the piercing sound bewildered the unprepared. Her allies followed suit, their cries echoing into a grand chorus, scaring many Elustrians into panic. The soldiers began falling back and tumbling down in their sudden fear.

Once she and others dealt with the retreating Elustrians, ending their lives with ease, they continued their advance. Hearing a scream and a crash resound over the battlefield, Zelina's head snapped to see several of her soldiers fall from the sky, hurtling down to the ground below and thudding against the hard, unforgiving earth. The mighty cries above were the telltale sound of two Wynverians engaged in aerial combat. The din started filling her ears as she looked up and saw her men engaged in combat with a flight of Wynverians bearing the red flags of the Elustrians.

Flying in Zelina rammed one dragon at full force, her golden body knocking aside the green one, injuring their wing and sending them crashing towards several Elustrians below. She watched as the soldiers were crushed by the dragon's body, while its injured wing and added injuries kept it from taking flight to retaliate.

With the enemy vulnerable, other Wynverians swooped down to attack the traitor. Once they finished with him, Zelina looked for the other as she flew, only for her to catch sight of the dark violet scaled dragon. The large dragon was biting the tail of one of her allies, trying to weigh them down. Baring her fangs, Zelina darted towards the enemy, flying near its beating wings before lunging swiftly, taking one, powerful bite at its wing. She felt the crunch of snapping bones inside her maw and tasted the hot, thick flow of blood before she spat it out, her victim crying out and falling rapidly to his demise as he lost his ability to fly. She saw reinforcements for Elustria draw near, though.

Preparing herself, Zelina and those still able to fight went ahead, engaging them. As the queen continued her battle, she hoped the others were holding their own in the conflict.

Markus felt the weight of an injured Wynverian lift from his shoulders as he handed off the wounded warrior to his fellow rescuers, before turning back to survey the battlefield. Markus and his squad had served to provide support, assisting possible and trying to save as many fallen Wynverians as they could, carrying the wounded from direct combat and slaying any Elustrians who tried to stop them.

Markus was shocked to see a wing of errant Wynverians, armored like the Elustrians and each bearing a rider, armed with lances and wickedly barbed spears. Surprised, Markus flew to assist his allies who were engaging the enemy, only for the riders to impale their opponent's wings while the dragons clashed. The sounds of the Wynverians' cries rang out, along with the sight of blood gushing from each piercing attack the Elustrians performed. Once Markus was nearer, he saw the ropes tied to the spears were weighted by large anchors, the wounds and weight both sending the Wynverians plummeting down. When he flew in to assist, signaling for his men to follow. He had to halt midflight enemy forces opened fire, a wave of arrows keeping him back.

Markus was unable to retaliate until others came to assist him, seeing Ericsen and Alya attack the archers targeting him. Both flew in, landing heavily before they attacked, crushing and slashing the archers before they could strike.

Breathing a sigh of relief, Markus flew to them. "Thanks for saving me."

"You can thank us after we save the others," Alya said, looking up and directing Markus' attention back to the matter at hand.

Realizing he needed to cut the rope, Markus reached for his battle-axe. Lifting it, he took flight. "Right, let's go!" Markus shouted, taking flight and speeding towards the foe as fast as he could possibly go, Alya and Ericsen joining him. As they got close, Alya and Ericsen engaged the foe, giving Markus a chance to free their allies.

With a mighty swing, his axe severed the rope attached to one spear, sending the attached weights tumbling down below and freeing the trapped dragons. While injured, the freed Wynverians were able to rejoin the fray, assisting their rescuers in taking down the Elustrians. In the chaos of his allies turning the tables on the Elustrians, Markus realized the Elustrians were losing their composure, their formation becoming more erratic; the trained soldiers falling back when faced by the raging Wynverians.

Soon, Markus freed more Wynverians, and their small forces had been bolstered. With his maneuverability and precision in flight, his foes at last noticed him, attacking at range or trying to fly in with errants while his allies engaged the rogue Wynverians. However, Markus' focus was sharp, and he felt an intense awareness, now used to the intensity of battle. Soaring towards his attackers, Markus struck, chopping or hacking them when he could, each individual blow more than enough to kill the unsuspecting Elustrians. Markus' speed was enough for him to close the distance between most archers, the stream of arrows less intense than before. Once he had killed a few bowmen and attacking riders, he saw the remaining Elustrians were falling back, attempting to escape the fray in retreat.

Pressing the advantage, Markus flew in to close the distance, when he saw two enemy Wynverians and Elustrians were upon him with nets to trap him. He tried to look for an escape, but he was surrounded on all sides until Alya, Ericsen, Captain Grey, and Audny all swooped in. Each of them struck an enemy, felling them and saving Markus. The Heofonite sighed in relief as he was saved.

"Keep your guard up," Grey said gruffly, looking at Markus. "Victory is at hand...You need only hold out awhile longer."

"Right," Markus said hastily.

Grey nodded before she went back on attack and coordinating, while Audny continued to assist with saving their allies.

Slowly, despite the harshness of the struggle, all was going back into the favor of the Wynverians. As the battle went on, a great number of the Wynverians were badly wounded, some hit by arrows, others by spears and axes desperately thrown aloft. Markus, Audny, and several squadrons of Wynverians were still focused on taking the injured allies from battle, carrying them to safety.

The pattern of rescue continued with several squads of Wynverians also fighting to keep their allies alive, however many perished even before they reached land again. The losses were heavy, but not for naught.

Zelina felt her wings ache and her lungs burn from spewing so many plumes of fire and flying, but she also saw Raleigh, standing high among his men and glaring directly at her. The queen's gaze did not turn from his as she knew she needed to end his life and do away with his accursed blade. Her attention was turned from him, however, when she saw that Raleigh's personal guard and the warmonger himself entering battle, she was staggered by how even after all of the combat they were involved in, Raleigh's elite were still able to press on. No less than twenty transformed Wynverians and even more in their human state were spread among them on the ground, killed by the peerless warriors.

Given how fierce the Elustrians proved, Zelina worried about a protracted battle; Aside from her own limited time, if the battle dragged on, more of her own people could die. The worst possible outcome would be Raleigh slaughtering more Wynverians, absorbing their souls into the blade. She could not afford to wait, for her sake or for the sake of others.

Slowly, though, the battle's intensity died down. Zelina could see the Elustrians were moving, but not in retreat. Instead, they were making way, as a troop of soldiers came, heralding Raleigh's approach with fanfare. The Elustrians were also carrying banners with white flags, and the Elustrian soldiers stopped attacking.

"Send word to hold off on our assault," Zelina commanded, having her soldiers carry the message. Looking at Raleigh as he approached, not letting her eyes off her would-be killer. She had no idea if he was surrendering or asking for ceasefire, but she needed to know.

Flying down to him, Zelina stood before the vanguard, who parted as Raleigh approached. Zelina waited for Captain Grey and others to come to her side. As she approached, Raleigh did so too, a smug smile on his face. "Queen Zelina, I'm pleased to see you here again. After our last battle I expected we wouldn't meet again."

Zelina stood firm, staring at Raleigh undaunted. "I had unfinished business. Besides, I felt it only fair I return the favor to you."

Raleigh smiled. "Many have made that claim. Still, I cannot deny you and your followers fight well, yet they failed to see how you fell during our prior battle." Raleigh's tone was confident, taunting. "However, you survived."

"You will find us Wynverians a hardier lot than you imagined." Zelina looked down at him, matching his gaze as she thought of her mission, and even a chance for vengeance for both herself and her fallen people.

"You are, however, I wouldn't want to waste the blood of my potential allies and current subjects. I came to offer you one final chance for graceful surrender, and the opportunity to serve under me willingly."

"I don't think that'll be necessary," Zelina said firmly, keeping her cold look of defiance.

"Oh? You appear confident while your men and women die in droves and my people hold the advantage. Meanwhile, Wynveria is no longer yours, considering my victory." Raleigh stood tall, his imposing figure looming over her as he cast a shadow. Swollen with confidence and pride, Raleigh stepped nearer still, his gaze lingering on Zelina's face. "You know, I told your insipid Guardian that I had considered negotiating a wedding. Perhaps to allow you to save face and to quell your peoples' concerns...Though it seems that is a bit much to hope for now."

Zelina's expression remained the same. "A bit is a gross understatement, and while my people have taken on losses, so too have yours. I can see that no matter who wins this war, and trust it will be me if I see this to its conclusion, there will be heavy losses and much rebellion."

Raleigh laughed. "Bold talk, but I already know your men and women would fight futilely to oust me, just as mine would not surrender if I were to fall."

"And you know the loss of life will damage this kingdom you wish to add to your empire. What's the point in wasting such a precious resource when we can conclude this here and now?"

"So you wish to challenge me again?" Raleigh asked, smiling. "I savor the opportunity to best you twice, though I fear there's little I would gain there..."

"Maybe not, but by Wynverian law, the ruler can be challenged for their claim to the throne, and as you said, you are ruler by rite, so why not accept?" Zelina asked. "Do you fear the competition?"

Raleigh stared at her blankly, pondering her words before laughing. "Hahaha! Trying to rile me? No need,

Zelina. While there is little you can offer me, I believe my forces would enjoy the spectacle. A ceremony to mark the dawn of a new era and the fall of the old. I accept, and you have no choice but to follow through."

"Of course I will. After all, I posed the challenge, and this time no distraction will save you, Raleigh,"

Zelina said firmly.

"I didn't take you for an excuse maker, but the stakes remain the same as before. Should you survive again, you will follow as a loyal enforcer of the Elustrian Empire. Should you refuse, you'll be spitting upon the word and tradition of your people...And let's not forget that I hold the advantage in this bout of ours. Perhaps you will be motivated to provide a challenge worthy of my time now. One final struggle, where the defeated yields to the victor...Just remember, when you are bested again, I offered you a chance to walk at my side and you rejected it, so now you can at least serve beneath me."

Zelina nodded; While Raleigh's terms were unsavory, she knew the odds of defeat were sadly more likely than victory, and the challenge would spare the lives of her people. Better the queen suffers than the whole of her realm, Zelina thought. "Very well."

To make a show, Raleigh turned before he presented his sword and looked to his followers. "Everyone, the queen of dragons doubts my word…However, I will give it to those who deserve it. I swear upon the lives of our allies that have been lost and all the blood that has been spilled on the field of battle by us that I will follow my word. Should I lose, I will respect Queen Zelina's edict and leave this nation in peace, as shall you all. Still, she forgets I bested her once, and I will best her yet again! When I do, the Wynverians will join us, the cold mountains will yield to the strength of our spirit, and we shall all run the rivers red, until the blood of our enemies is all that slake this continent's soil!"

There was a thunderous cacophony as the warriors yelled in approval of Raleigh's words. Their cries echoed loudly, filling the air as they raised their weapons, chanting his name as they recognized their leader and champion.

Zelina went wide eyed, seeing how even the most injured and tired among them cheered his name, drawn to the man even as their allies, enemies, and innocent bystanders died around them and fires raged.

Raleigh's presence was commanding and his sway over them absolute; It was indeed true they would never surrender so long as that man lived.

Clenching her fist, feeling anger at how the warmonger and his underlings used the field of battle to further aggrandize their cause, Zelina stepped forward, glaring daggers at her foe. For a moment,

Zelina felt the urge to transform there, but held back, though flames escaped her mouth for a moment before she composed herself "Raleigh, your arrogance is staggering. It will be a pleasure to defeat you," she spoke, a clear edge of aggression evident in her restrained words.

Raleigh chuckled at Zelina's defiance. "And it will be an honor to have you serve in my new contingent of Wynverian warriors."

Zelina looked to her own followers before her generals and captains flew to her side. Once they were there, she spoke. "Instruct everyone to cease fire and hold their ground. Do not attack the Elustrians, but if any make a move against you...Slaughter them, without reservation."

Afterwards, everyone moved out, Zelina flying back to the wall's top and taking a moment to herself. She felt the rush of fury welling up within her die down, at least to the point she could think calmly. She began to realize the weight of her decision, feeling doubt settle in as she remembered last match, how she had lost when the whole of her nation counted on her, and how she had failed. Since then, more had died, and she was more worn from battle now than she was before.

Caught in her thoughts, Zelina didn't notice Grey or Markus touch down near her, with Grey speaking.

"Queen Zelina, have you lost your mind?" "Excuse me?" Zelina asked, caught off guard by her frankness. "My decision was a calculated risk, I've learned from our last battle and am better aware of how to beat him."

"I'm not so sure it was," Grey said quickly her gaze focused on Zelina.

The queen's eyes widened a bit before she turned to Grey, standing straighter. "Captain, is there something you wish to say to me?"

"Yes. Why would you throw away our chance at victory like that? Was your last brush with death not enough for you?"

"Grey, you're out of li-" Markus began.

"I am speaking to Zelina, Markus! After all the Aurah accursed work we went through to keep her alive, after her foolhardy deal with Dante, she insists on risking all of us on a grudge match." Her anger was clear, though it stemmed from worry for Zelina.

"Captain, your Queen is right here, and you will obey the chain of command," Zelina said, maintaining composure.

"*Former* queen." Grey's words came out like venom, before she saw the anger on Zelina's face and calmed some, her expression of anger becoming concern. "A...Apologies. I'm just asking, why? We could have won."

"Maybe, but not without heavy losses. Raleigh's forces were dictating the tide of battle and they're too many. This war would have been dragged out longer than I can afford to fight it."

Captain Grey grew quiet. "Are you sure that you can win?"

There was a quiet, tense moment before Zelina replied. "I am." Zelina felt a flicker of guilt at her lie, but knew she had no choice but to believe in herself. "One way or another, I am ending this war today."

"We'll be at your side in case he tries anything," Markus insisted.

"Thank you, Markus, but I need both you and Captain Grey to patrol the area, in case his men try to sneak in. Please...Arachon is the heart of Wynveria, and I am trusting you with it."

"Thank you, Queen Zelina, but this city is not truly the heart of this nation, you are, as are the people living here. I know you will be fine, but I want to be here to support you," Markus insisted.

Zelina began to think it over before she smiled. "Very well, if after your search you see no trouble you can come. All I ask is that you promise not to interfere."

"I wouldn't dream of it." Markus returned Zelina's expression as he anticipated seeing her second and final match with Raleigh.

"Captain Grey, will you be fine holding watch with your troop?"

More collected, Captain Grey nodded, her gaze expressing full confidence in Zelina. "It would be an honor. Please, Your Majesty, win for us all."

"For all of us who yet breathed and especially for those who have ceased to." Zelina then transformed before roaring and taking flight, her wings bringing up a gust as she flew. Soon, Markus and a few others Zelina instructed to follow her took flight behind her. As the Wynverian army rallied, the Elustrians and errants also followed suit.

* * *

For her part, Zelina, back in human form walked near the center of the battlefield and surveyed the area, seeing the faces of both allies and enemies nearby. The air grew heavy, and suddenly, Zelina felt a shock of agony, the sharp stab of phantom pain as she remembered the wound Raleigh had inflicted upon her. The pain was so intense she gasped, but then it was gone just as quickly. Part of her wondered if it was a true feeling or if it was imagined.

Taking a calming breath, Zelina gripped the handle of her sword and stood tall, her head held high as she locked eyes with Raleigh; It was the final battle and the war would only end when Raleigh's life did. As she looked ahead, she saw the fierce warrior drawing near, his great sword carried upon his shoulder as he took heavy, powerful steps; He maintained a confident smile, one that anticipated victory. She would enjoy seeing his smug smile become an expression of fear.

Raleigh took a deep breath, as if inhaling the tension in the air itself. "Remember this day well, Queen. Today you will lose your crown, but you and your people shall gain purpose. Take comfort in that and the opportunity to become a legend."

"I will remember this day, Raleigh." Zelina raised her blade, pointing it at the warmonger as he lifted his ruby red sword. "It will be the day that this war ends…Along with your life."

Raleigh sneered. "Bold words from a proud warrior, but now I will humble you!" Swiftly, faster than any warrior Zelina had seen, Raleigh lunged, his sword singing as it sliced through the air, directly at her throat.

Instantly, Zelina blocked with her sword, a mighty clang produced as she locked eyes with her foe. She glared intently as his smoldering, scarlet eyes fixed on her, before she pushed him back and attacked, striking twice.

The warlord ducked the first blow before backtracking, avoiding the second entirely as he gathered his bearings. Raising his sword again, he struck using a downward slash, only for Zelina to avoid it entirely and go back on the offensive.

Zelina lashed out at Raleigh in a furious storm of steel but try as she might the warlord parried every strike, exploiting every opening she left with powerful, controlled and precise strikes. As Zelina mustered all of her strength, she felt Raleigh falter, even as he blocked each of her intense strikes, but he was not alone. Soon, Zelina felt herself starting to tire out as she bled from several small wounds, while the warlord looked none the worse for wear. She had thought he was just a mad berserker, but it dawned on her that unless she could find some way though his defenses, her hopes of victory were slim. She grew more wary, slowing the pace of her attacks and watching for an opening. When Raleigh opted to raise his sword again, she struck in a flash, cornering him as he stumbled back, the edge of her sword slicing the man's cheek, opening a deep, bloody gash.

Attacking again with quick, precise stabs, she pushed Raleigh back, the pressure and rapidity of her moves making him retreat again and again. She could see Raleigh growing sloppier, leaving more openings. Finally, a chance came when he swung his sword far out and he was backed against the wall. Drawing back and lunging, Zelina knew her attack would kill him. However, Raleigh managed to sidestep it. She realized him drawing his sword was a feint, and as she attacked, he rammed into her with his shoulder, winding the blonde warrior and knocking her aside.

Zelina gasped as she fell to the ground, trying to catch her breath as the dust of the battlefield rose around her. Above her, she saw Raleigh raise his sword, the sun at his back. His shadow loomed over her like the certainty of death.

* * *

As the Elustrians and Wynverians continued their path towards the battlefield, where Zelina and Raleigh struggled, Markus kept watch. While he trusted Queen Zelina and knew most the Elustrians dared not act out against Raleigh, he also knew from personal experience how even the most loyal of people could deviate from their leaders' orders.

While Markus kept watch from the skies, he caught sight of Tiernan, surprised to see Raleigh's second-in-command slip off from the main crowd into a back street. Flying nearer, Markus saw he was meeting with others, the lot of them heading away from the masses and in their own direction.

Feeling a pit form in his stomach, Markus gained a sense of foreboding and knew that he needed to keep an eye on Tiernan, though he heard the beating of wings beyond his own grow louder as he saw Alya and Ericsen drew near.

"Guardian, why are you headed away from your post?" Alya asked.

"It seems we have a few Elustrians deviating from the path. I want to keep an eye on them," Markus explained.

Ericsen looked on, tracking the small group from afar. "Are you going to alert Captain Grey or the others?"

"I would, but I worry that'd attract too much attention," Markus said. "If too many Elustrians think we're breaking our word, the battle will break out again. So far as I can see it's only ten of them."

Alya considered what Markus said. "I agree...I think us three will be plenty, provided we follow at a distance. We'll assist you however we can."

Heartened by the offer, Markus smiled despite the dire situation. "Thanks...Glad I can count on you both."

As they remained in the sky, trailing the rogues but keeping their distance, they saw they were making their way towards the castle of Arachon, though each had a grappling hook and rope ready, throwing them up and testing them before they scaled the fortification walls.

"They're invading the castle!" Markus shouted, anger welling within him. He clenched his fist, realizing their deception.

"They're not the only ones." Alya pointed out another five drawing near, also ready to scale.

"Are there any more?" Markus asked.

"Not that I see," Alya replied, scanning the area.

"We'll take care of these ones, then go after the others, quickly!" Markus decided.

Flying to intercept the second group, Markus, Alya, and Ericsen all landed in front of them, both dragons crushing two each, while Markus tackled another, pinning him to the ground.

The five Elustrians were dealt with quickly, with Alya and Ericsen crushing them beneath their weight, dispatching them quickly, while Markus pressed against the other's throat, waiting until he had passed out from air loss.

Sighing, Markus rose, stripping him of his weapons before restraining him with rope. Once he finished, he turned to Alya and Ericsen. "Are others here?"

"No, these were the last ones," Ericsen stated.

"Alright, now we go after Tiernan..." Markus said bitterly.

The trio went back to the castle, going inside. With so many people focused on the war, and then the duel between Zelina and Raleigh, few were there to guard the castle itself. While Markus, Alya, and Ericsen were trying to warn the few guards around, only to instead discover that there were several bodies on the floor.

Markus stared on, feeling anger at the scene while Ericsen swore as and knelt down to look at the bodies. The three looked on grimly, seeing many had slit throats and more had been killed in a surprise attack.

"They broke the ceasefire...but why?" Ericsen asked in disbelief.

"To loot this place, no doubt," Alya said. "This probably wasn't Raleigh's plan, but we need to handle this. Now. Those fiends can't possibly know about the castle interior, so they can't have gotten far." Alya looked about for a hint or clue as to where Tiernan and his people could have gone.

"They're probably just looting what they can, but stay wary," Markus said. "The guards are already looking, but we need to keep our wits about us too..."

"Right," Markus agreed. "We need to warn anyone who's still alive, but them leaving a bloody trail should make them easy to follow." Looking around for clues, it was easy for Markus to see evidence the stairs, scarlet droplets of blood on the stone and carpet, along with the banister.

Following the trail, the trio saw a few more guards along the way, there were three bodies, but two were wounded. Quickly, Markus went to their side, looking them over. He was grateful to see that, while hurt, they were stable. "What happened?"

"The Elustrians...They stormed in. We heard a commotion but were too late to save the others. Aft-" The guard coughed, clutching his wound near his abdomen, blood spilling from it before he could finish.

"Sir, don't talk," Alya said, kneeling to look at his injury.

The guard shook his head. "No...He took lady Delys. He's forcing her to take them to the treasury room."

"Delys?" Markus asked, remembering Zelina's handmaiden. "Where is the treasury? We have to save her."

"D-down the hall..." The guard looked to his wounded fellow who was still breathing. "We'll be fine, go!"

Markus nodded before looking at Ericsen. "Listen, we need you to find the other guards and come this way. We'll go after them, but we can't afford to let them escape."

"Alright," I'll be back before you know it," Ericsen said quickly before he went on his way.

Going ahead with Alya, Markus continued to follow the trail and found his way to the treasury, the large, double doors open while Markus readied his axe and Alya drew her broadsword. The two were ready to fight when they heard a scream.

"Pl-please! I showed you where the treasury is, just take what you want and leave!" Delys' voice came, panicked and strained.

Markus and Alya saw that Tiernan's four men were standing there, each with a sack filled to the brim. The others filling their pockets, coinpurses, satchels, and whatever else they could use to contain their ill-gotten riches, while Tiernan held the edge of a dagger to Delys' neck threateningly. The rogue Elustrians were picking up whatever they could from coins and rings to jewel-encrusted armaments and other finery.

Tiernan gave a confident laugh, grinning from ear to ear. "Oh, we will, girl, but that's on the off chance Lord Raleigh does lose. If he wins as I expect him to, well, he can't miss what he doesn't know he has, right, men?"

"That's right, sir!" one said. "These will buy me a fine villa here."

"But in the cold?" another asked. "Save it for when we conquer another land, someplace more pleasant."

Delys gulped, clearly afraid, but not willing to cower. "Whatever you plan, you can't possibly think you'll get out of this unscathed."

"Young woman, after all the time I put in for Lord Raleigh, I'll be surprised if I don't wind up with a dukedom....and if I don't, I'll consider this my severance pay."

Markus gripped his axe harder and looked at Alya; the two had to strike while the men were distracted.

Markus took a moment to steady himself, to focus before he sprung into action. Rounding the corner, no words passed his lips, no moment was wasted before he swung his axe at a thief admiring a gem. Seconds later, Markus' axe cleaved his skull, splitting his helmet before Markus kicked his dead body down, landing and spilling riches and blood to the ground.

By then, all eyes were on Markus, while Alya jumped out, stabbing another as he readied his own sword. Her blade plunged into his side before she withdrew it, letting his body drop to the ground.

The two remaining thieves and Tiernan backed away, while the leader held his blade to Delys' neck tighter, drawing blood.

"Ah, looks like we have some unwelcome guests," Tiernan said. "Hello again, Guardian. Here to finish stabbing us Elustrians in the back?"

"My nation gave Raleigh an alliance, not me," Markus said. "Besides, you're the traitor here, disobeying your leader's word."

Tiernan smiled. "A pious hypocrite, a common sight...But one I don't have time for. I propose a negotiation, quickly, one that suits us all."

"Really? I think we all know you break word easily," Markus said, not willing to hear him out.

"I shed blood even easier, Guardian," Tiernan said, emphasizing the blade against Delys' throat. "Now...My compatriots and I drop our bags, we take the girl with us a short distance, and when we're a far enough away, we'll let her go and she makes her way back."

"What proof do we have you'll keep your word?" Alya asked.

Markus grit his teeth, he knew they only had to hold out until Ericsen and the guards arrived, but there was no guarantee Delys would live.

Tiernan shook his head. "You have none, but trust me...If I have nothing to live for, why not take what I can?"

Markus sighed. "Fine...We'll let you go."

"Markus!" Alya shouted.

"Trust me, Alya, this is the only way." Markus then dropped his axe. "My only condition is that you take me instead."

"Oh?" Tiernan asked. "I think the Wynverians would be more willing to listen with one of their own at risk."

"Yes, but your master will forgive any transgression if you take me in to face his punishment...Delys didn't earn this terrible fate, I have."

"Ah...How chivalrous." Tiernan nodded. "Boys, escort him here, I'll let the wench go once he's here and bound."

Stepping forward, hands raised, Markus waited until the men bound his wrists. He could tell they were tense, desperately trying to think of how to escape, but not focusing on other factors.

Once Markus' wrists were bound, he was roughly carried to Tiernan, while Markus watched the man slowly release Delys, pushing her aside dismissively.

"Markus, you idiot, they'll kill you!" Delys cried.

"We will, but not just yet." Tiernan put away his dagger and then drew the same sword he had stolen from Nersel. Pointing it at Markus' chest, he spoke. "Now, we'll be leaving. If anyone moves, you'll be joining my late friends and those worthless guards on the floor."

Markus nodded, hoping that his plan would pay off. Walking ahead with a wide berth, Markus could hear Tiernan breathing heavily, along with his own heart beating fast in his heart. Carefully, tentatively, he walked ahead, until he heard more footsteps.

Markus immediately jumped ahead, his sudden move earning two attacks from Tiernan. Markus felt the sting of cold steel on his wing, but managed to get away from Tiernan's range, just as a dozen guards and Ericsen arrived.

"Are we too late?" Ericsen asked.

Markus could feel blood trickling down the feathers on his wing, wincing before he poured his might into snapping the rope binding him. Feeling the knots and fibers rend after he moved, Markus glared at Tiernan, who gave him a rueful look. "You're just in time." After, Markus looked to Delys. "You may wish to leave."

Nodding, Delys backed away from the conflict as the guards drew nearer, to block the exit from Tiernan and his men. Once the path ahead was blocked, Tiernan began to scowl with rage.

"Hmph...Once a liar and a trickster, always a liar and a trickster."

"I think you should blame me less and more your own greed and desperation," Markus said before he retrieved his axe. Raising it, he pointed it at Tiernan. "You may wish to surrender."

"I'll die before I surrender to you," Tiernan said, taking out his sword.

"Looks like that won't be a long wait," Markus retorted before drawing near, Alya, Ericsen, and the guards doing the same.

Grimly, Tiernan stepped ahead, his fellows following suit. "No quarter and no surrender, men. If we die, we die as we lived...Warriors."

With loud, unified cry, the three attacked, though the guards repelled them with raised shields, forcing them back. While Tiernan struck, wounding a few by stabbing between their shields, he was getting cornered.

"Captain Tiernan! Help!" one shouted as he was pierced in his shoulder, unable to wield a blade anymore.

Markus saw Tiernan grow frustrated, grabbing his own man and shoving him forcefully towards the guards, making a few stumble as his underling fell upon them, causing them to falter even more as some backed against the already dead bodies. Tiernan wasted no time using the chaos to run past the guards and toward the exit, while Alya, Ericsen, and the guards left standing set upon the last warrior.

Not willing to let Tiernan escape, Markus ran after him before taking flight, wincing as he started to flap his wings, but his anger blocked out the pain. Seeing the slain guards in the hall again only fueled Markus' fury. His breath grew hot and his mind clouded as rage took hold of him. "Tiernan! Get back here!" Still clutching his weapon, Markus closed in on Tiernan, rounding a corner before throwing his axe at the man. With a yell, Markus watched as his axe spun in the air quickly, the blade singing and shining in the light, though Tiernan dove, landing on his front and avoiding injury as the axe buried itself in the wall with a loud thud.

Not deterred one bit, Markus tackled Tiernan as he scrambled to get up, pinning the warrior down before grabbing him by both wrists. Grabbing them tightly, Markus could feel his enemy's bones preparing to give way, along with Tiernan's pained cries.

"Aaagh! Mercy, Guardian, mercy! I yield!"

"No. You don't deserve it..." Markus grunted, grabbing harder until he heard a harsh, crunching noise. Markus heard Tiernan's screams of agony continue, not minding his strength as he continued to crush the man's wrists, until Markus felt Tiernan shift.

For all his strength, Markus was still fairly light, even with his armor. As Tiernan bucked beneath him, Markus tried to force him back down, until Markus felt the man knee him in the groin.

Stunned by the low blow and overcome by pain, Markus reeled, only for Tiernan to reach for his stolen sword. Markus mustered his strength, pushing himself before he punched Tiernan in the chest fiercely, hearing more cracks as the man's armor gave way, along with his ribs. Markus could hear Tiernan gasp and wheeze, before he realized what was happening.

Rising, Markus saw Tiernan struggle to catch his breath, his body on the ground as the man reached to his chest, only to keep coughing and sputtering. Standing there, breathing heavily, Markus watched as Tiernan turned blue. Wordlessly, he reached down, noticing the wide-eyed Tiernan reach to him, trying to clasp Markus' hand.

Coldly, Markus swatted Tiernan's hand aside, reaching for Nersel's blade and taking it. "This belongs with these people." Turning, Markus walked back to the others as Tiernan's last breaths were taken in vain, and his hand fell to the ground.

Walking back to the others, carrying Nersel's sword with him, Markus rejoined his companions.

"Guardian, what happened to Tiernan?" Ericsen asked, concerned. "Did he escape?"

"No...His luck ran out," Markus said. "We've won here...But Queen Zelina needs us. We have to get back."

"We will, Markus," Alya said. She then turned to the guards. "Will you all be fine here?"

"Yes, of course. We'll keep an eye out for other invaders and tend the wounded, but know we send our support with you," the head guard said.

"Great, then we'll get going," Alya began, when she saw Delys. "Oh, Lady Delys. I thought you left for safety."

"I did, but I need to go with you three, please!" Delys implored.

"But it's not safe, especially for someone who isn't trained," Alya said. "Lady Delys, you needn't-"

"Please!" Delys cried, tears forming. "Queen Zelina is my best friend. If I'm not there for her when she needs me most, I'll never forgive myself."

Markus turned to Delys. "We'll take you. Just promise to stick close to us," Markus said.

Alya turned to him. "Markus, are you sure?" "Delys is right we can't afford not to support Zelina now. Even if we can't fight with her, we can be there for her and remind her just what she's defending and how much we all need her." Markus looked at his allies. "This is the moment we've all struggled for, all of us, we can't afford to miss it."

"Markus, thank you," Delys said, "For saving me and...For this."

"You don't need to thank me, but...I appreciate it, very much," Markus said before standing tall. "We need to get going."

"Right, will you be able to fly?" Delys asked, looking at Markus' wing.

"I will," Markus said, moving his injured wing. However much pain he was feeling, he could put it out of his mind. Nersel had been avenged, but with the pain of the lost allies somewhat assuaged, Markus wanted to focus on the people he could still help save.

* * *

Time slowed to a crawl, Zelina feeling her heartbeat grow louder and stronger, but she felt something aside from fear...Resolve. She couldn't fall, and doom Wynveria with her. It didn't matter if she lived or died, but Raleigh couldn't win, he couldn't consign her people to life as oppressors and servants. Their lives would mean little more than being pawns in Raleigh's twisted war games, and stripped of freedom to choose their meaning. Praying to the Arbiter for a last flicker of strength, Zelina found it was already within her, and she'd use every ounce of it. In denial of loss, in a great surge of righteous anger, she rose, holding her sword steady and slashing.

She grimaced as the warmonger blocked the attack before laughing madly, clearly enjoying the contest as he pushed her back using his massive weapon.

"Enough of this game!" Raleigh roared. "You will hold nothing else from me, Zelina! Fight! Show me what you can truly accomplish!"

Though it was a struggle, Zelina pushed him back, her might overcoming him even with Raleigh bearing down on her with his great sword. She could feel herself standing shakily after his assault, but she soon regained her confidence.

Raleigh's laughter stopped as Zelina fought to her feet, every swing of her blade and every time she deflected his attacks resulting in him losing ground. Zelina saw his surprise, grinning as she gained momentum, pushing him back inch by inch. Finally, with a loud shout and a mighty shove of her shoulder, she managed to throw the warlord off her, yet even then, his glare never wavered. Staring him down, she saw her opening and took it, thrusting downward again and again, capitalizing on the opportunity.

Raleigh desperately blocked her first two strikes, bracing his great sword against his arm like a makeshift shield, but Zelina's strikes wrenched it to his side, her third slash cutting deep into his arm before he could recover.

Zelina raised her blade to strike him while he was weak, but Raleigh kicked her leg out from under her, making her stance weak and causing her to fall briefly. The opening was just long enough for Raleigh to rise and retreat to a safe distance, with Zelina gritting her teeth in anger. She watched the blood run down his arm, smiling at the progress she had made. Seeing Raleigh's face, though, she was surprised he wore a grin on his. Eager to rid him of it, she attacked again.

However, the queen was too hasty and Raleigh was still calm enough to use his wits to his advantage. Scooping dust from the ground below in his palm, Raleigh cast his hand out, before it spread into Zelina's eyes. Blinded, Zelina barely had a moment to register what had transpired before he stabbed her, his sharp blade piercing her side and making her groan in agony.

The queen of the dragons would not be stopped, however. Fighting through pain and gritting her teeth, even as she felt intense pain she hacked into Raleigh's body, severing all resistance as she took off his right arm entirely. She heard a deafening cry as Raleigh backed off, immense satisfaction as she saw his arm hit the ground. She had made undeniable progress, but had to remain vigilant. Even short an arm, Raleigh could still end her life if she let her guard down. Zelina smiled, feeling the situation turn in her favor, yet she knew she could not count Raleigh out yet.

Zelina warily approached as he hefted his sword up with his remaining arm, she was stabbing again when Raleigh parried immediately. Instinctively, she pulled back and swung her sword again, but again Raleigh was ready, swinging to intercept, throwing his weight into the strike. The clash of the swords was loud, shaking Zelina's bones and testing every muscle in her body.

Over and over, Zelina defended against his wild assault, blood from Raleigh's wound still pouring out until some splashed onto his blade. Every time they clashed, Zelina couldn't help but notice the sword glowing a vibrant red color, growing brighter with each strike. Zelina was able to defend, but each time her sword's mettle was tested, the edge chipping and metal bending, until Raleigh's sword took on a deadly glow. She blocked another powerful swing, but only barely as her sword broke. Once Raleigh's blade decimated hers, she narrowly threw herself out of the way as the pieces of her sword went flying.

Holding a handle to a broken lump of metal, Zelina felt her advantage disappear. With him down an arm but wielding a weapon and her holding a broken blade, she realized she had to consider her moves carefully. The warrior queen considered transforming into a dragon, but knew he would attack her mid-transformation, just as he had before. It was down to her skills and her broken blade, a lone opportunity to save her kingdom and herself, however slim.

"Now you will die, Zelina! Your body will soon be just as broken as your sword!" Raleigh bellowed, his lust for battle keeping him from registering even his own grave wounds, his sword's light raging like a fire, as red as the blood littering the battlefield.

"Never! I may die on the battlefield, but it will never be to you!"

"Bold words, but I assure you we'll see if you will return from death twice!" Raleigh shouted, challenging her as he swung his sword again horizontally, planning to split her in two.

In desperation, Zelina managed to jump above the attack, remaining in the air just long enough before landing again and stabbing him through the abdomen with her broken sword.

The bloody warrior coughed, hacking up blood, but tried to raise his sword again, not relenting for even a moment.

Furious, determined, and emboldened by her righteous cause, Zelina's arm shot out, grabbing Raleigh's wrist and twisting as hard as she could manage, hearing several painful cracks. After intense struggle, she wrested his blade from his hand, just as he had done to her before. She then wielded the blood-hued weapon. As she gripped it in her hand,

Zelina felt something, a sudden rush of power as something within the blade, several somethings, cried out. The cursed weapon empowered her, a new strength flowed into her, one that tempted her with power, with glory. She took it in before visions flooded her mind in a brief flash that felt like an eternity. She could see so many faces she had never encountered, so many trapped souls wailed in her mind as the blade offered her power, yet the queen of dragons refused to let another fall to such fate, especially by her hand. As she quieted the storm, she noticed one face grew stronger...It was her own self, the fragment of her soul that had been stolen.

Reaching out, Zelina touched it, her finger on her spirit's form before it returned to her, and she felt a sense of renewal, one that made her feel whole. Her lungs rushed with air as she felt stronger, her pains fading. The power offered by the blade was rejected...It was her own strength she would rely upon.

With a final, great yell, Zelina drew back the sword that had nearly ended her life, that had ended the lives of her kindred, and used it to stab through Raleigh, the sword finding its home next to the broken one that impaled the warrior. With a cold, detached calmness, now cooled from the rage of the fight, Zeina stood there, gripping the sword's handle fiercely as the sands soaked up her and Raleigh's blood and sweat. The defeated warrior stood, coughing again, but his eyes were fixed on Zelina. The queen looked up at him, seeing not anger or disbelief on his face, but acceptance, almost joy as he chuckled, blood spluttering from his mouth.

"Well done, Queen of Wynveria..." Raleigh managed to whisper before his last breath escaped his lips. Even after Zelina released the sword piercing his body, it did not fall. Raleigh's corpse remained standing, as if the warrior's own spirit refused to let its body rest.

The magnitude of Zelina's actions finally sunk in as she saw that Raleigh was truly dead. For a long time, Zelina held her breath, before finally letting out a sigh of relief, making herself still for a brief time. Raleigh was dead, the war was over...She had won. She had won! Then, once it finally registered, she cheered loudly. "WYNVERIA! WE ARE VICTORIOUS!"

"ALL HAIL THE QUEEN!" her people cried, many weeping tears of joy as they stood scattered around the battlefield. As cheerful as the Wynverians were, the Elustrians contrasted them, all in shock, some falling to their knees and mourning, others trying to run.

There was fear and disbelief, just as there was joy and cheer, with Zelina's long struggle finally ending.

* * *

A sudden relaxation came over Zelina as the Wynverians crowded around her, her body loosening up and a smile coming over her face. In spite of all the bloodshed, she felt far better than she had in quite some time. As she tried to walk ahead, she faltered, before falling unconscious, the crowd barely catching her body while her mind and spirit traveled elsewhere.

When Zelina woke again, she was in the same realm as when she last saw the Arbiter, the great dragon standing before her and staring at the queen.

"Arbiter."

The spiritual dragon stood tall in the Astral Mountain, his gaze one of warm pride as he looked at her. "Queen Zelina. You have defeated your foe, as we agreed."

"Yes, Arbiter. I even took claim to the sword that almost took my life, the soul stealing blade." Zelina looked to see that a manifestation of the sword was with her. She was shocked to see the aura from before, although now she could hear the wailing of souls and could see the outlines of many faces, the victims who fell to the blade. She grew more solemn as she heard them crying for freedom, looking at the weapon and absorbing the magnitude of how much harm it had truly done.

"So you have, but I loathe to consider that creation's origins." The Arbiter gave a disgusted groan as Zelina set the blade down between them. "Such a foul blade and with such dreadful power...I fear even its wielder was not aware of its full might."

Zelina stared at the weapon, concerned. "What do you mean?"

"It is not my place to tell you, however the blade almost claimed your own soul when you nearly died from its wound. The fact that you were guided to me instead was fortunate indeed. But I must cleanse it as best I can." Taking a deep breath, the Arbiter inhaled before blowing out a white stream of fire that soon covered the sword. The blade's glow faded under the Arbiter's gaze as countless souls streamed forth, ascending like stars around them, soon becoming one with the realm or escaping to their final resting place.

Looking down, Zelina saw the flames around the crimson sword slowly disappear, though the sword remained where it was. "At last, this blade's curse has ended."

"That's not true, sadly. I was able to free all the Wynverians who died by this blade and many other souls, but there are many more that weapon has too much hold on, hundreds at least." The Arbiter seemed concerned. "I underestimated the force you had to face."

"With all due respect, my foe was a man, not a tool; I used that sword to kill him," Zelina said firmly.

"Then his soul is likely still within. A foul sword like this bonds deeply with its wielder. It would not let him go so easily even with my influence. Still, this weapon won't pose a threat so long as you keep it under close watch."

"Very well. I will take it with me into the Astral Mountain," Zelina said, gripping the blade firmly.

"No, you won't be, Zelina. You are not bound for this place today."

"But aren't you going to take me into the afterlife now?" Zelina asked, confused.

"No, I think you have more than earned a second chance at life. You gave everything you could to spare your people. You spent your life trying to be a ruler your people could rely upon, and you've succeeded. However, you have duties left to fulfill."

"To whom?" Zelina asked. "To you, Arbiter?"

"No, to yourself. I think there is much more you can do in life for the good of others, yes, but you deserve to also be happy. One cannot live solely for their duty or their calling. While all who live have purpose and drive, life is to be lived to its fullest, as it is a gift like no other. I want you to make the most of that gift, of that time. For those you love and yourself. However, if you do wish to take your rest, I would say you have earned it well."

"I agree with you whole-heartedly, Arbiter. It will take time but I'll learn to do more than toil with my life. I will rest here someday, but today I'll accept your offer."

To Zelina's surprise, the Arbiter chuckled. "Very well, young queen. I am sure that you will see much in your life and I hope to hear of it when I see you again. Just promise not to make it too soon." The great dragon winked coyly at the queen.

Zelina nodded and found herself aglow with a strange, yet familiar warmth as she soon faded from the realm of the Arbiter.

When Zelina awoke she was still warm, however, it was a different kind of warmth. Slowly, she opened her eyes, looking up at the ceiling and seeing she was back in her room, laying in bed and covered by sheets and blankets. Sitting up, her body still ached, but far less than it had after the battle with Raleigh. Smiling a little, Zelina gave a contented sigh. "I'm home."

"Queen Zelina! You're finally up. I was starting to wonder if you would ever get up," Delys said, her tone warm and playful.

"Delys?" Looking about, Zelina saw she was back in her chamber, where the hearth was aflame and everything was as she remembered it, from her mirror to some of her favorite carvings placed nearby. The queen smiled happily as she felt nostalgia fill her heart. It had been so long since she had been home, and she finally was back. "You're here!"

"Of course. I tried to be there during your fight too, but we arrived after you had finished." Delys continued to grin as she drew nearer to Zelina. "Still, I figured I could keep things cozy for when you returned."

Sitting up straighter, Zelina looked around the room, noticing how tidy and neat it was, seeing even her bed was immaculately kept. Looking at the perfectly made sheets and feeling how fluffed the pillows were. "You did well. So then, how long have I been unconscious?"

"Three weeks since your battle with Raleigh," Delys explained more seriously. "The war has officially been declared over and majority of the Elustrians have been sent home."

"Not all of them?" Zelina questioned as she managed to stand firmly. Looking down, she saw her leg wound had healed well.

"Some asked for a chance to serve in Wynveria, while others are trying to fight on despite Raleigh's declaration...Which didn't go well for them." Delys looked like she wanted to stay more but changed topics. "Some good news, though, is that the errants who served with them are also leaving too."

The queen nodded as she pondered those words. "Hm. I will need to hear more of those who want to serve. They were so loyal to Raleigh, I can't imagine they want to serve the person who killed him."

Delys shook her head. "Maybe they saw the loyalty you inspired, or perhaps they wished to show respect to someone their own leader seemed to respect so much. As vile a man as he was, it seemed to be that he inspired many. A trait he possessed almost as well as you."

Zelina thought about Delys' words for a moment; It almost made her sick to imagine having anything in common with the warmonger who had killed so many of her people. She shook the thought from her mind. "Thank you, we have much healing to be done and rebuilding to do. If I am to be a worthy leader to anyone, I must care for my followers."

"Yes, that is true, but I think you're forgetting to care for someone else," Delys said, folding her arms.

Zelina tried to think, when she remembered her conversation with the Arbiter and felt the aches of her body once again. Sheepishly, she laid back in her bed. "Right...I forgot myself."

"I'll say. You've worked so hard, Queen Zelina, and you haven't been home in so long. Take a moment to rest. You have us to help you get there when it's time," Delys said to her softly, placing the covers over Zelina.

A small part of her wanted to object, but Zelina knew Delys and the Arbiter were right; It was time to live for more than just her duties, to truly find a balance between her station and self. "A week's rest won't kill me, I suppose."

"At this rate, I doubt anything will," Delys replied jokingly. "One last thing, the Sovereign sent a few messengers who say that he will come if you wish to hold audience with him."

"How long ago did they arrive?" Zelina asked.

"A week ago," Delys said

"Is Markus with them?" Zelina asked, concerned.

Delys smiled. "Yes. They seemed rather impressed by his stories of what happened in the war. To be honest, I am too after he and the others saved me."

"He did?" Zelina asked, surprised. "When were you in danger?"

"Oh, one of Raleigh's men and his underlings came to loot the castle during your duel," Delys explained. "Markus, Alya, and Ericsen all came to stop them, and he made sure I was safe. I admit, he's made a much better impression than his first one."

"Markus has grown," Zelina said, smiling. "We both owe him a debt, but I can only hope his people know how well he represented them. In any case, please inform the messenger that I will meet with the Sovereign after I've had a week to recuperate. Otherwise, where is Captain Grey?"

"She has been helping to oversee the exodus of the other Elustrians. She'll be at her post looking to make sure their vessels leave and all the stragglers are rounded up," Delys explained, looking at Zelina like a parent about to scold a child.

"And has a man named Dante come?" Zelina asked, ignoring Delys' focused gaze.

Delys gave Zelina a look before clearing her throat. "Are you sure you're trying to rest, Queen Zelina?"

"This is my last question, I promise," Zelina said hastily.

Rolling her eyes, Delys spoke up. "No, he hasn't, but we were informed by Captain Grey to allow him to await you should he arrive. However, I think that is all the news I have, my queen...At least until tomorrow." Delys winked. "Now, I'll let the others know you're well and have your advisors and the nobles handle things. You did order me to let them know you're delegating to them...Yes?"

With a nod, Zelina agreed. "I am...Thank you, Delys."

"You're welcome, Your Majesty. I'll have the cooks prepare you a meal. Brunch in bed should be suitable." With a bow, Delys opened the door and watched Zelina leave.

* * *

The week between Zelina's rest and her resuming her duties felt like it passed in a blink, but nonetheless, the queen of Wynveria was able to slowly gain her bearings. After what felt like an eternity of fighting, fretting, and planning over the war with the Elustrians, she was able to fully relax, letting herself catch up on sleep and soak in the respite peace provided.

While she knew in the back of her mind there was much left to do, Zelina knew she could face it best once she had taken time to let herself recover, one issue at a time. Once she was well enough, and the day of the meeting came, Zelina decided to make rounds and familiarize herself with the Heofonites before she saw the Sovereign.

Walking out into the hall, Zelina began to wonder what awaited her. Eventually, she made it down to the castle's great room, seeing Markus talking with two other Heofonites. One was a woman who seemed a bit older than Markus, the other a young man with dark skin and curly black hair, his expression cheery.

Wanting to catch them by surprise, Zelina spoke. "Had I known we would have more Heofonites here I would have arranged for you three to have your own wing."

"Queen Zelina!" Markus cried, rushing to her side. "You're awake again."

"Yes. Hopefully this will be the last time I take an extended break for a long time." Zelina turned to the other two Heofonites. "Who are these two?"

"This is Adara and that is Simon. The two of them are also Guardians," Markus said, still elated as he stood among his people before gesturing to Adara.

"Adara is one of my oldest friends, she and I became Guardians around the same time."

"Though I became Virtuous first," she said with a wink to him. "Maybe if you put in a bit more work, you'll be promoted too."

"Who knows, maybe I will," Markus replied playfully.

"I would second that," Zelina said, amused by their exchange. "You must have worked hard, though I think Markus is well on his way."

"So do I, Your Majesty," Adara said more seriously as she bowed to Zelina. "Also, it is an honor to see another nation, especially a surface one." The woman's tone was reverent, yet giddy. "Perhaps after I finish my training as a Virtue I can return and become a liaison between our two nations."

"Adara, maybe you should wait for Markus to leave the post first," Simon laughed good-naturedly, poking fun at his companion, Adara and Markus chuckling with him. Simon then turned too Zelina, bowing. "Your Majesty, thank you for allowing us here."

"It is no trouble. Wynveria is home to all of its allies," Zelina said. As she tried to kneel to shake his hand, she winced, her back still pained after all of her battling.

"Queen Zelina, is it your back wound?" Markus asked worriedly, drawing nearer to her.

Zelina shook her head and raised a hand as she stood straighter. "No, no. That's healed, save for the scar. Just some soreness. It'll pass, I'm sure."

Simon looked at Zelina. "You said you were scarred, Your Majesty?"

"It's one of few I've picked up during this campaign," she said, trying to downplay its importance."

"If you like, I can make it go away," Simon offered. "I am particularly gifted in healing, though I say that with utmost humility."

"Thank you for the offer, Simon, however that will not be necessary," Zelina said appreciatively. "I'm not too bothered by them."

"Of course, Your Majesty. My apologies," Simon said quickly.

"No need to apologize. You meant well. Regardless, I will need to converse with Markus alone. The two of you will not mind, will you?" Zelina asked them.

"Of course not," the two said in unison.

"Good. By the way, Delys, my handmaiden, has a message for you both regarding your business here. She'll seek you out shortly. That is all."

Nodding, the two bowed before departing hastily. By then, Markus and Zelina were alone in the room.

"I wanted to ask if you have been well in my absence," Zelina said softly, trying to gauge his state of mind.

A bit solemnly, Markus nodded. "Yes, but I have to admit that I felt uneasy when you fell unconscious again. At first I worried you had died, given you were unconscious when I arrived to the battlefield."

"Had I, I would have died allied with a worthy Guardian, and an even worthier friend." Gently, she placed a hand on his shoulder, offering a small smile. "Thankfully, I am here and well, and I wanted to ask you a question."

"A question, Your Majesty?" he asked, surprised. "Yes," Zelina said as she walked towards a window and looked outside. "What do you think of Wynveria?"

"I think it is a beautiful country, one full of strong people," Markus replied honestly and almost wistfully as he looked outside. "I saw quite a bit of it during this whole war, but I wish I could have seen those places and people in a more peaceful time."

"As do I, yet you may someday if you choose to stay," Zelina offered, looking at him earnestly and with a welcoming expression.

Kneeling, Markus bowed his head. "Only if you will allow me to stay. I know I was not chosen to by you to be your Guardian, but I hope I can continue to serve you well."

"Of that I am certain. Please, rise." Zelina's expression was soft and sincere, but for a moment she remembered what Delys had said about inspiring loyalty and the comparison to Raleigh. The flicker of doubt did not go unnoticed by Markus.

"What's amiss?"

"It's nothing important, not really. I was told I inspired loyalty in my followers, much like Raleigh has... That comparison made me think of him and how I could not help but be worried that I might become a warmonger like him or worse."

"Queen Zelina, forgive me for being so blunt, but that's ridiculous. Raleigh was despicable, but very few people in this life are purely good or purely evil. I imagine once he was a normal, but charismatic man. He let his power twist him and his desires rule him, to a point where he forgot that those outside of his circle were people, at least that is what I think.

If you feel any good sentiment about his ideals and views that weren't destructive, then that's not bad, but so long as you don't walk his path and do what you think is just and moral, I doubt you will ever end up as corrupt as he did."

The Wynverian queen was silent as those words sunk in. She still felt pangs of guilt, but Markus' words made sense and ultimately, she agreed with them. "Thank you for sharing your thoughts."

"Thank you for listening. By the way, I heard among those who you inspired on Raleigh's side, a man calling himself the bibliognost wanted to try his hand at writing a play about what has happened. Maybe it will be your chance to get into acting after all."

"As flattering as it is, I feel a play celebrating my victory disservices the losses we endured," Zelina said as her mind traveled to the people who had died to help Wynveria not only secure victory, but defeat Raleigh's menace once and for all. "I am not sure if I wish to watch it, much less play myself in such a production."

Markus thought on Zelina's words, placing a hand to his chin. "True, but if you spoke to him maybe it could be a chance to show the tragedy of war instead of the glory of victory. Something to pass on to future generations and to memorialize those who fell, like General Nersel."

"A memorial play?" Zelina turned, thinking over Markus' words. "I will consider it if the playwright will…I forgot to ask, what happened to Raleigh's sword?"

"That cursed weapon? It was placed in a vault in the castle. I am not sure where the vault's located, but it is on the premises, at least," Markus explained.

"I'll bear that in mind. Thank you." Zelina smiled before yawning. "Well, I am sure I have much work to do organizing reconstruction and reparations, not to mention my normal duties, but I think I'll have some tea first. Care to join me?"

"It would be an honor," Markus said, as he followed behind the queen of the dragons.

Feeling confident, Zelina went on with Markus at her side. There would certainly be other challenges in the future, and even now the war ending did not mean that the vengeful Elustrians or other errants would not cause trouble, but even so she would face them with resolution and her valuable allies. It was her responsibility and purpose, but most of all her pleasure to protect the ancestral home of the dragons against all threats.

* * *

Later that day, Zelina and the Sovereign met again, the queen and the winged ruler both stood atop the highest tower, overlooking Arachon and the rest of Wynveria. From there, the two could see the clouds near to them and the mountains below. All around, Zelina could see the town and reconstruction efforts, as well as the wreckage that remained after the war.

Given she was meeting with a foreign leader, Zelina had the finest table, wrought of silver and perfectly polished, along with a silken cloth laid out, a pot of warm tea set between them. However, Zelina's mind was not on the drink, but how much Wynveria had changed since she met with the Sovereign last, how much she had changed.

"Even after war, Wynveria remains beautiful, Queen Zelina," the Sovereign said with a gentle voice. Drinking some of his tea, he placed the cup down before continuing. "I'm glad to see you continuing to rule it."

"I feel you would have been happy with either outcome, given you also allied with the Elustrians," Zelina said to him, her gaze firmly on his face. "Speaking of, I appreciate the aid you sent after the conflict was concluded."

"It was only then that I was informed of the extent of your hardships, Queen Zelina…And I must apologize that we of Heofonia did not intercede sooner. While we were and are your allies, as diplomats and peacekeepers, we weren't able to send any additional support, and given our alliances at best we could have mediated a retreat by Elustria."

"I'm sure you would have," Zelina said dryly, her tone sardonic. Zelina's blue eyes met the older man's silvery-gray ones, daring him to continue the line of conversation. For a moment it appeared he would, but he remained silent. After, Zelina continued, "I appreciate the sentiment, but it is past. I am glad to say Markus was a great asset to us."

"It makes me glad to hear that." The Sovereign gave a small, amicable smile. "So, I take it you wish for him to remain as your Guardian?"

"Yes, though I have a few plans to create my own sort of Guardians." Zelina turned to look out the window again, past the clouds and down to the nation she held dear. "If this war has taught me anything, it is that one cannot accomplish everything alone."

The Sovereign nodded. "I would like to offer Heofonia's assistance with reparations and rebuilding, to forge a stronger connection between our two lands. We'll be more than happy to provide this service all over Wynveria as recompense for our earlier misjudgment."

Zelina considered it. "If they are willing and can help with watching for rogue Elustrians or repairing Aurah's monument, I would appreciate it deeply."

"Then it is settled. How soon would you like them to come?" the Sovereign asked.

"As soon as possible," Zelina said. "I want to have reconstruction efforts underway before I leave."

"Leave? Where to, if I may ask?" the Sovereign asked, curiously.

Zelina smiled. "To the Lurion Islands. There's a festival I have been asked to attend, and I wanted to visit an old friend of mine there." The queen began to wonder how her friend, Kenta, was doing. She had heard he had left on a journey of his own up until recently during her week of rest. She hoped that whatever he had gone through it had been positive, and she was eager to share tales of her own, as well as introduce her new friend to her old one.

-The End-

Lorenzo Hall
Illustrated by Edgar Caballero

ALSO FROM THE WORLD OF ISAVOIRE

find more stories at www.isavoire.com

www.ingramcontent.com/pod-product-compliance
Lightning Source LLC
Chambersburg PA
CBHW060240100726
47907CB00003B/706